THE FLYING BEAVER BROTHERS
AND THE EVIL PENGUIN PLAN

MAXWELL EATON III

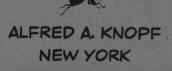

ALFRED A. KNOPF
NEW YORK

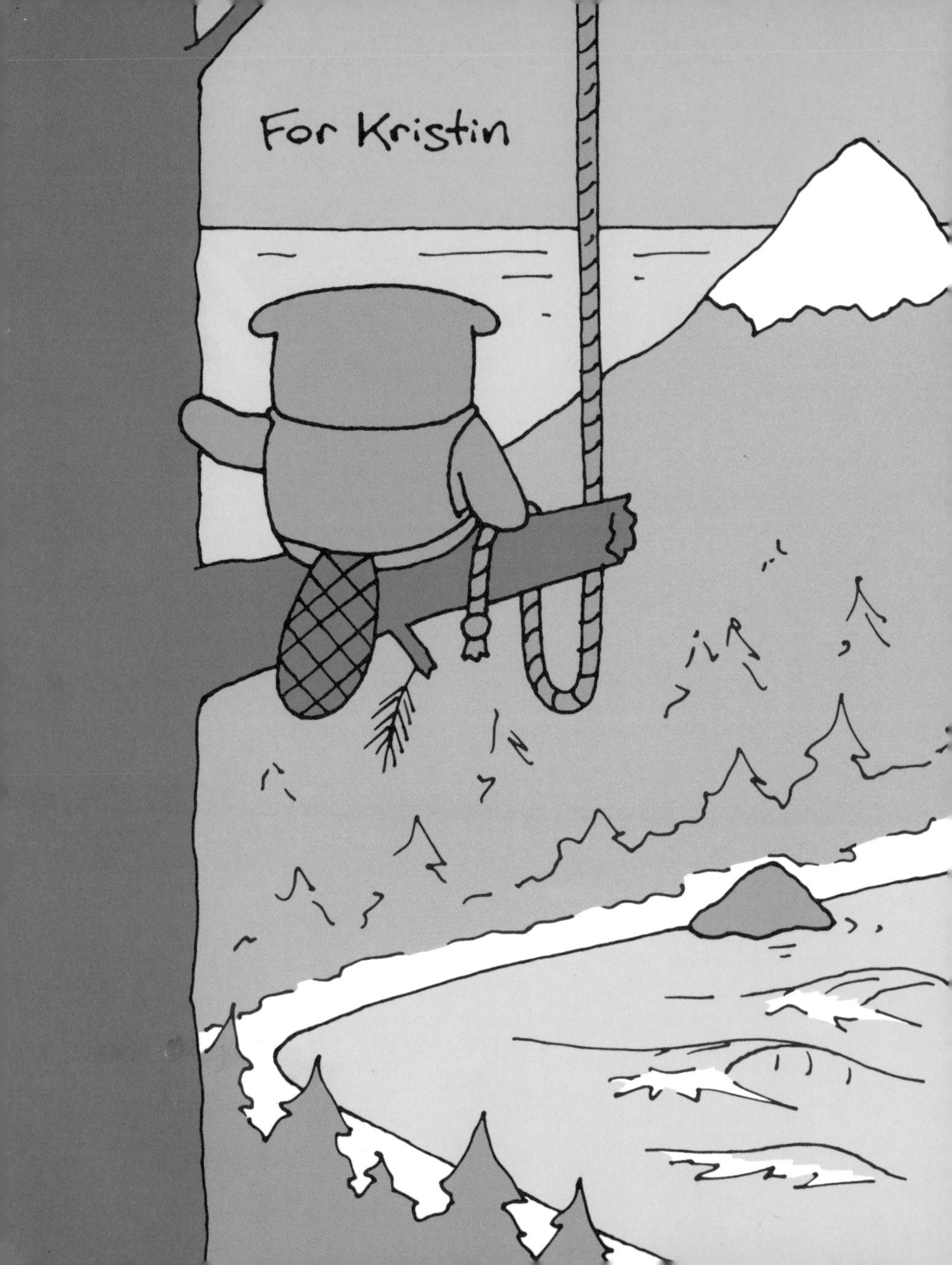
For Kristin

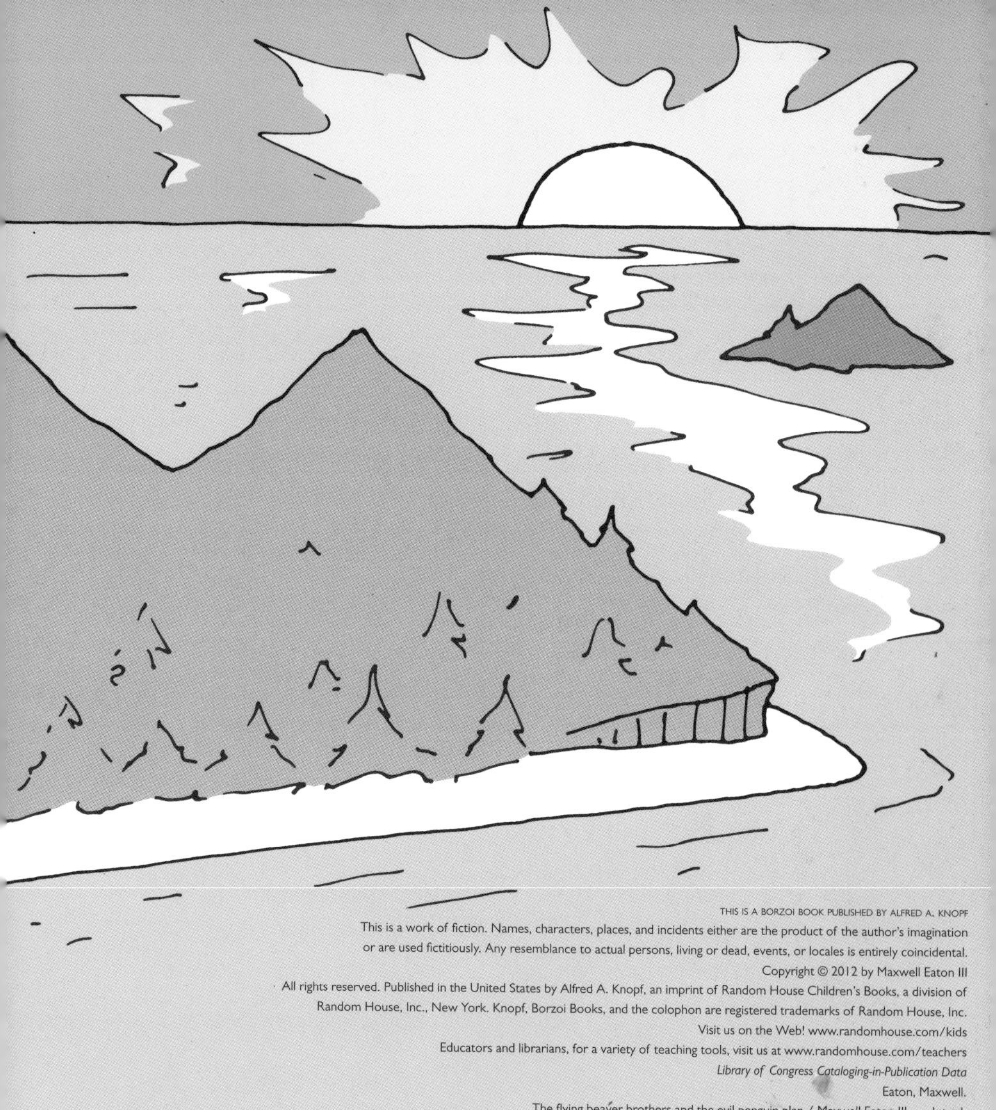

THIS IS A BORZOI BOOK PUBLISHED BY ALFRED A. KNOPF

Visit us on the Web! www.randomhouse.com/kids

Educators and librarians, for a variety of teaching tools, visit us at www.randomhouse.com/teachers

Library of Congress Cataloging-in-Publication Data

Eaton, Maxwell.

The flying beaver brothers and the evil penguin plan / Maxwell Eaton III. — 1st ed.

p. cm.

Summary: Two beavers thwart an evil plot by penguins, who plan to turn Beaver Island into a frosty resort.

ISBN 978-0-375-86447-6 (pbk.) — ISBN 978-0-375-96447-3 (lib. bdg.)

[1. Beavers—Fiction. 2. Penguins—Fiction. 3. Islands—Fiction.] I. Title.

PZ7.E3892Fly 2012 [E]—dc22 2010050652

The illustrations in this book were created using pen and ink with digital coloring.

MANUFACTURED IN MALAYSIA January 2012 10 9 8 7 6 5 4 3 2 1 First Edition

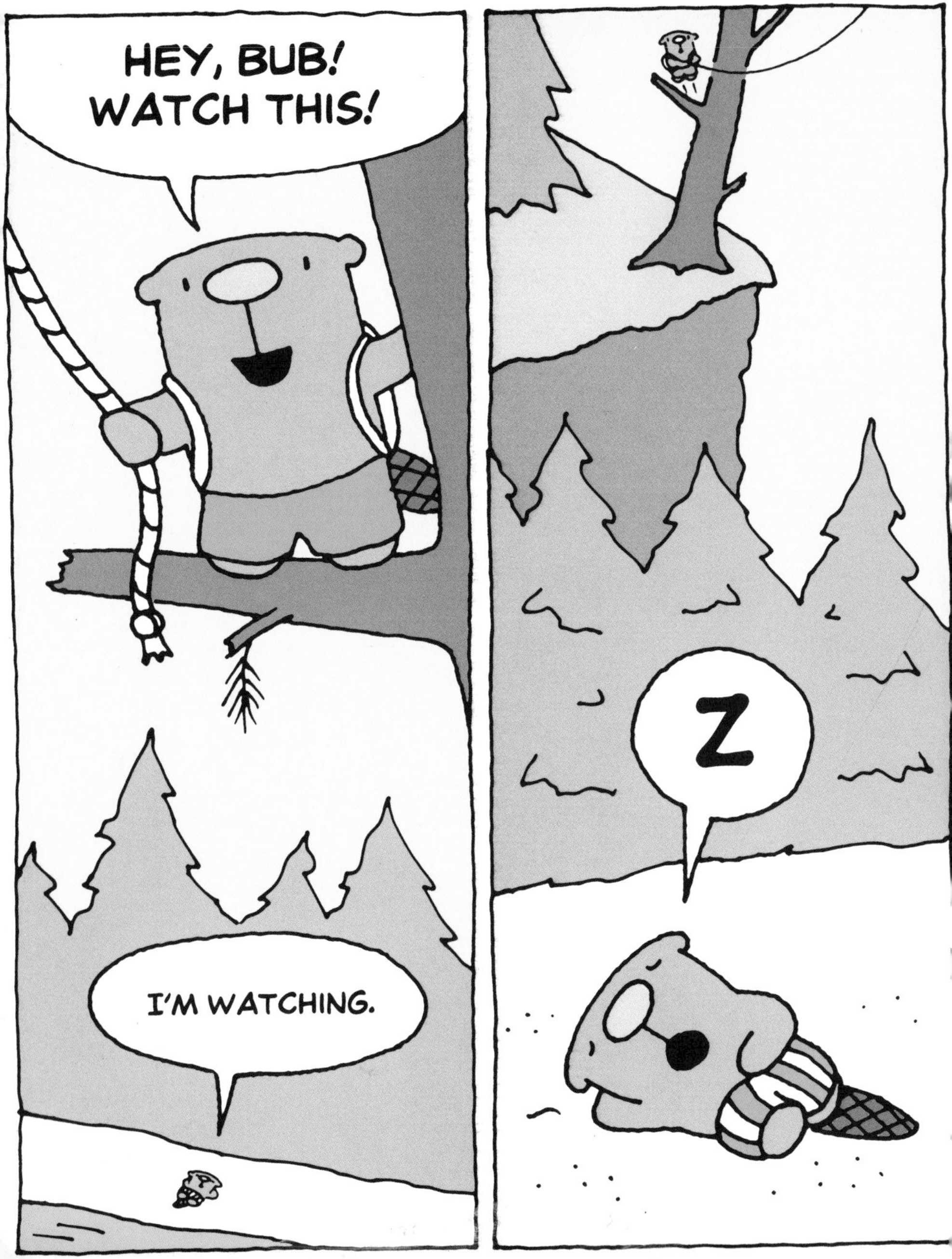
HEY, BUB! WATCH THIS!
I'M WATCHING.
Z

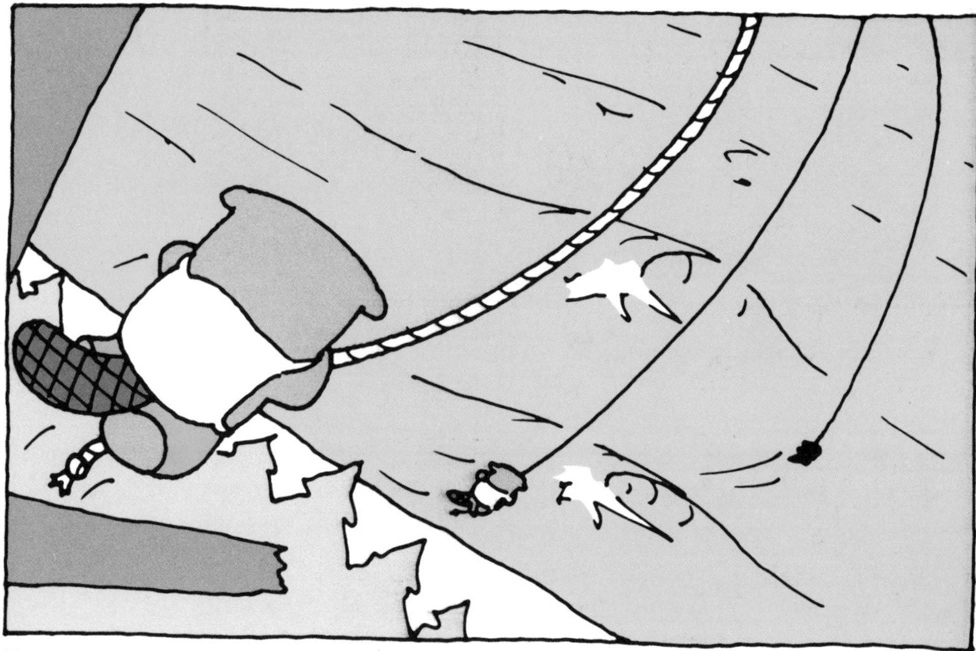

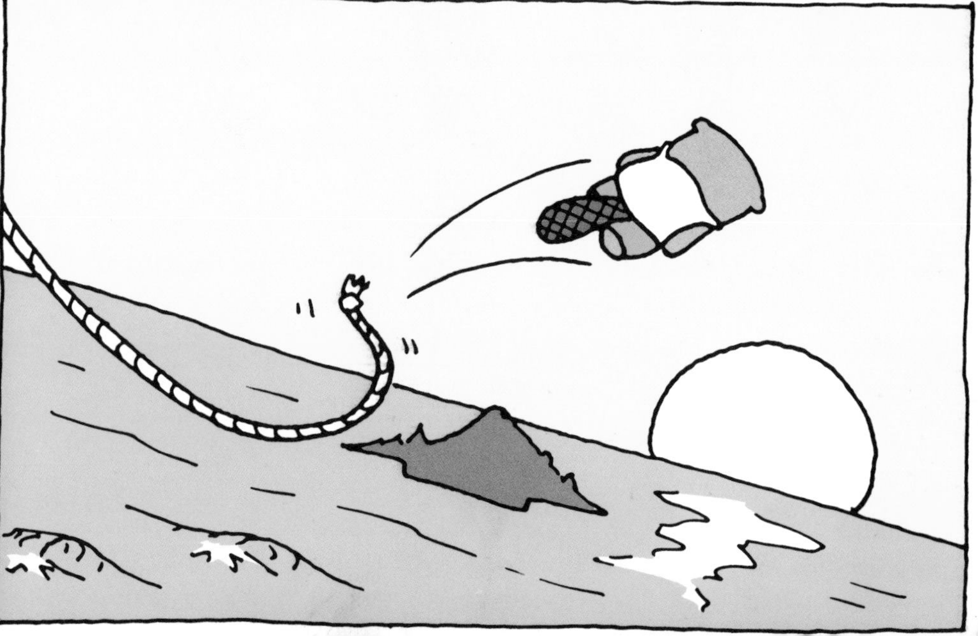

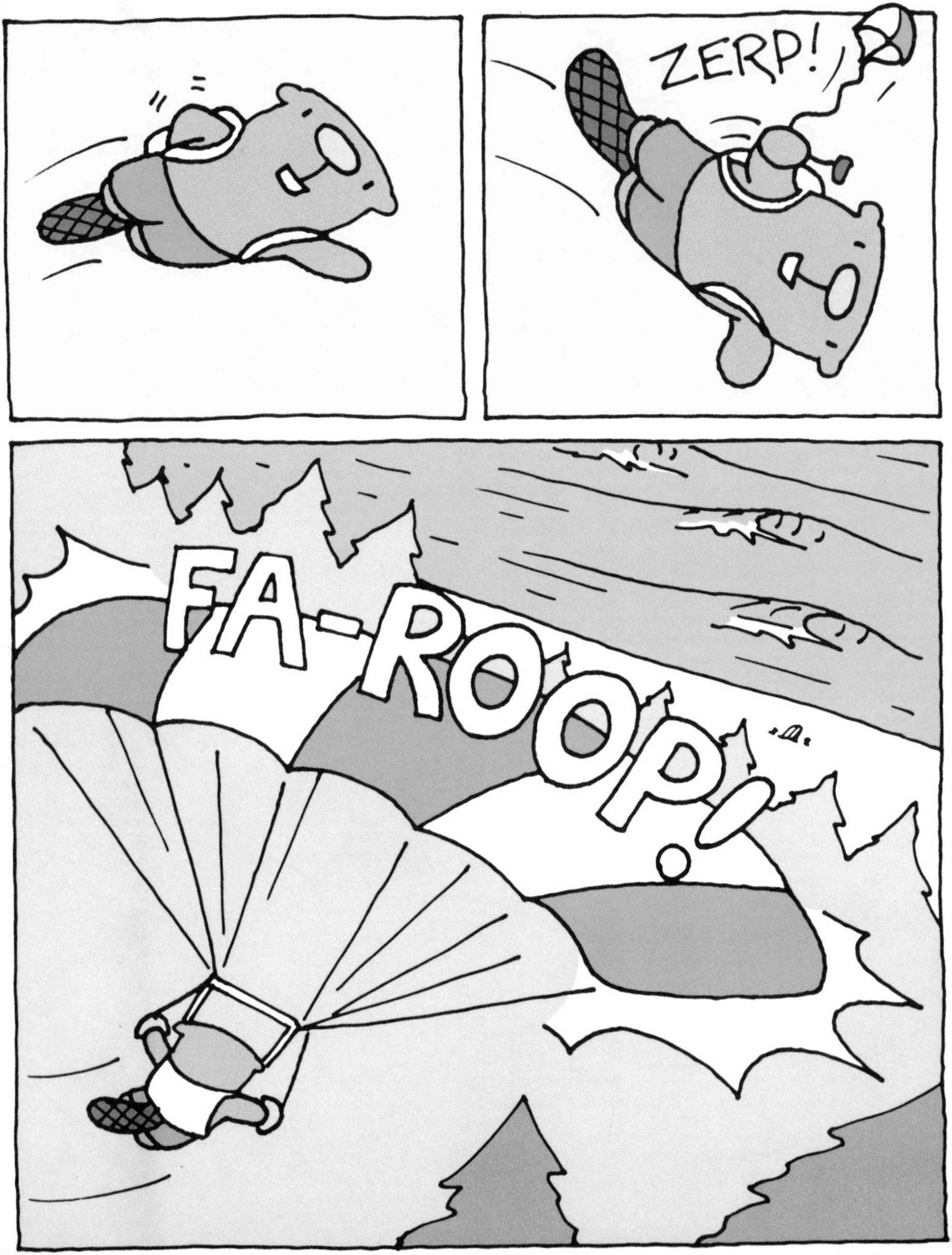
ZERP!
FA-ROOP!

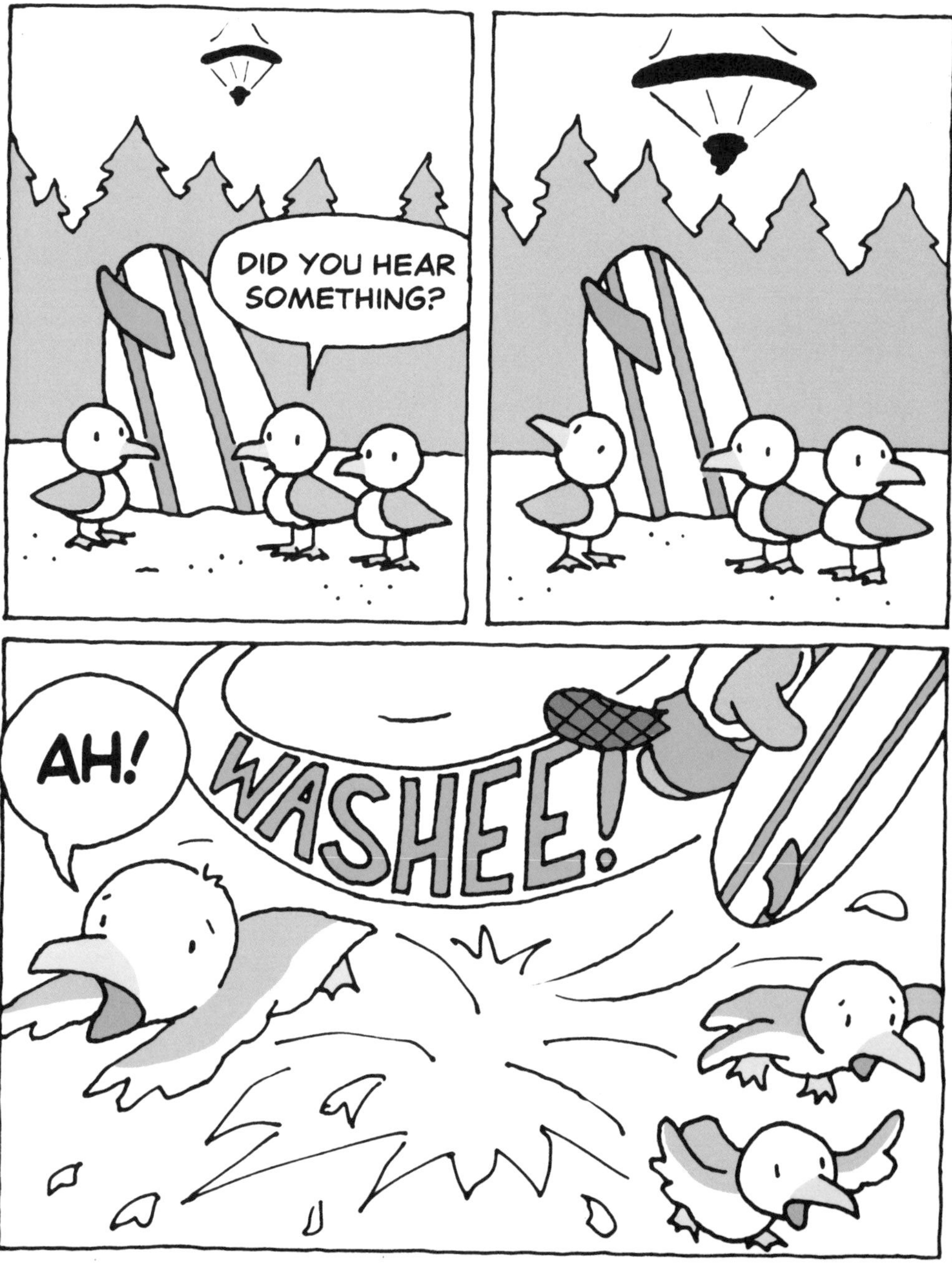
DID YOU HEAR SOMETHING?
AH!
WASHEE!

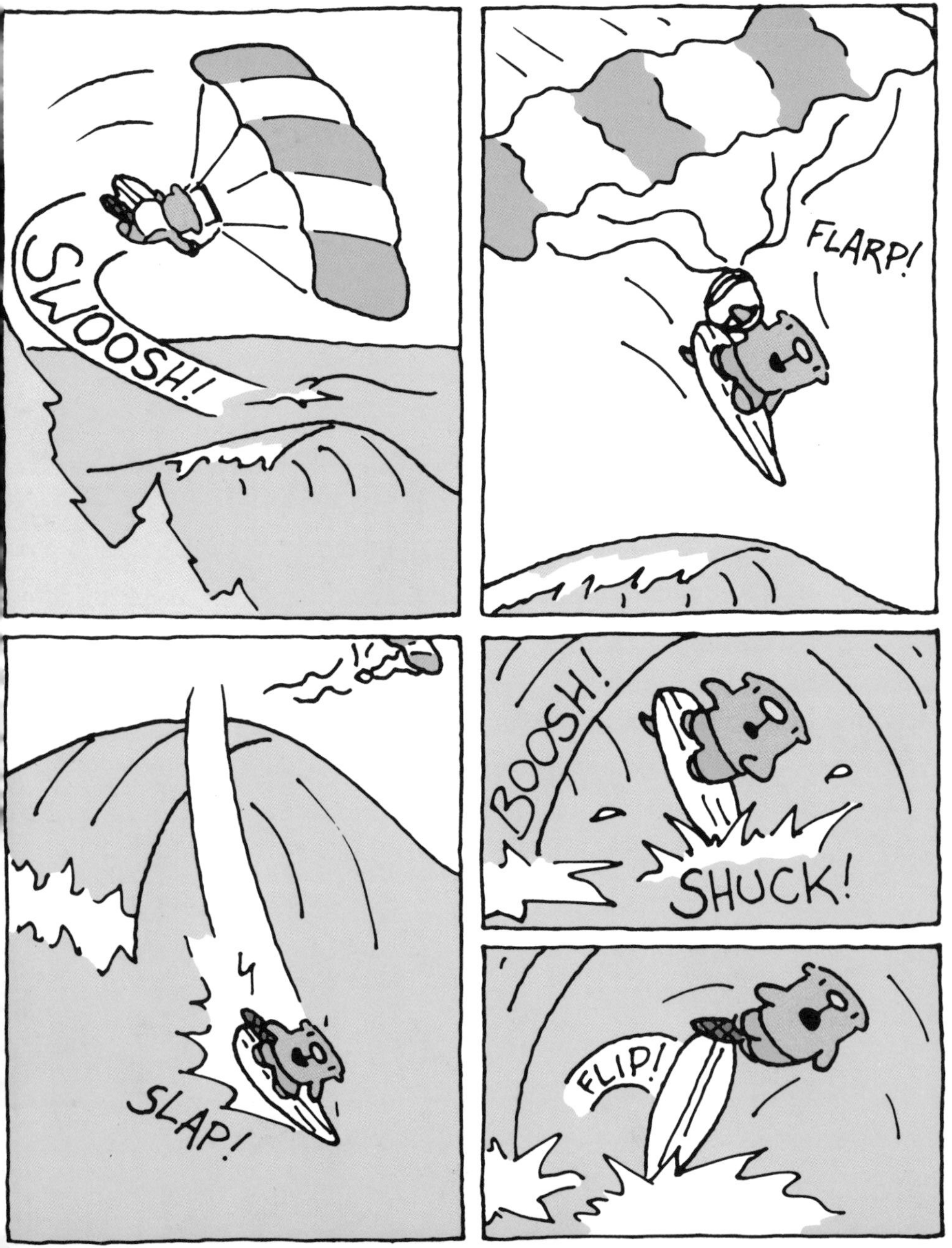
SWOOSH!
FLARP!
SLAP!
BOOSH!
SHUCK!
FLIP!

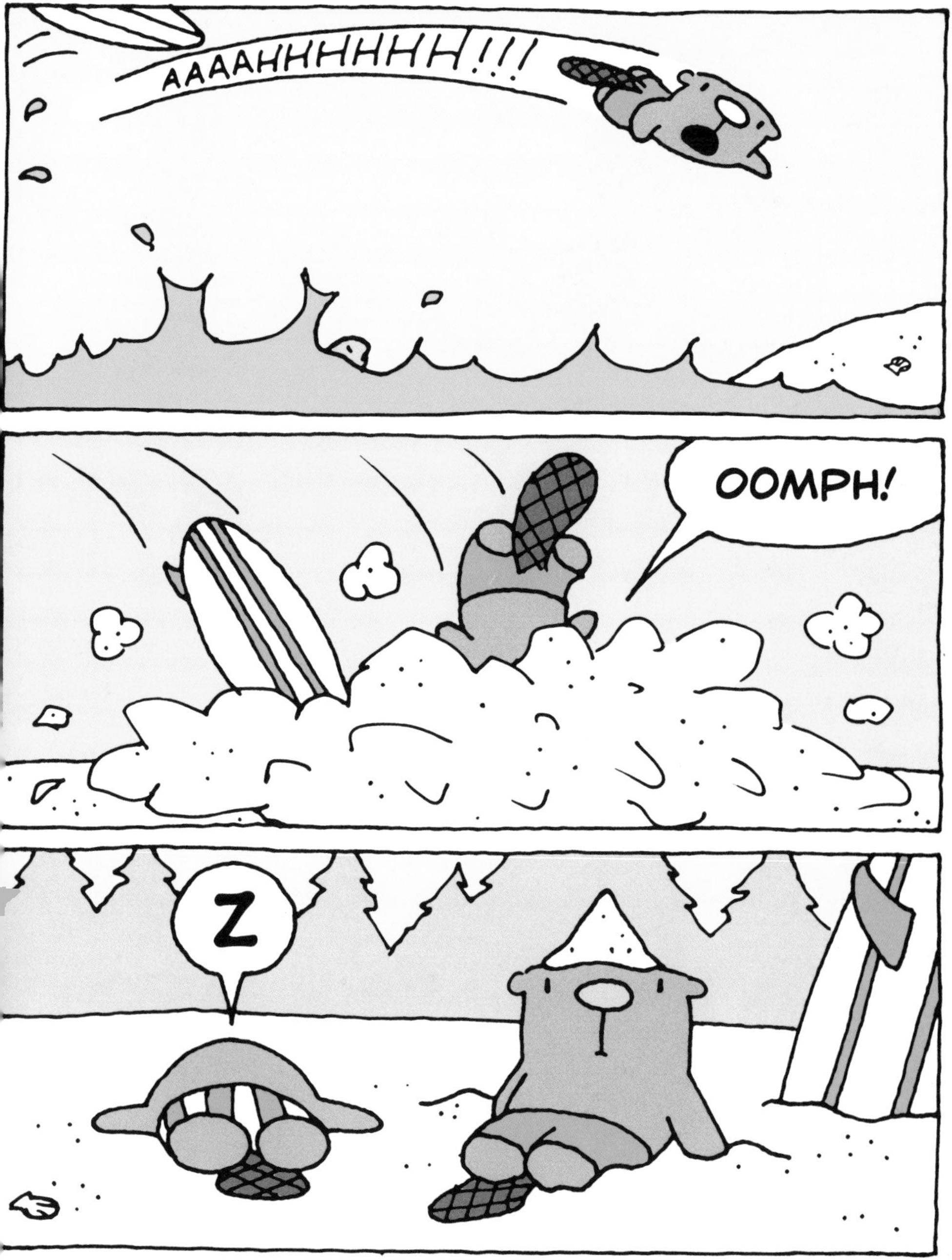
AAAAHHHHHHH!!!!
OOMPH!
Z

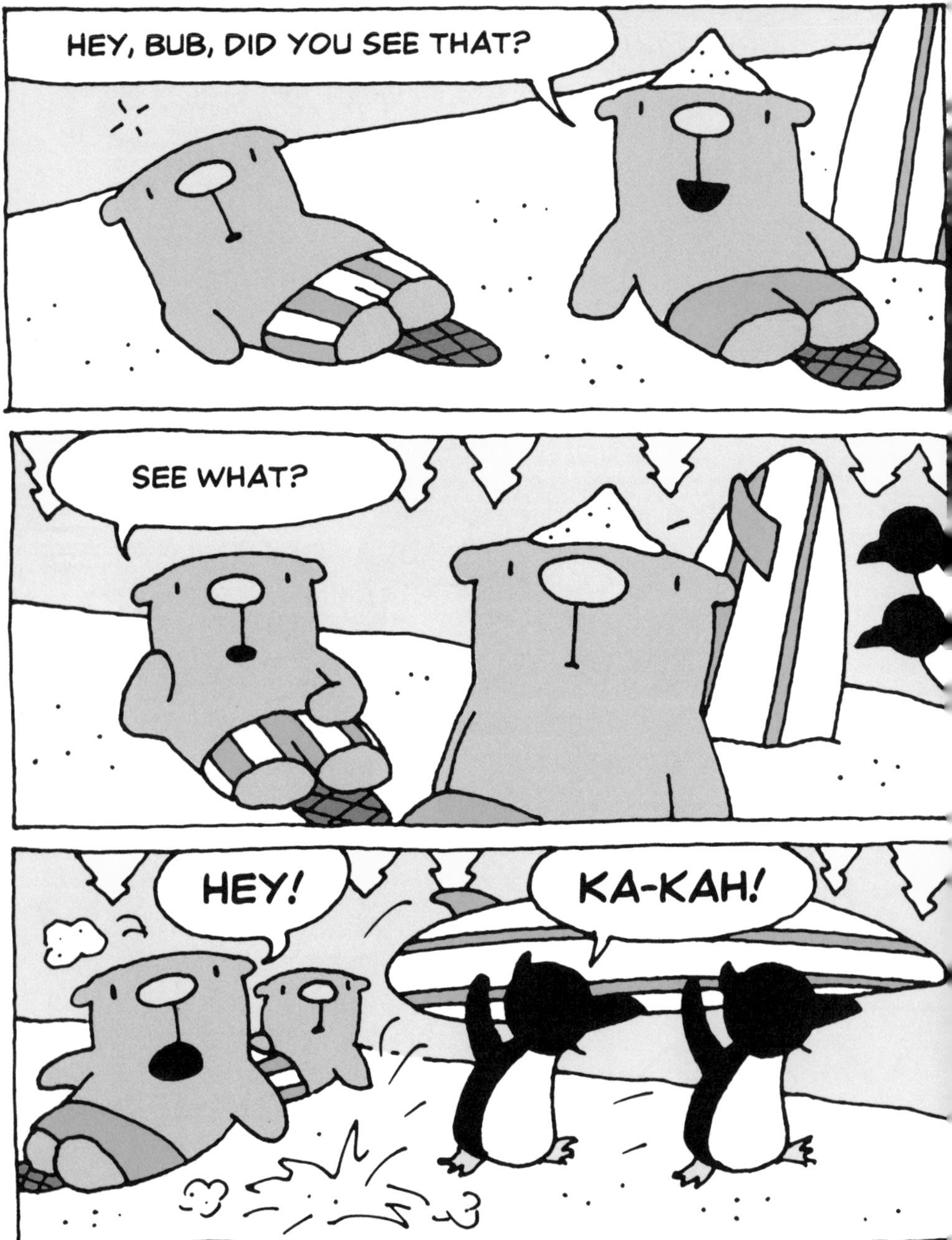
HEY, BUB, DID YOU SEE THAT?
SEE WHAT?
HEY!
KA-KAH!

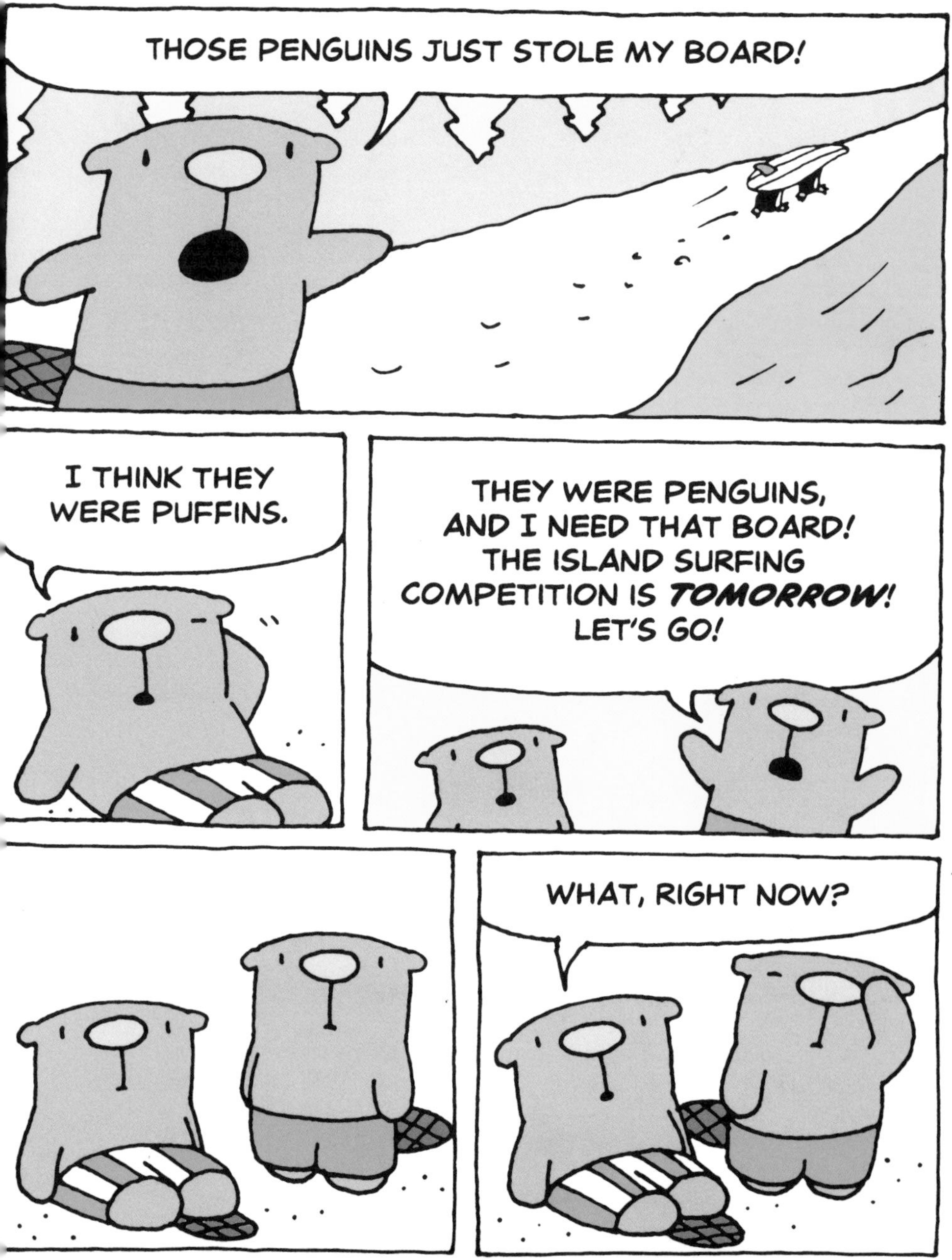
THOSE PENGUINS JUST STOLE MY BOARD!
I THINK THEY WERE PUFFINS.
THEY WERE PENGUINS, AND I NEED THAT BOARD! THE ISLAND SURFING COMPETITION IS *TOMORROW*! LET'S GO!
WHAT, RIGHT NOW?

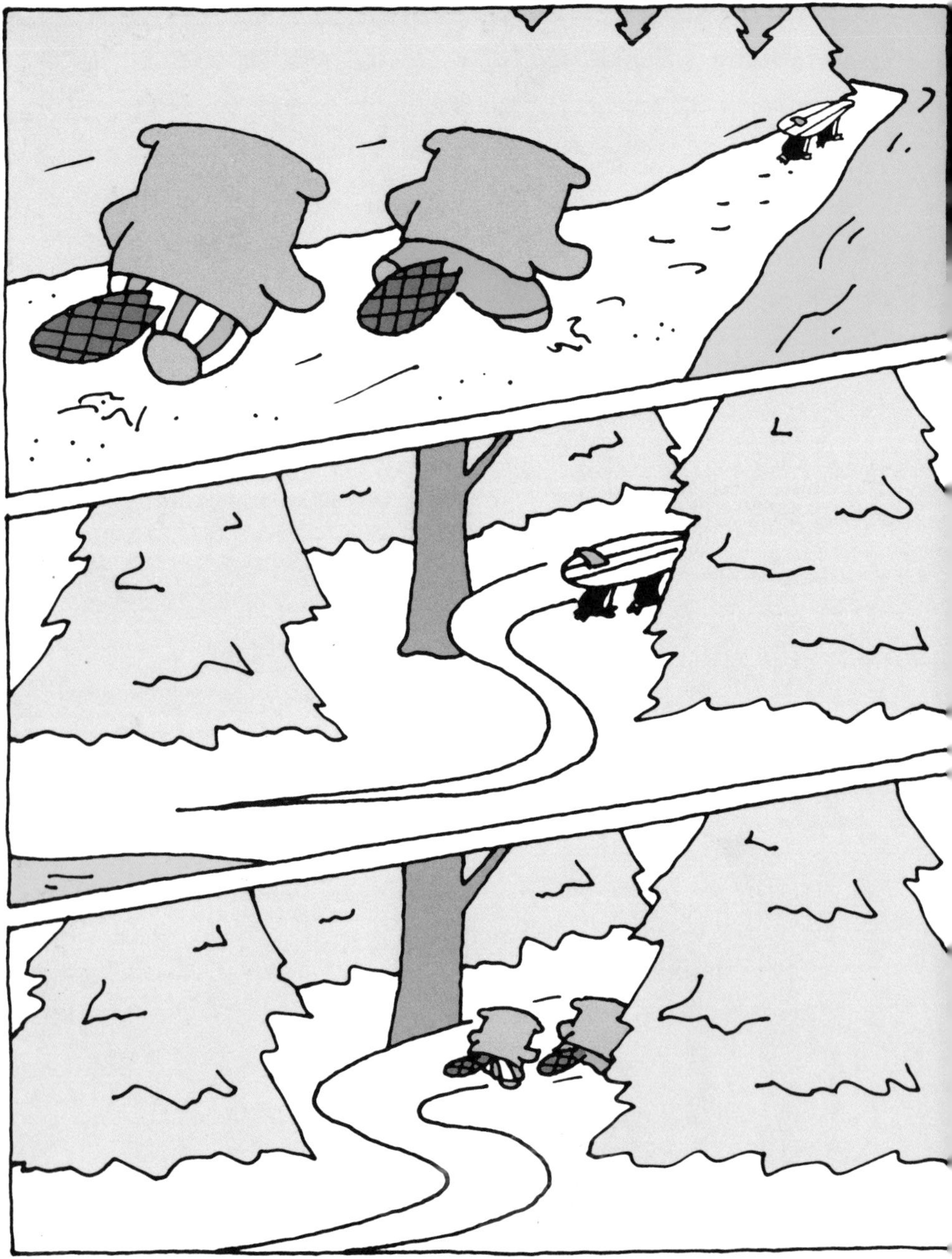

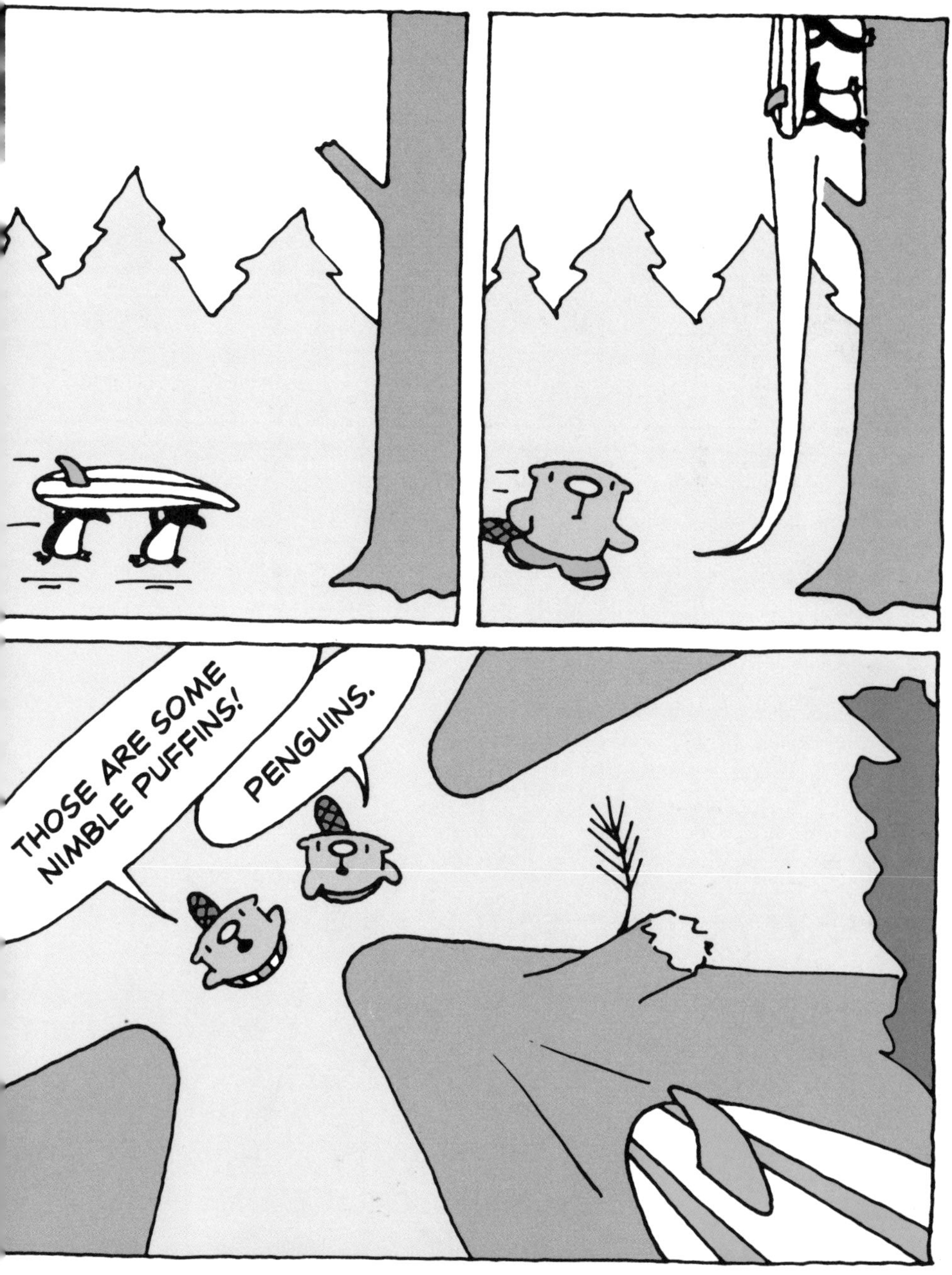

THOSE ARE SOME NIMBLE PUFFINS!
PENGUINS.

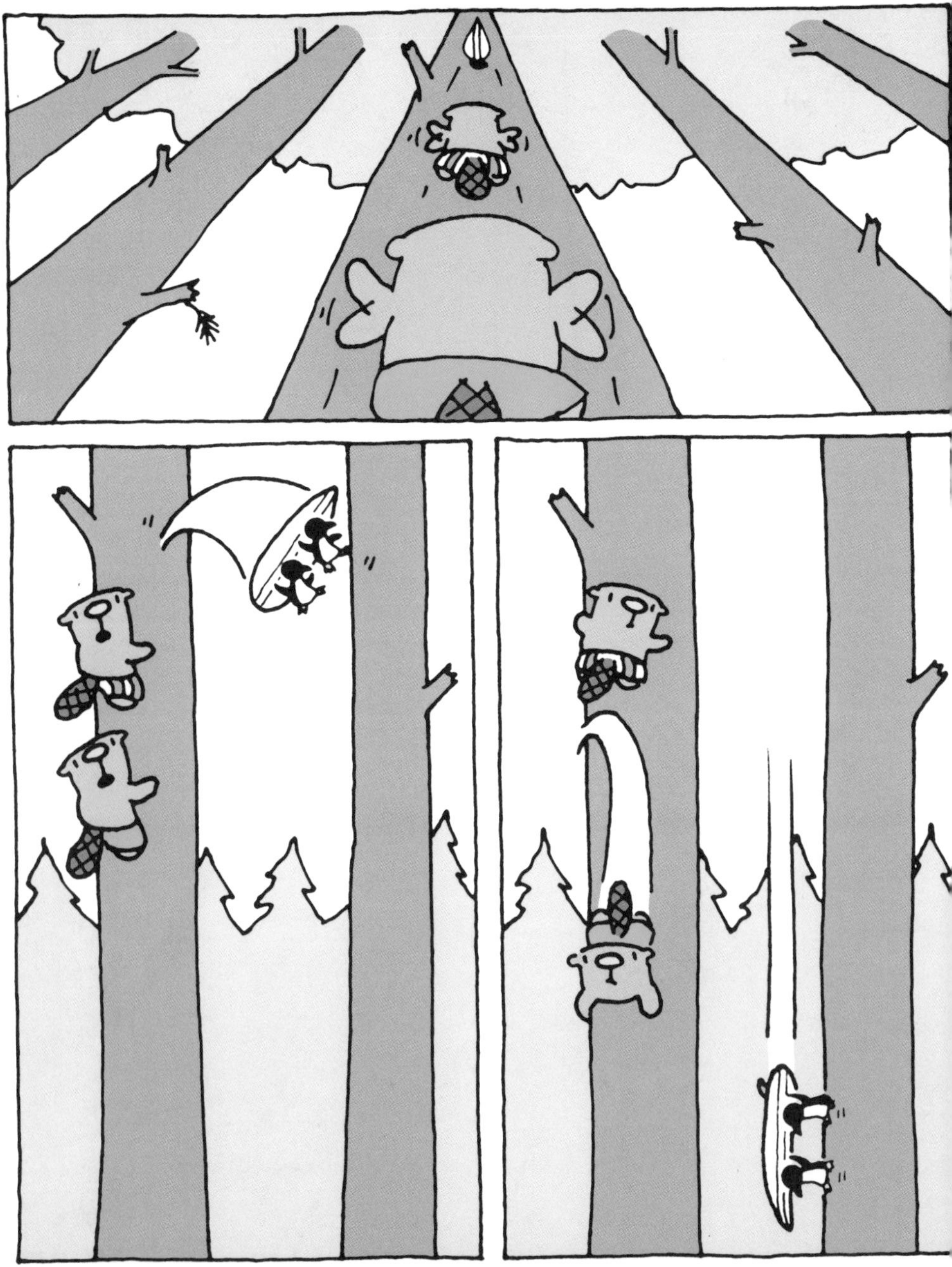

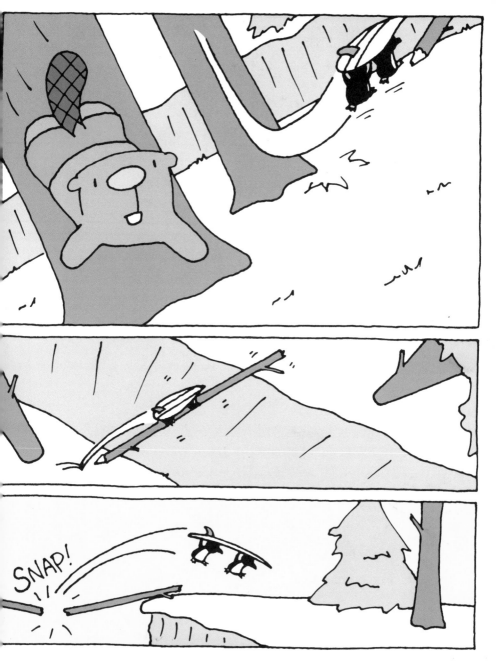

SNAP!

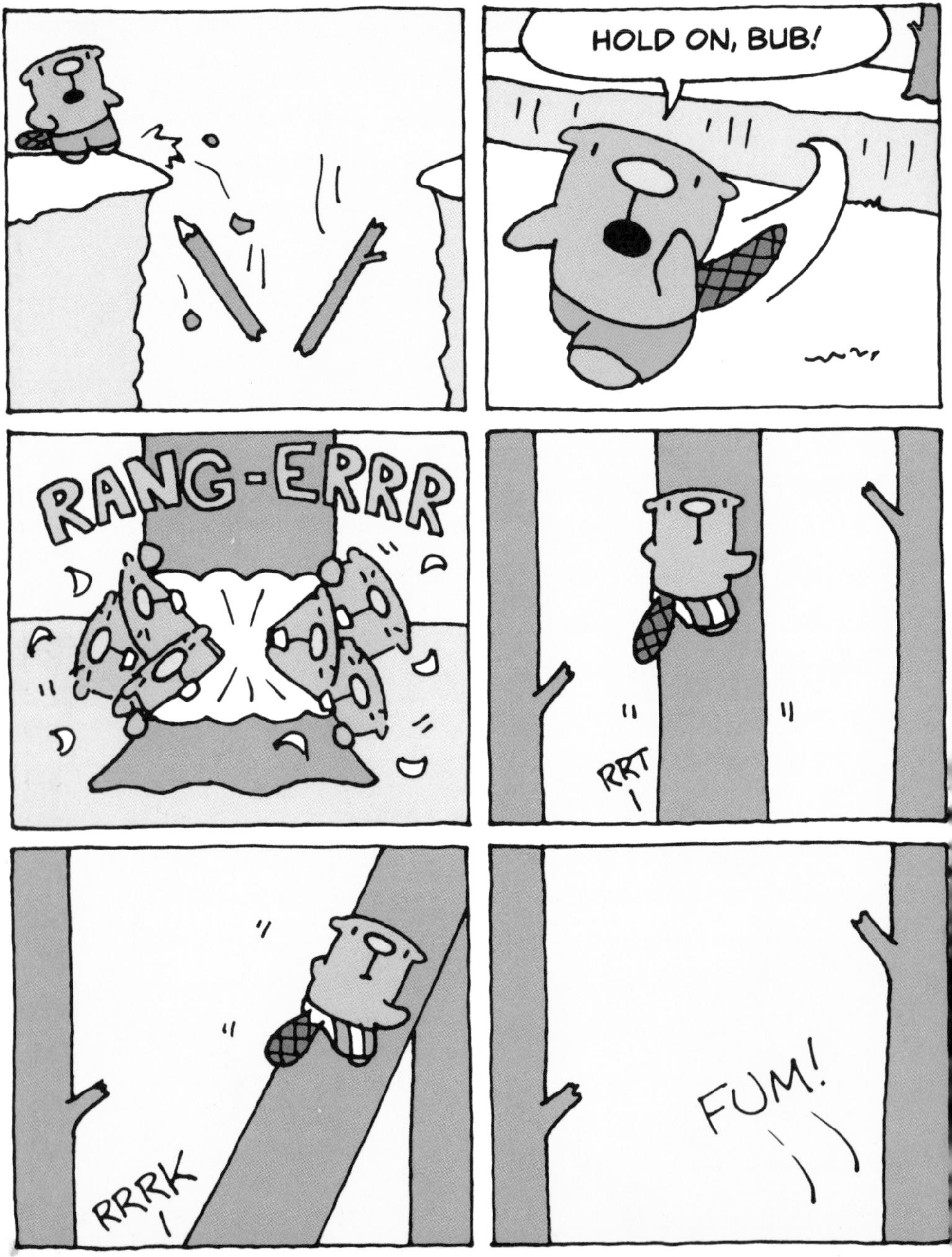

HOLD ON, BUB!
RANG-ERRR
RRT
RRRK
FUM!

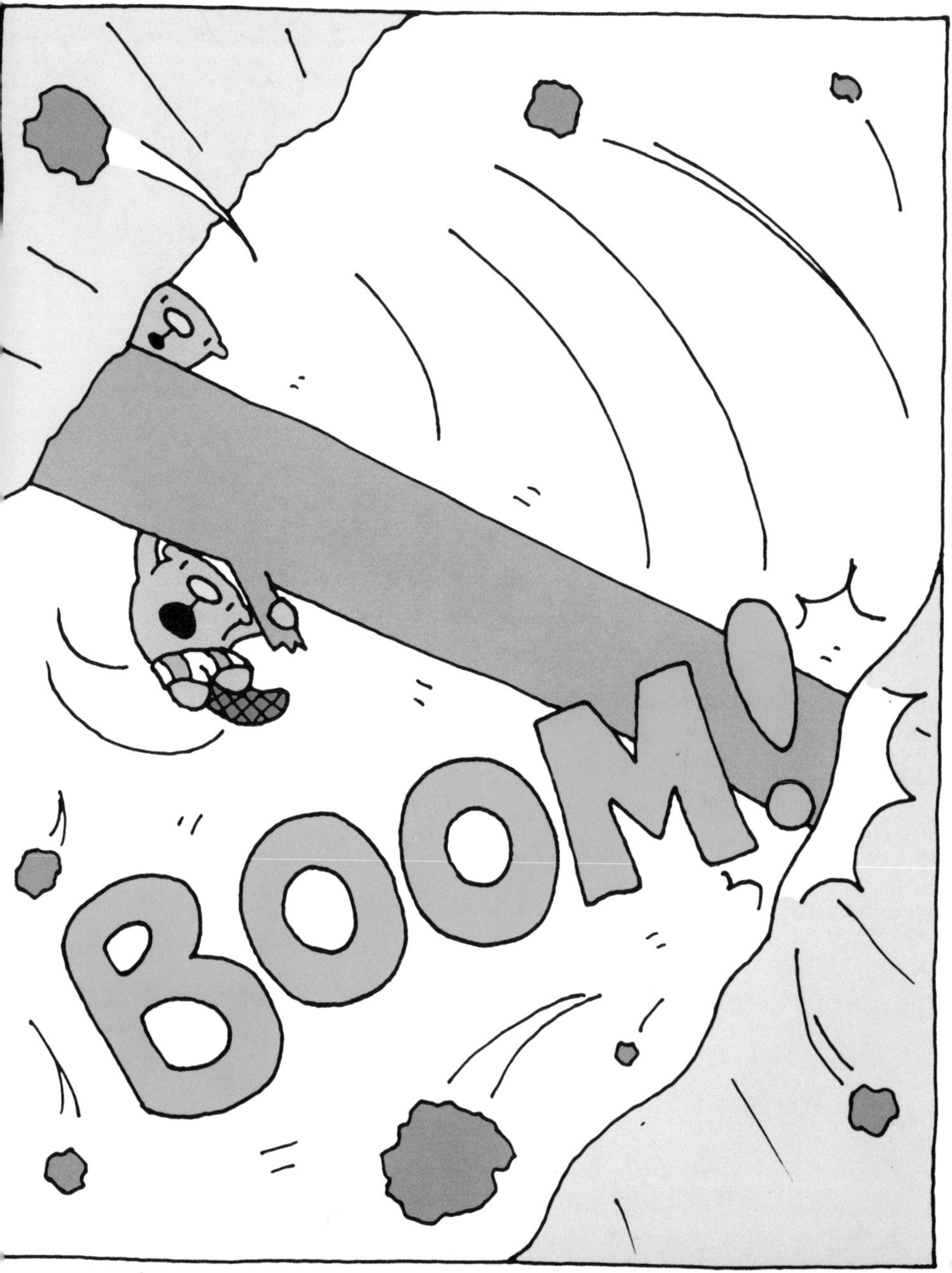
BOOM!

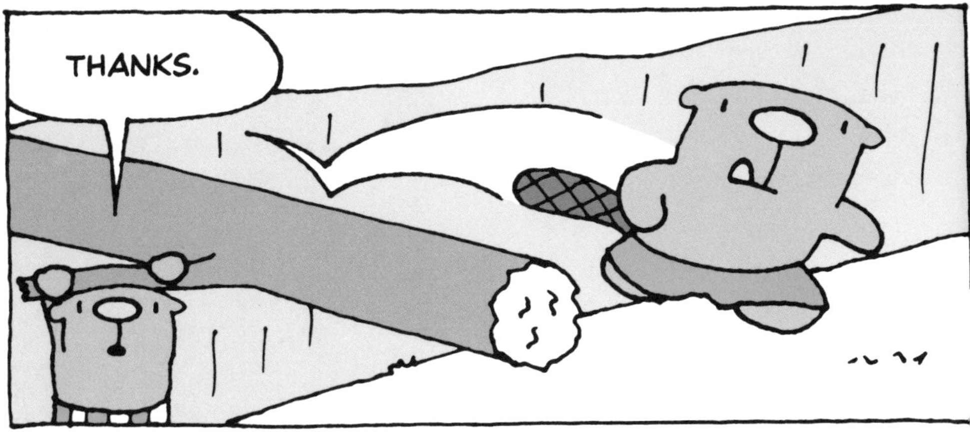
THANKS.

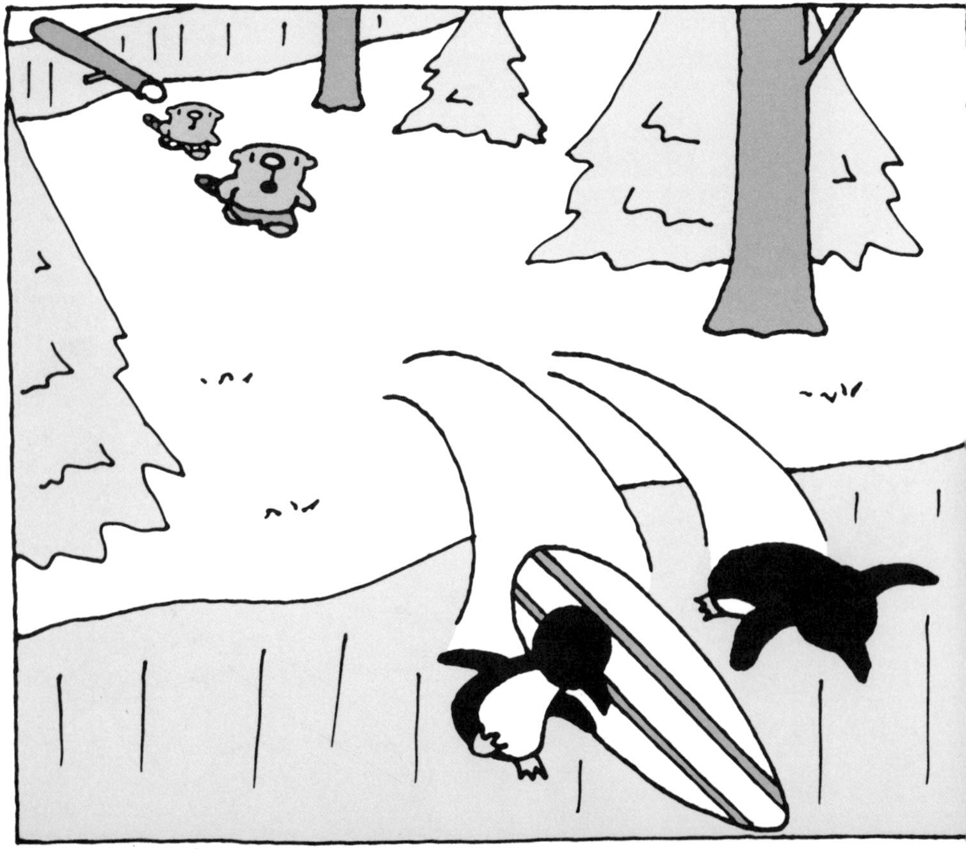

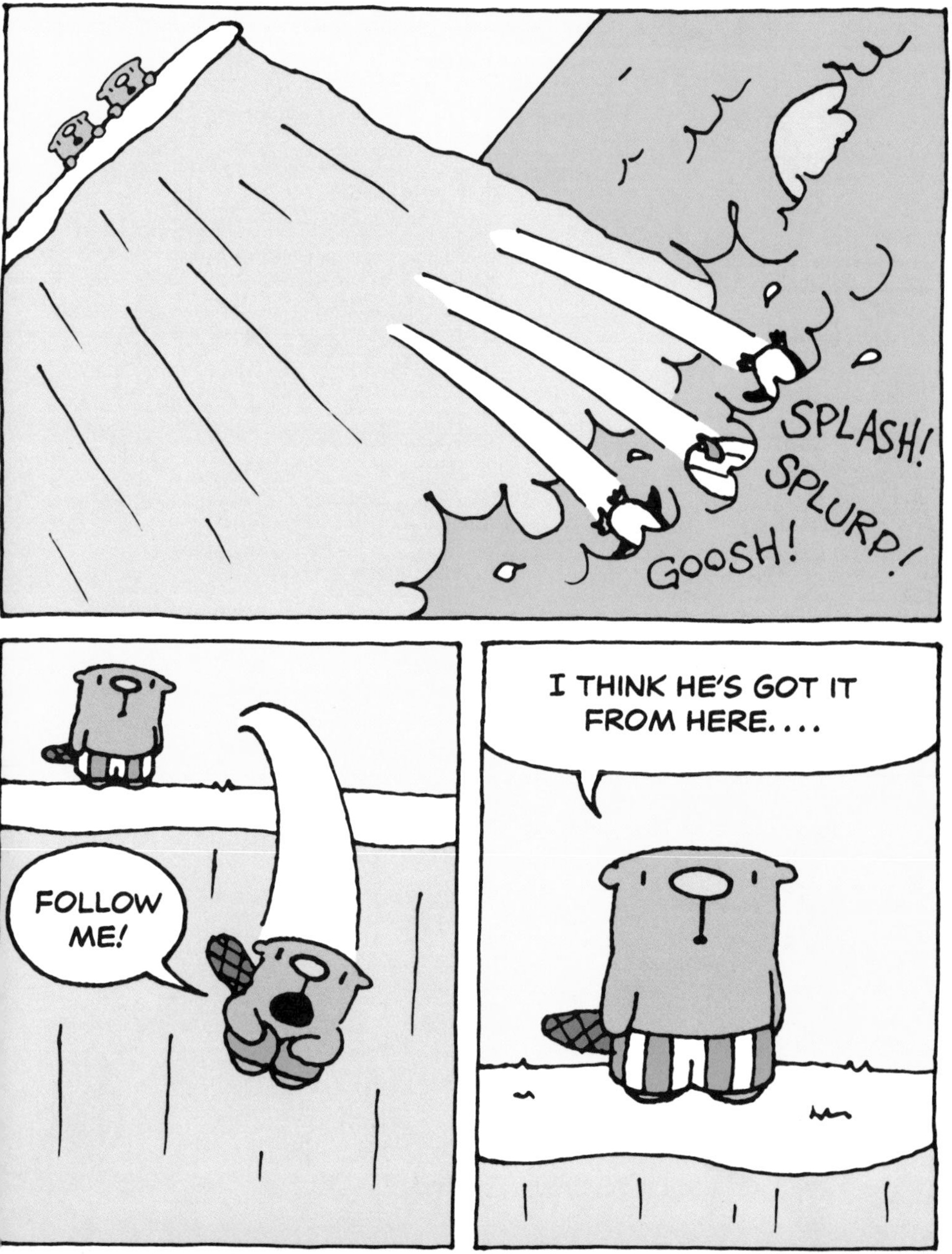
SPLASH!
SPLURP!
GOOSH!
FOLLOW ME!
I THINK HE'S GOT IT FROM HERE. . . .

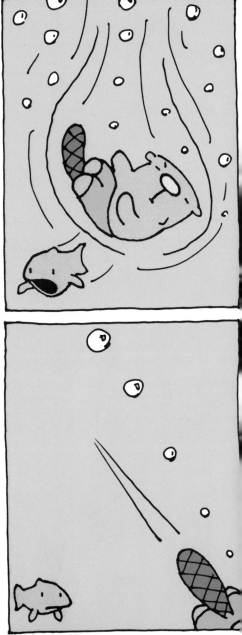

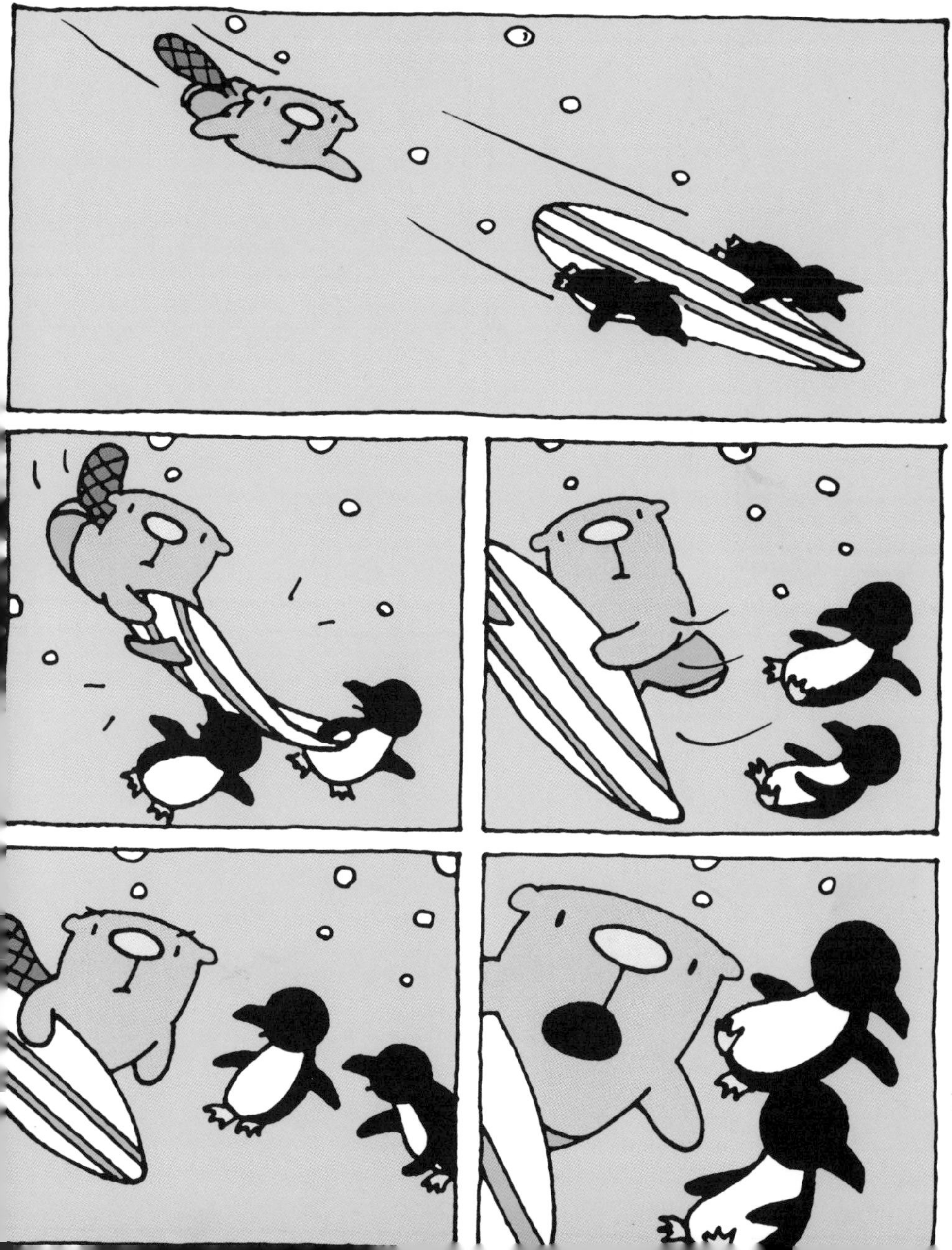

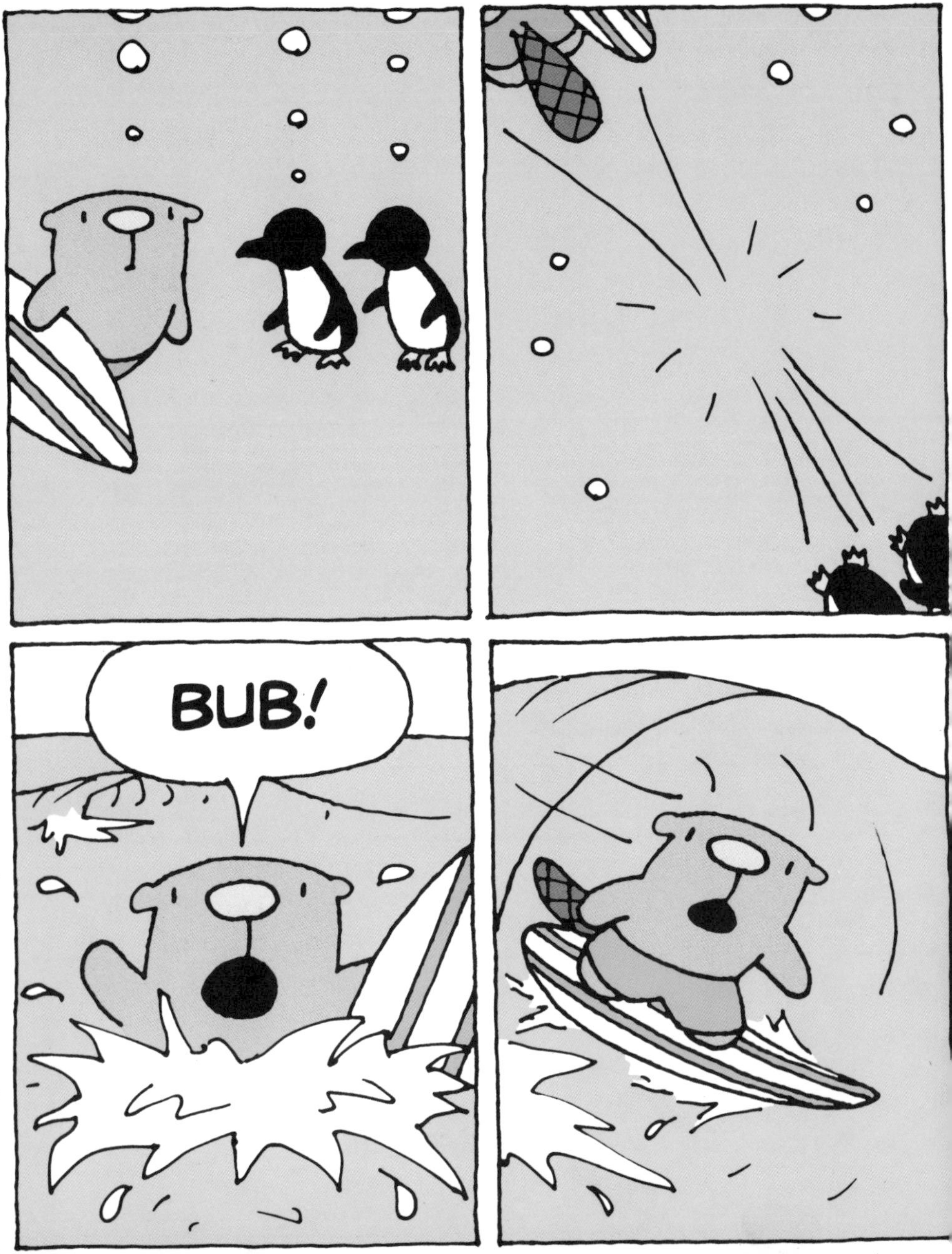
BUB!

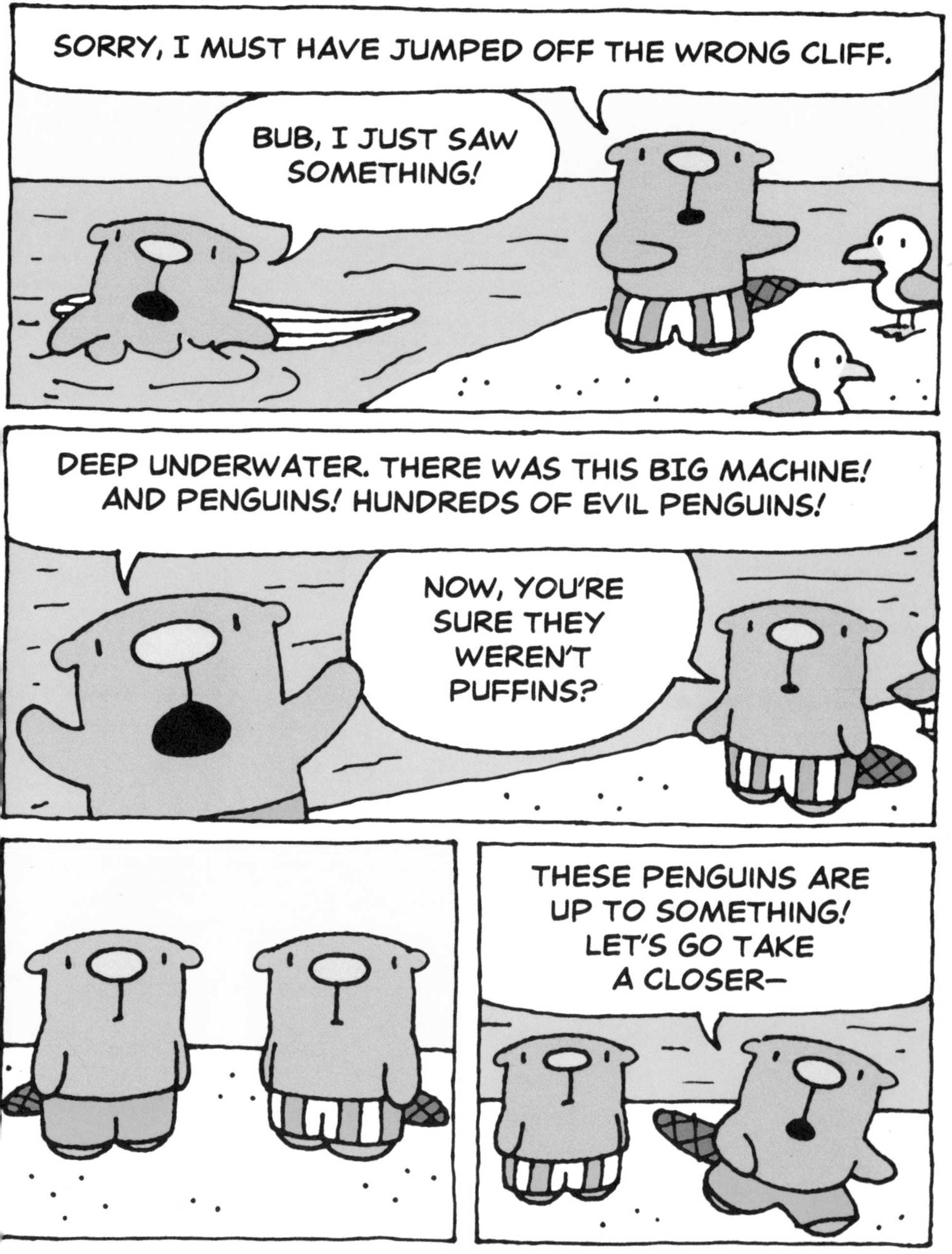
SORRY, I MUST HAVE JUMPED OFF THE WRONG CLIFF.
BUB, I JUST SAW SOMETHING!
DEEP UNDERWATER. THERE WAS THIS BIG MACHINE! AND PENGUINS! HUNDREDS OF EVIL PENGUINS!
NOW, YOU'RE SURE THEY WEREN'T PUFFINS?
THESE PENGUINS ARE UP TO SOMETHING! LET'S GO TAKE A CLOSER–

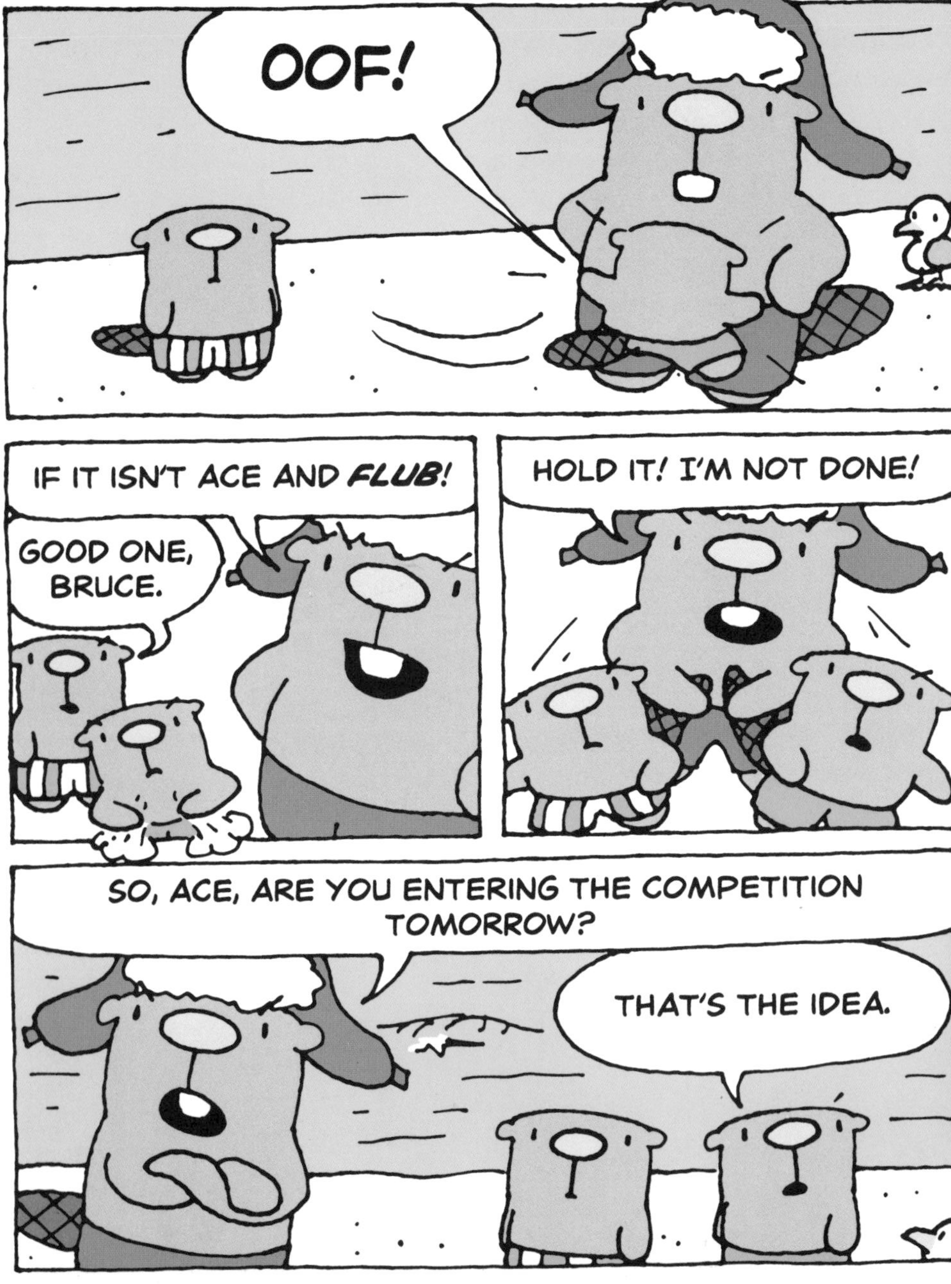
OOF!
IF IT ISN'T ACE AND *FLUB*!
GOOD ONE, BRUCE.
HOLD IT! I'M NOT DONE!
SO, ACE, ARE YOU ENTERING THE COMPETITION TOMORROW?
THAT'S THE IDEA.

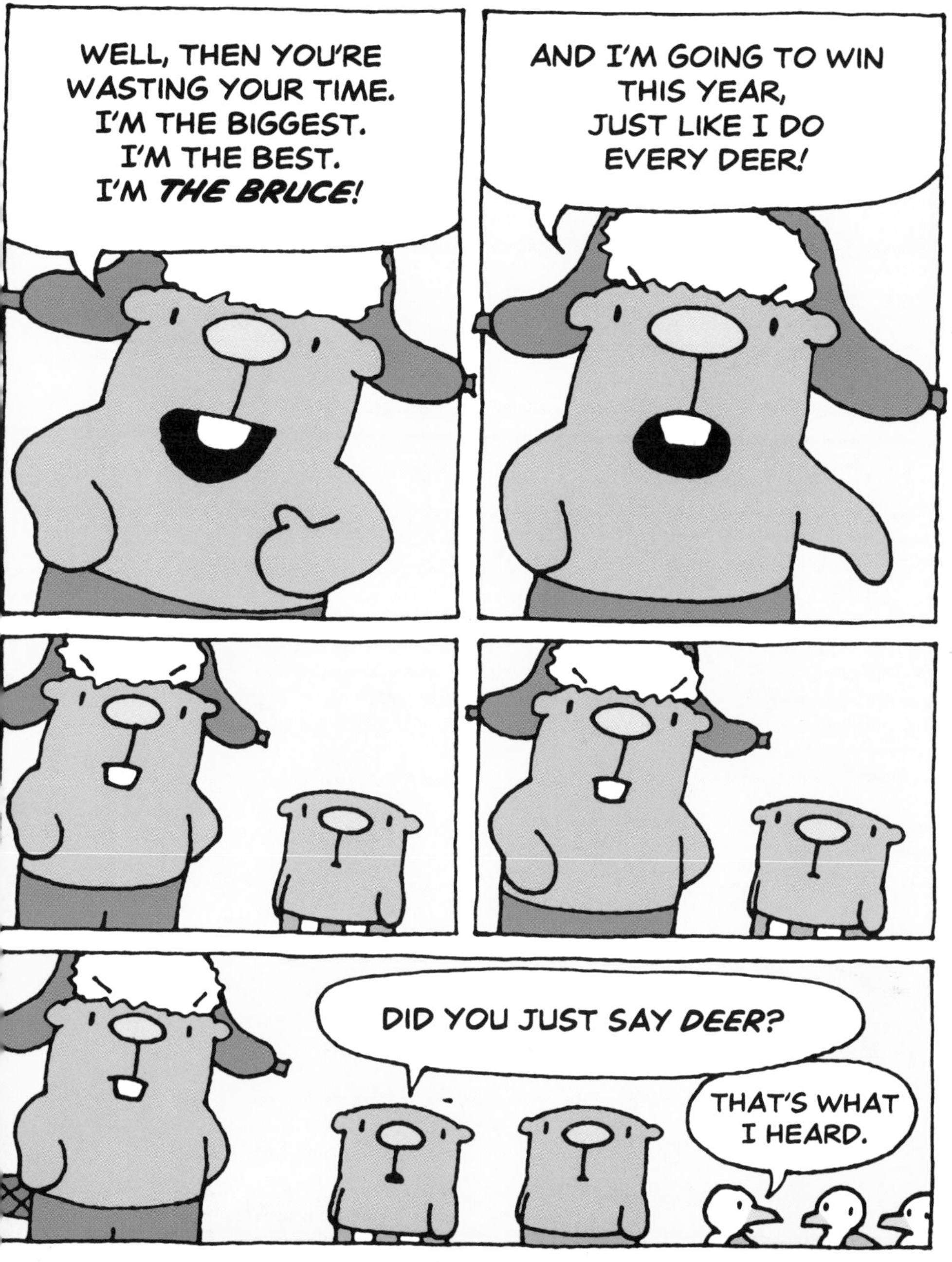
WELL, THEN YOU'RE WASTING YOUR TIME. I'M THE BIGGEST. I'M THE BEST. I'M *THE BRUCE*!
AND I'M GOING TO WIN THIS YEAR, JUST LIKE I DO EVERY DEER!
DID YOU JUST SAY *DEER*?
THAT'S WHAT I HEARD.

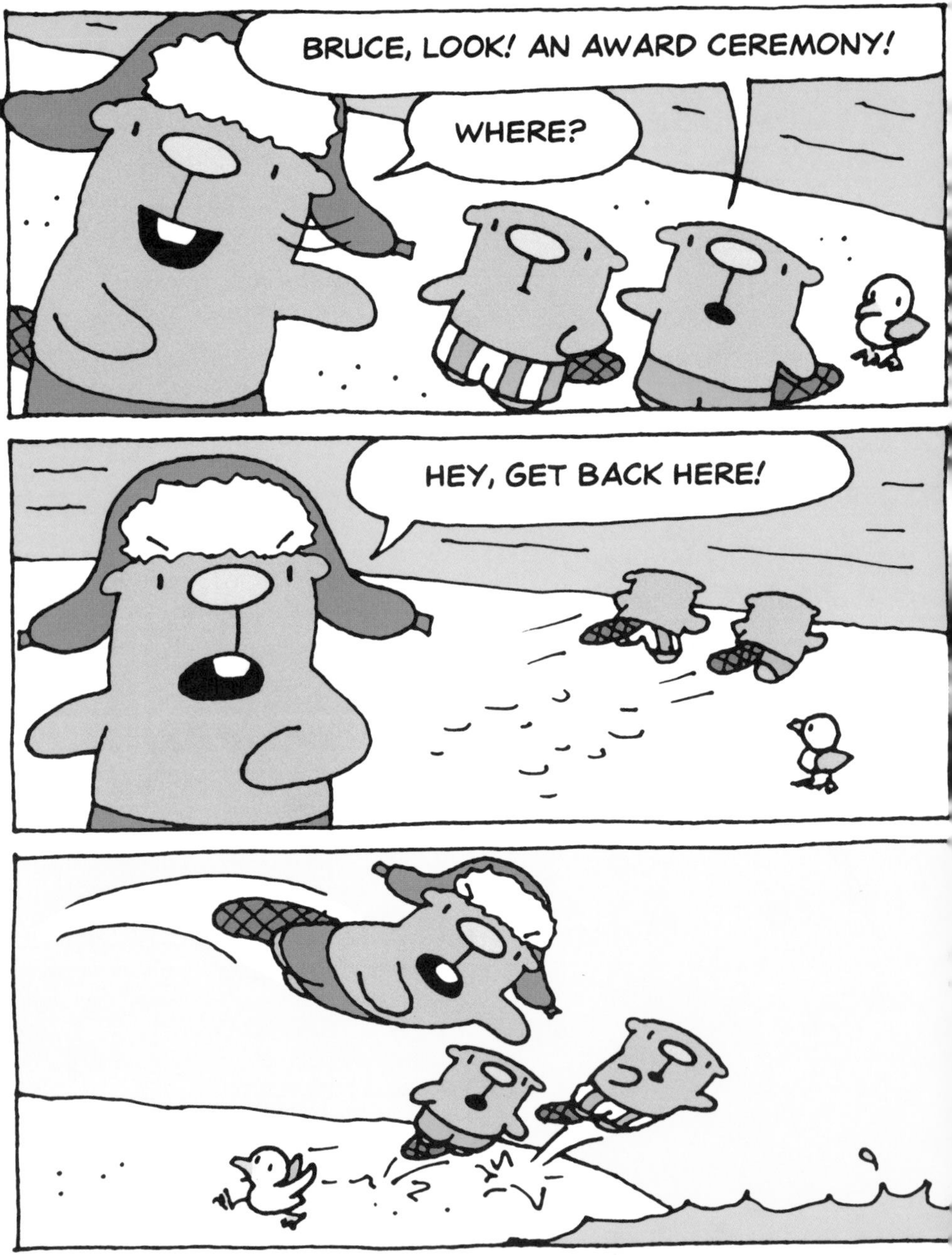
BRUCE, LOOK! AN AWARD CEREMONY!
WHERE?
HEY, GET BACK HERE!

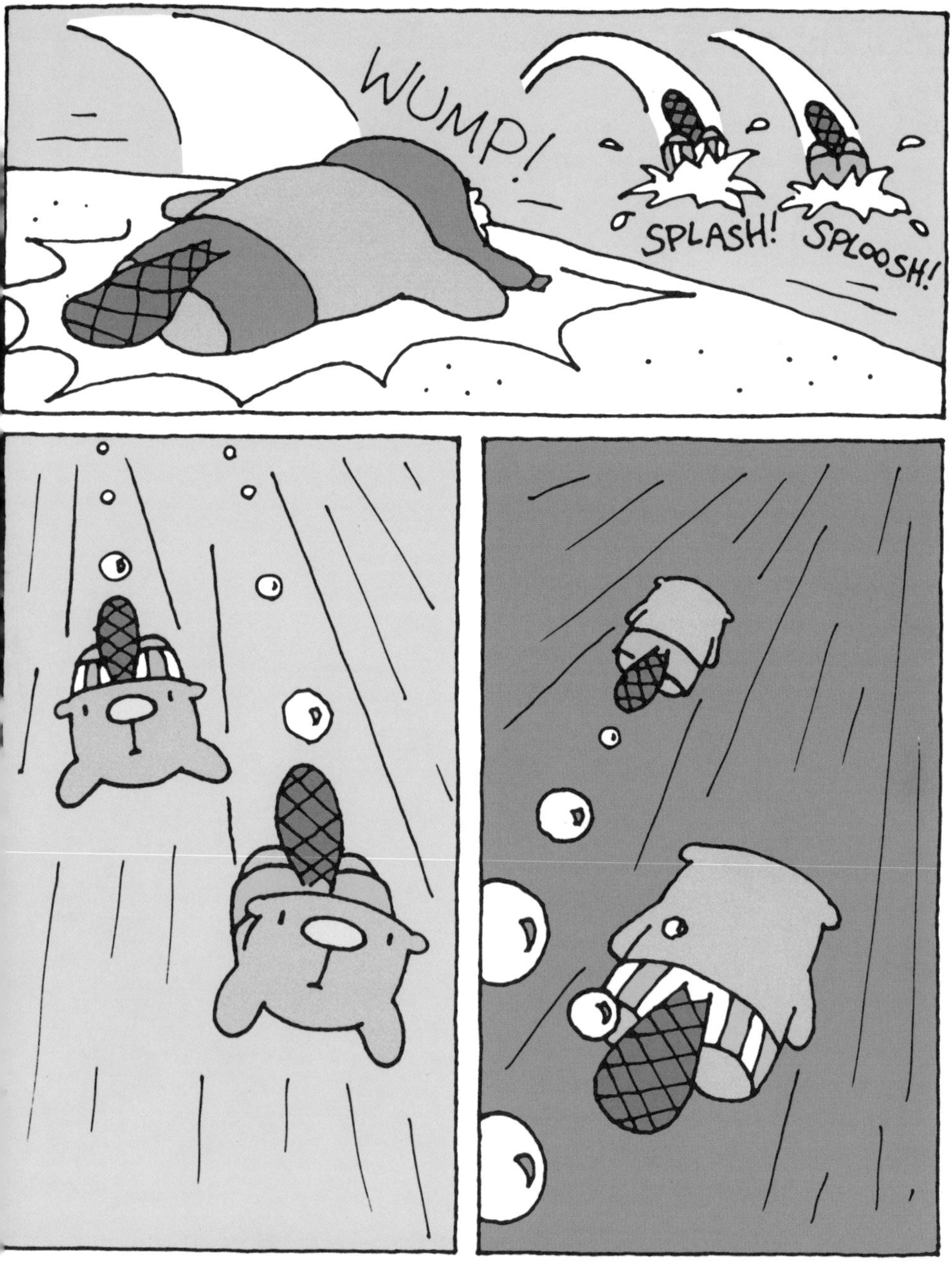
WUMP!
SPLASH!
SPLOOSH!

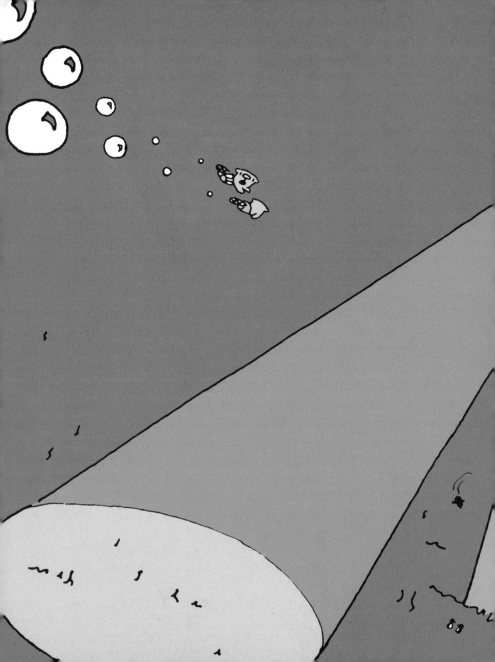

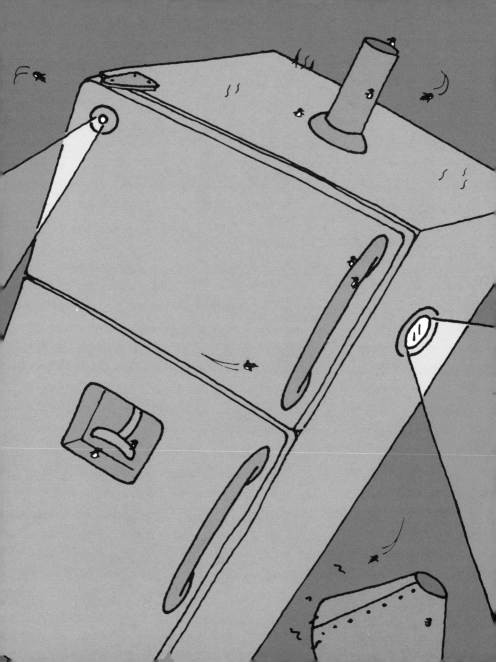

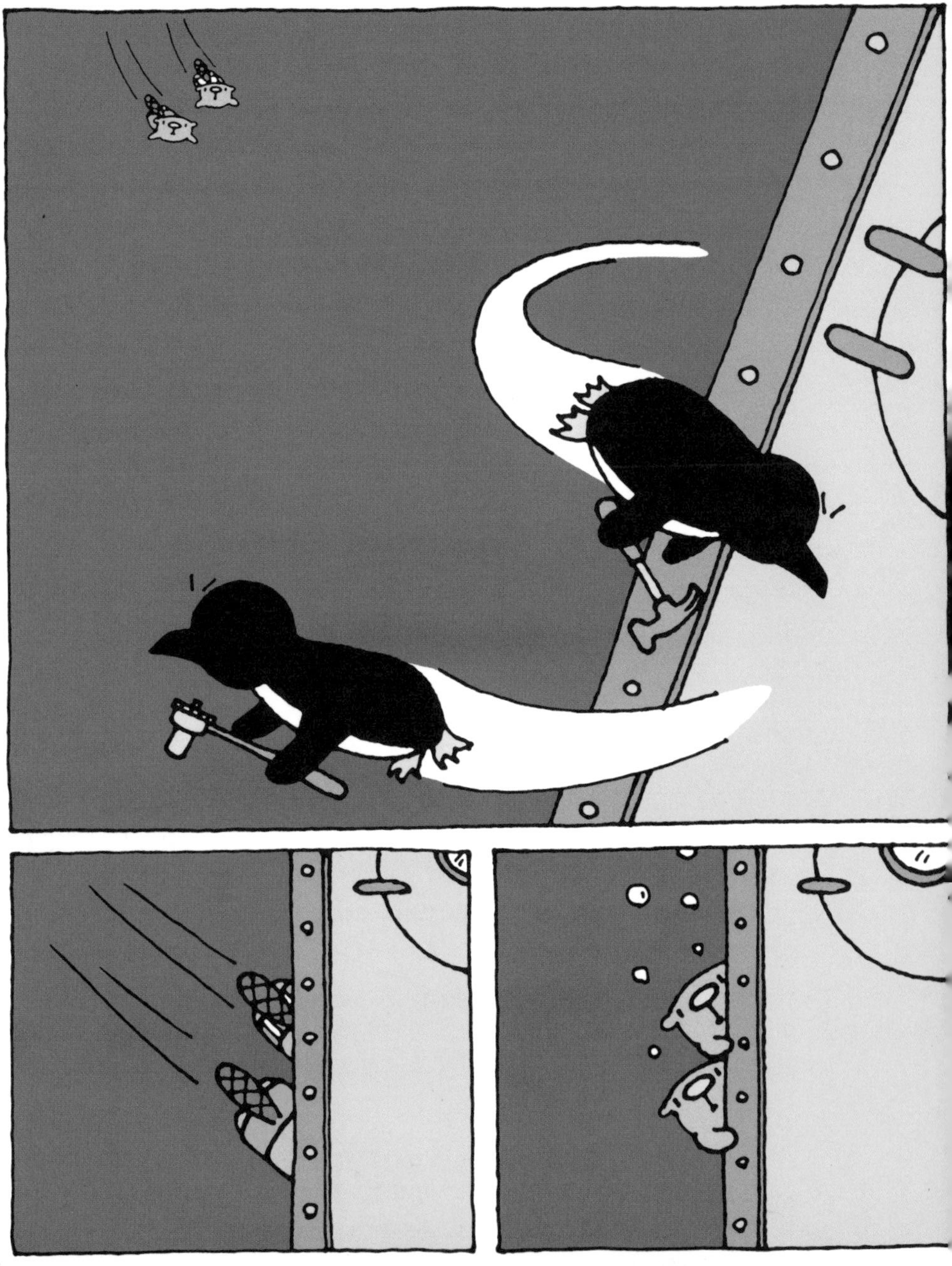

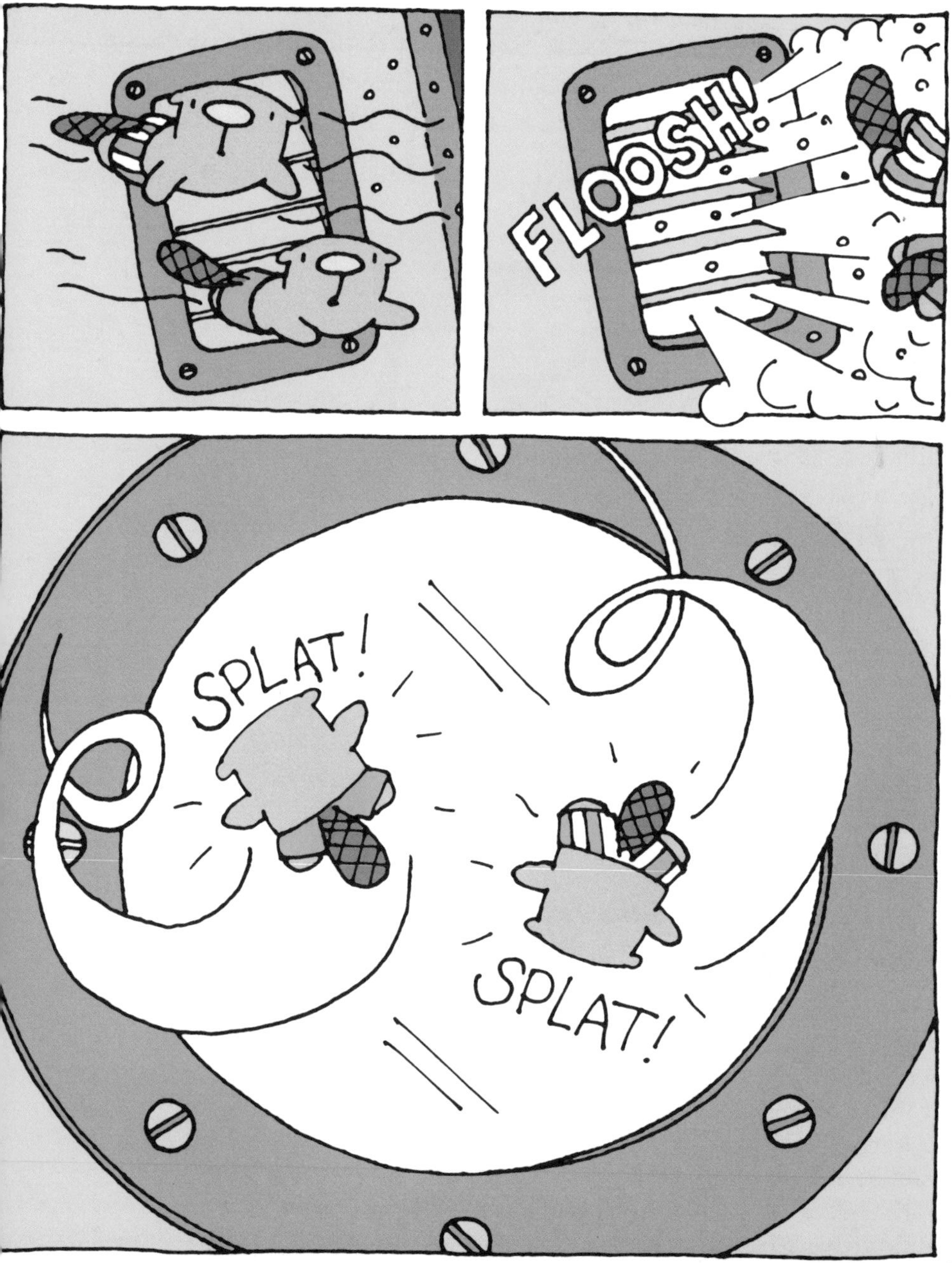
FLOOSH!
SPLAT!
SPLAT!

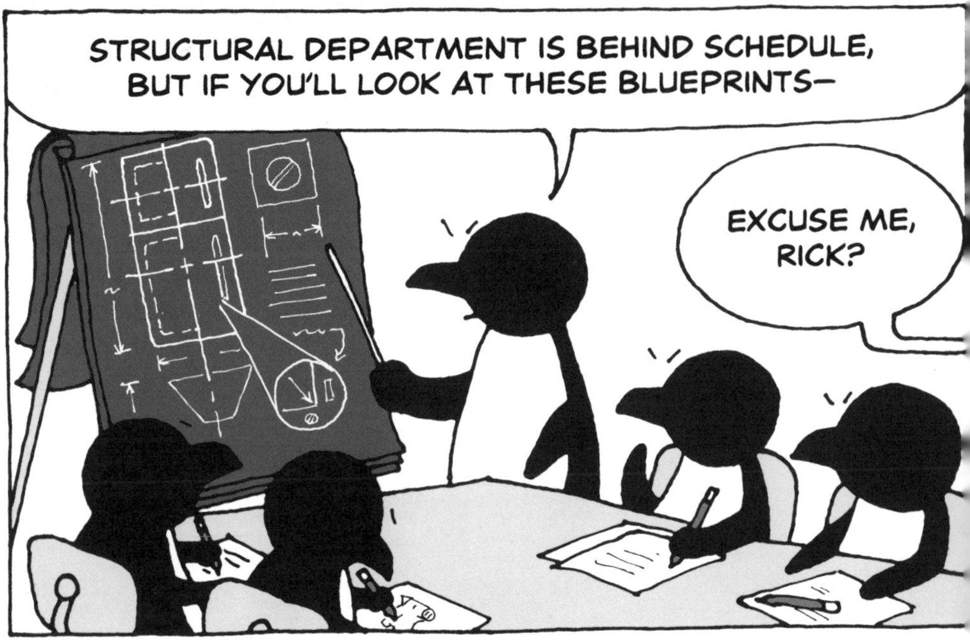
STRUCTURAL DEPARTMENT IS BEHIND SCHEDULE, BUT IF YOU'LL LOOK AT THESE BLUEPRINTS—
EXCUSE ME, RICK?

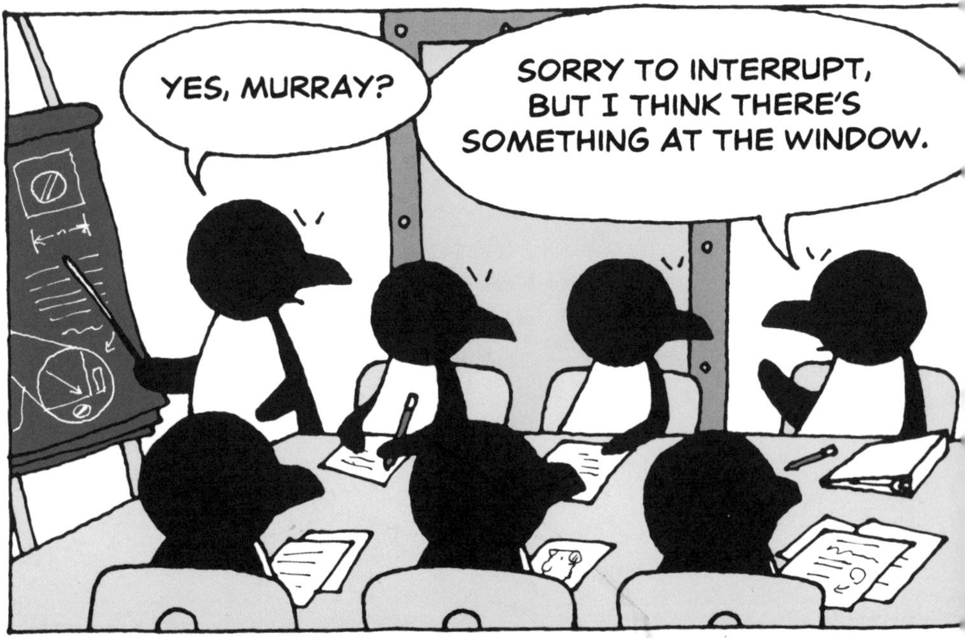
YES, MURRAY?
SORRY TO INTERRUPT, BUT I THINK THERE'S SOMETHING AT THE WINDOW.

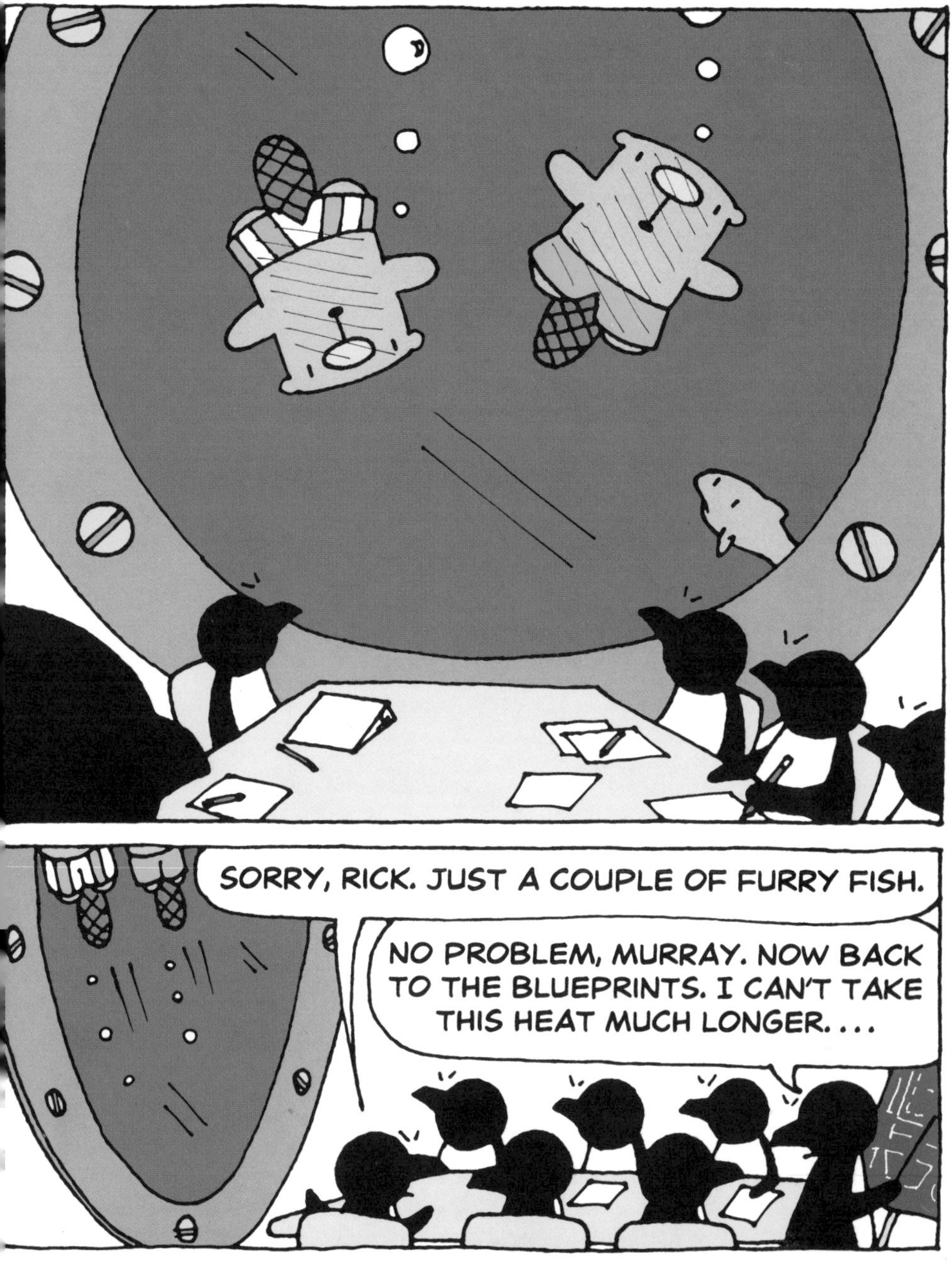
SORRY, RICK. JUST A COUPLE OF FURRY FISH.
NO PROBLEM, MURRAY. NOW BACK TO THE BLUEPRINTS. I CAN'T TAKE THIS HEAT MUCH LONGER. . . .

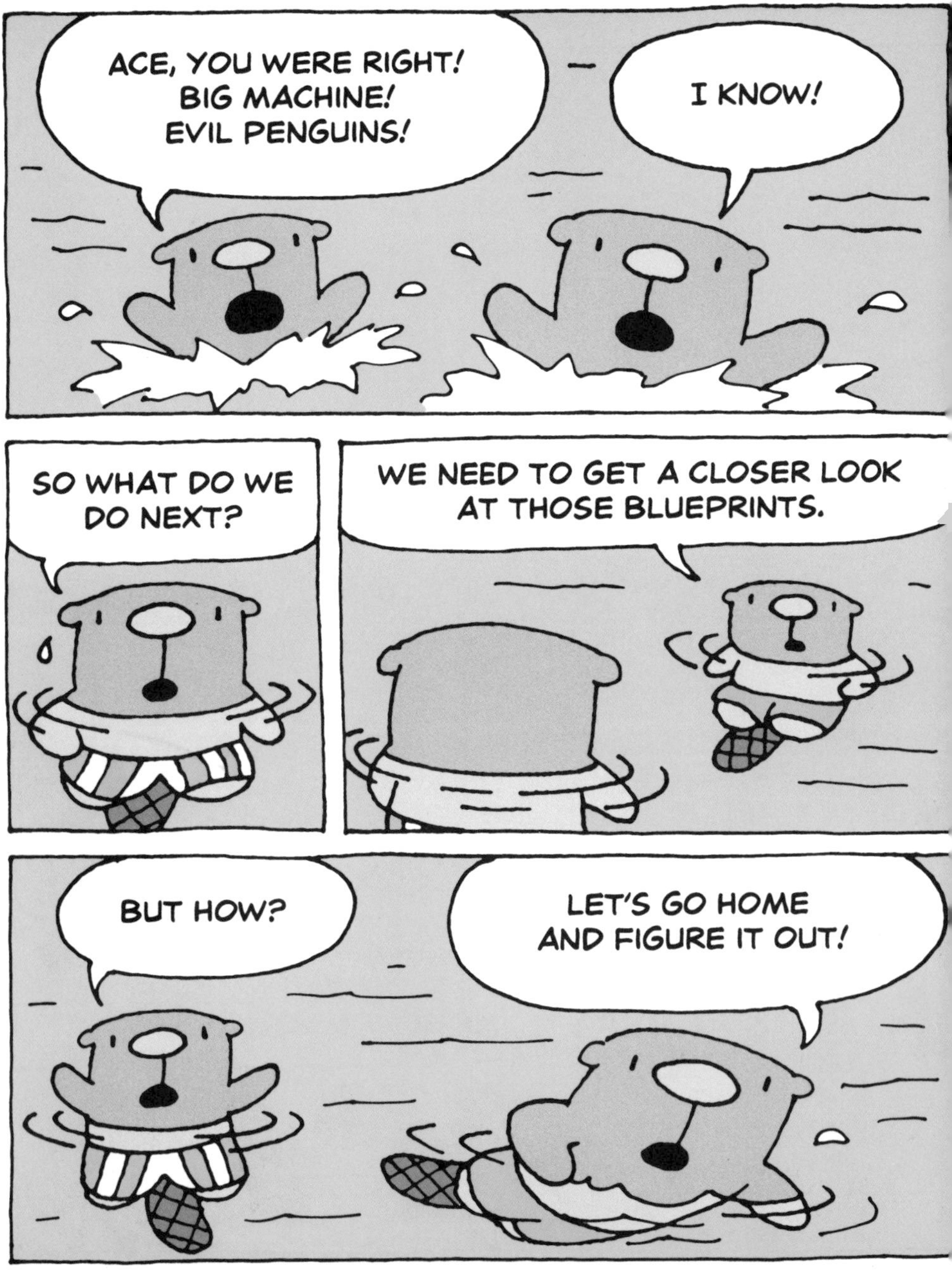
ACE, YOU WERE RIGHT! BIG MACHINE! EVIL PENGUINS!
I KNOW!
SO WHAT DO WE DO NEXT?
WE NEED TO GET A CLOSER LOOK AT THOSE BLUEPRINTS.
BUT HOW?
LET'S GO HOME AND FIGURE IT OUT!

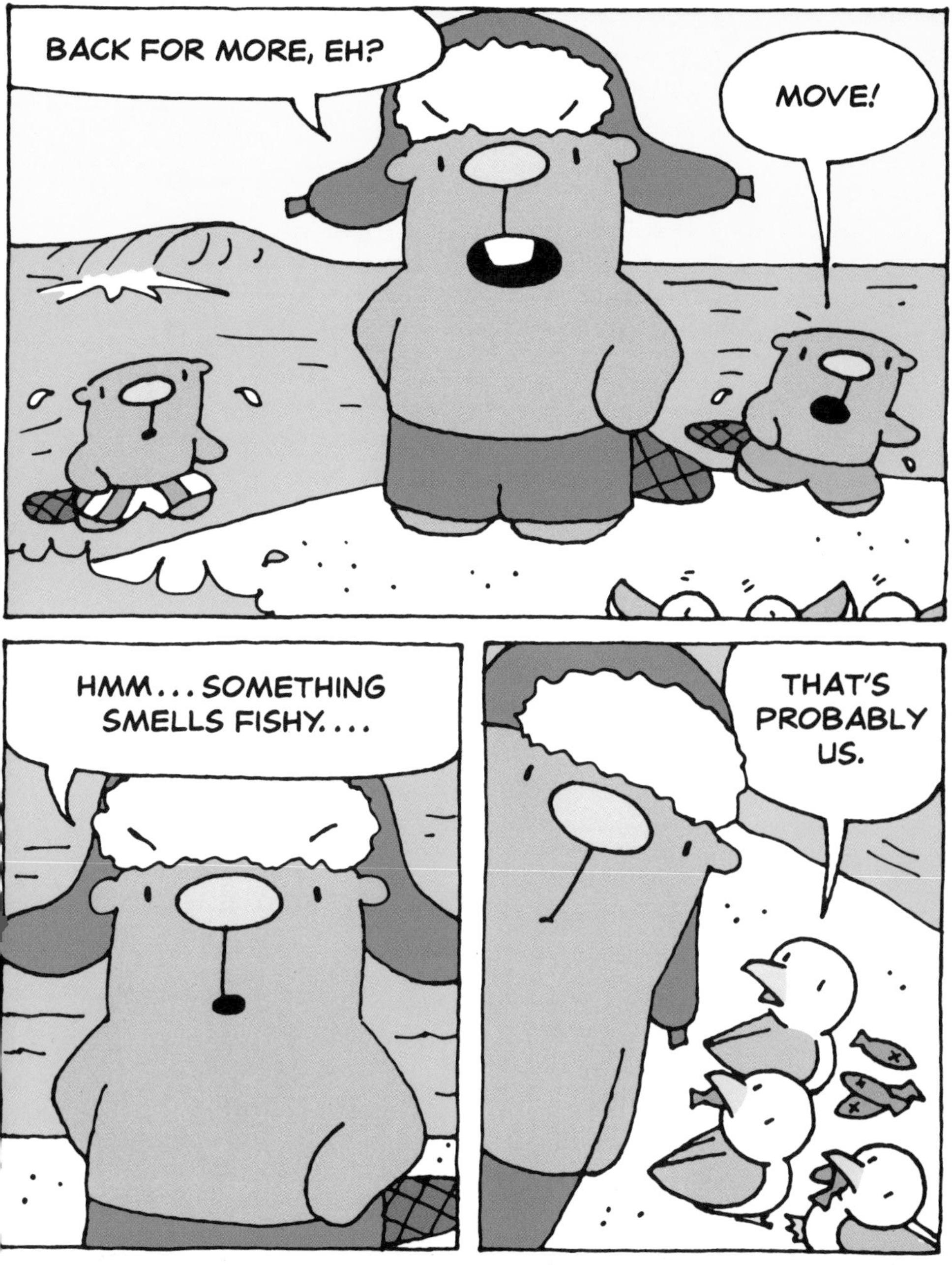
BACK FOR MORE, EH?
MOVE!
HMM...SOMETHING SMELLS FISHY....
THAT'S PROBABLY US.

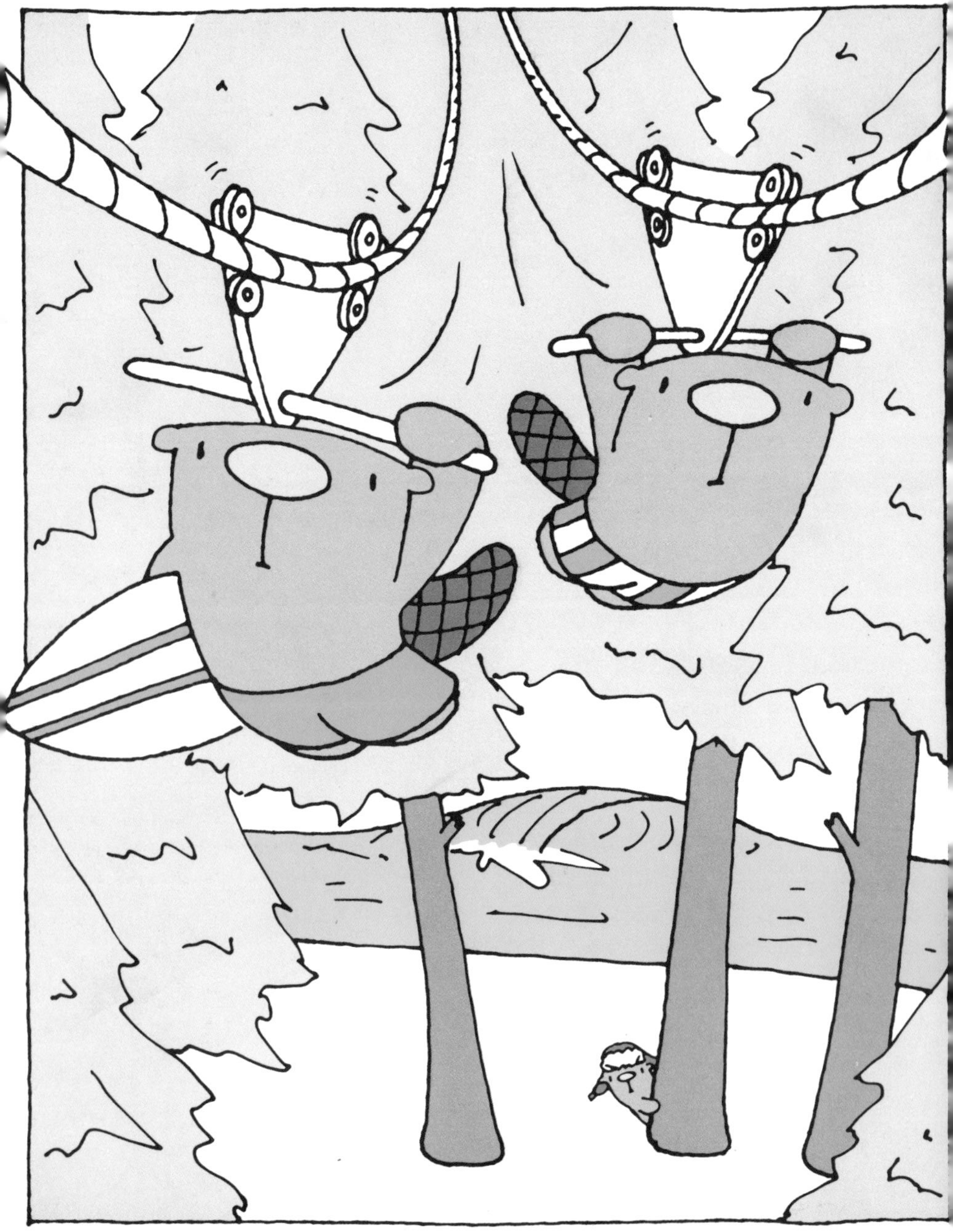

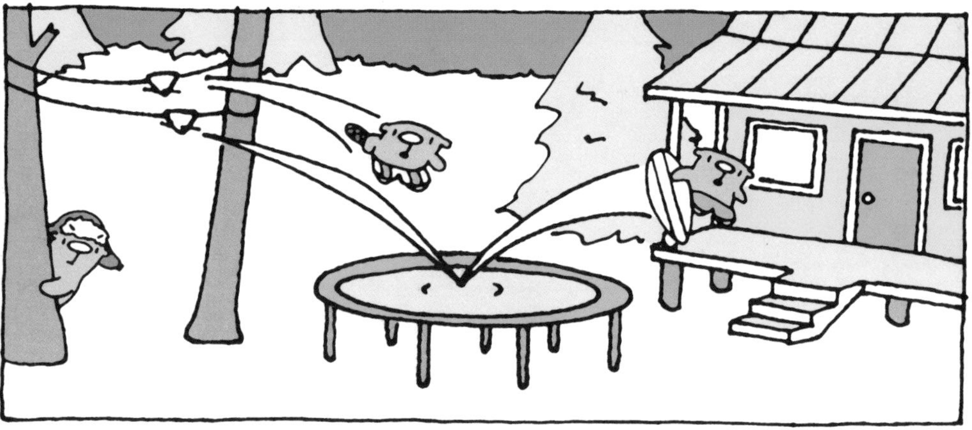

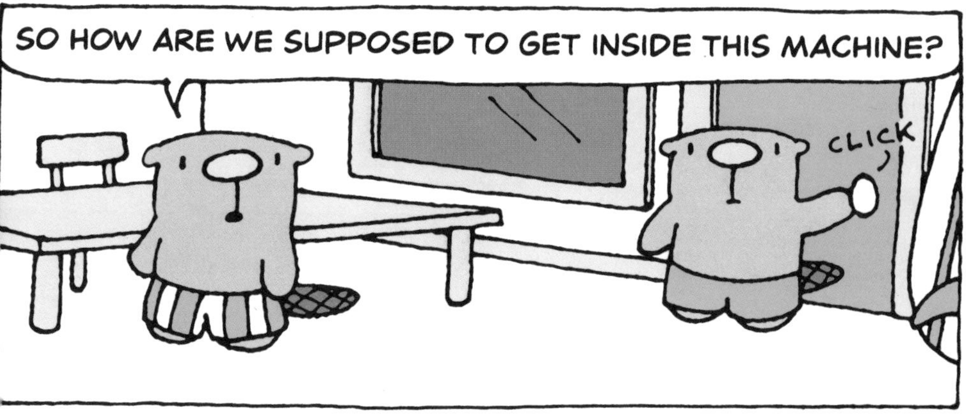

SO HOW ARE WE SUPPOSED TO GET INSIDE THIS MACHINE?
CLICK

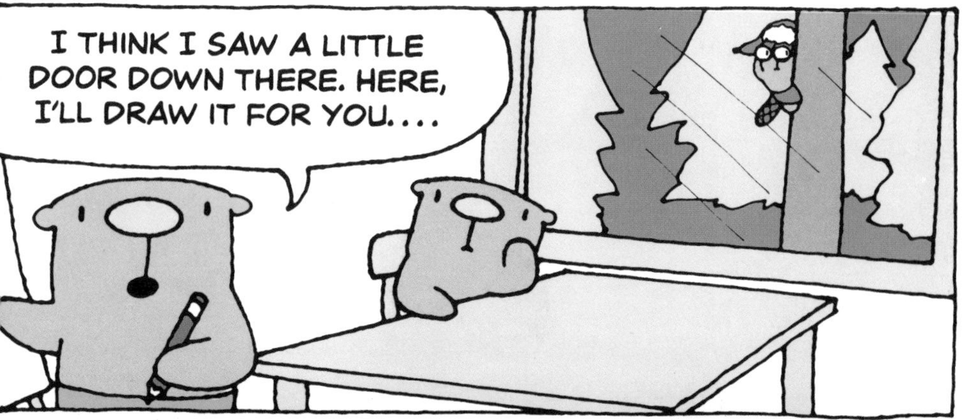

I THINK I SAW A LITTLE DOOR DOWN THERE. HERE, I'LL DRAW IT FOR YOU. . . .

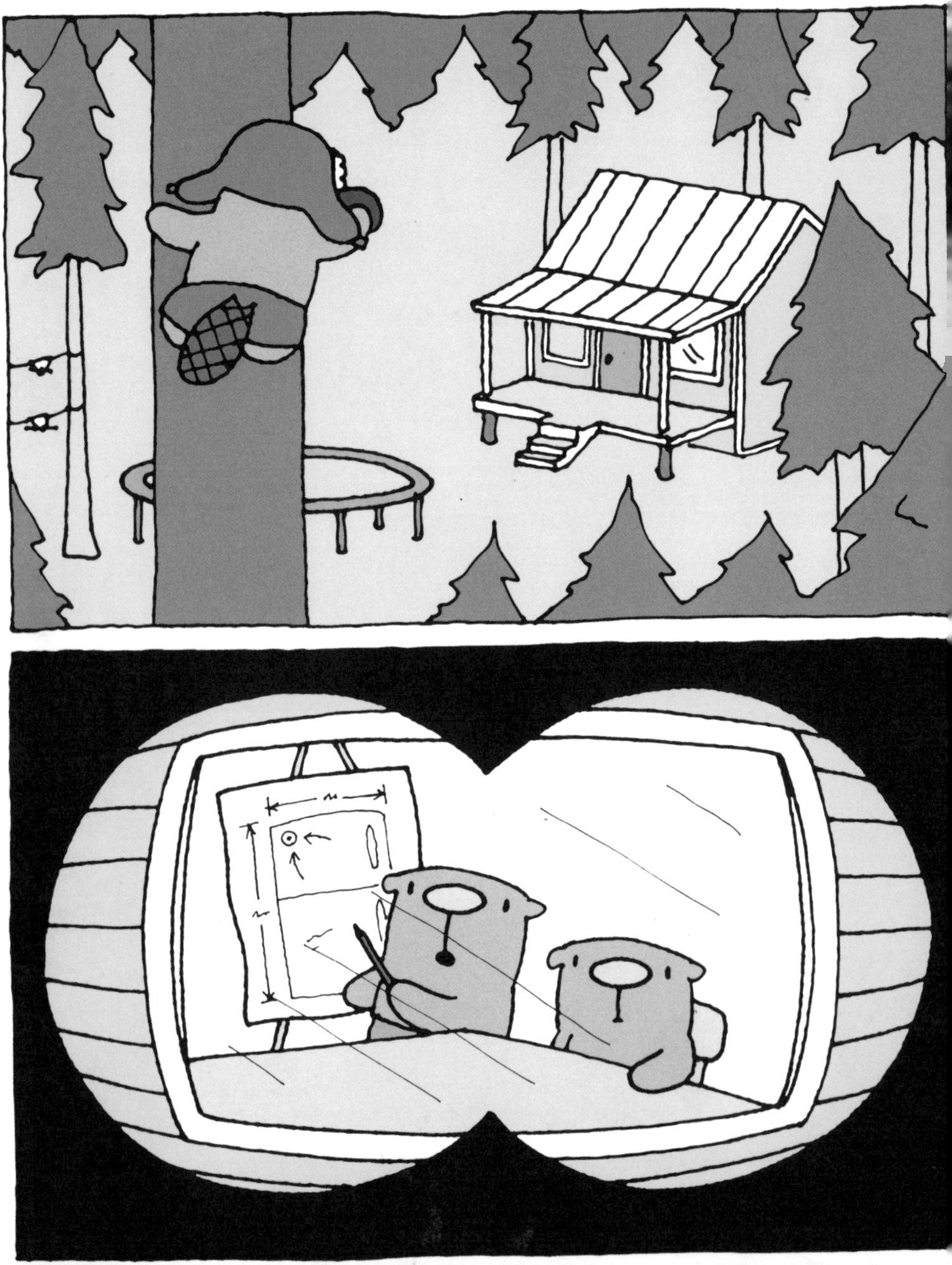

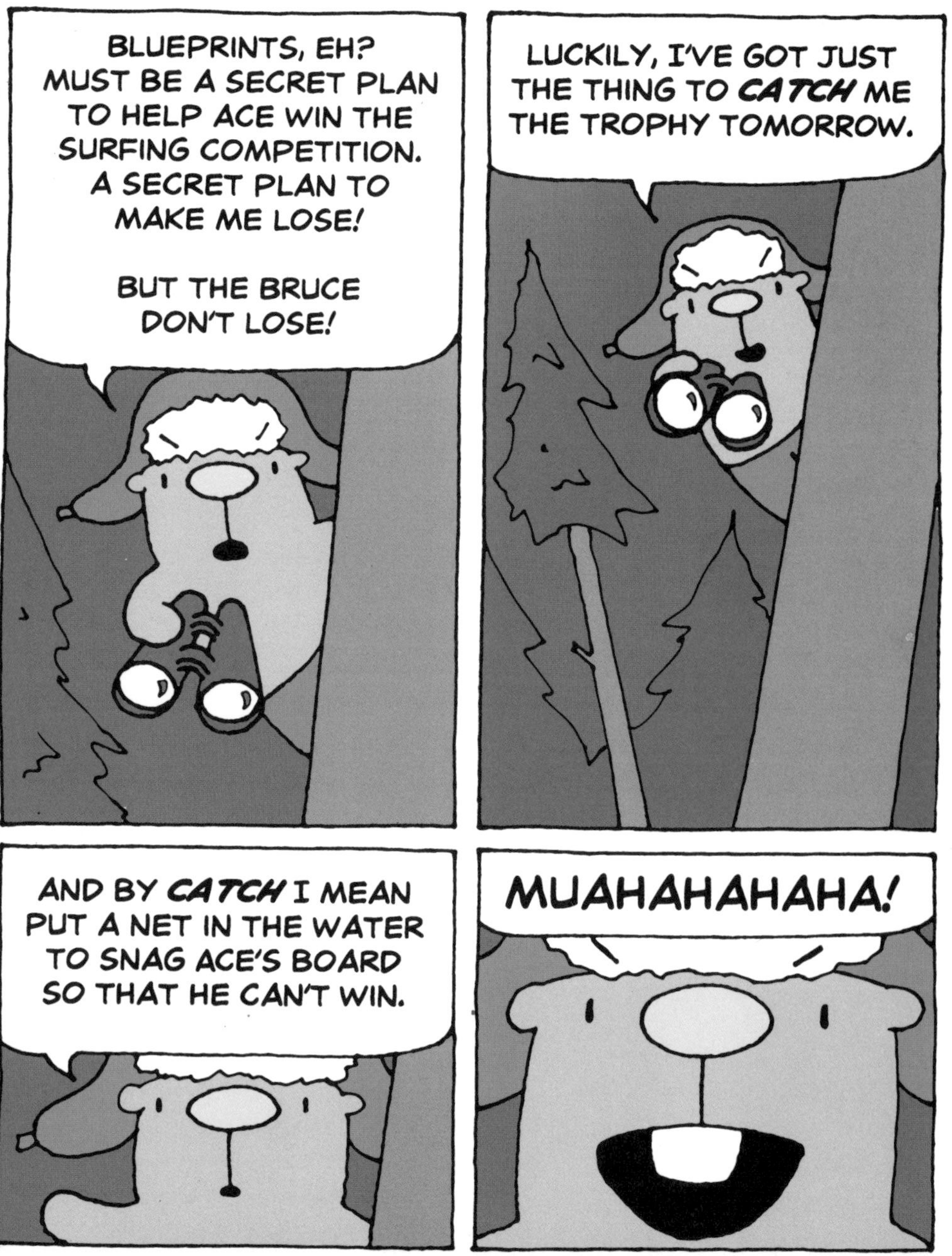
BLUEPRINTS, EH? MUST BE A SECRET PLAN TO HELP ACE WIN THE SURFING COMPETITION. A SECRET PLAN TO MAKE ME LOSE!
BUT THE BRUCE DON'T LOSE!
LUCKILY, I'VE GOT JUST THE THING TO *CATCH* ME THE TROPHY TOMORROW.
AND BY *CATCH* I MEAN PUT A NET IN THE WATER TO SNAG ACE'S BOARD SO THAT HE CAN'T WIN.
MUAHAHAHAHAHA!

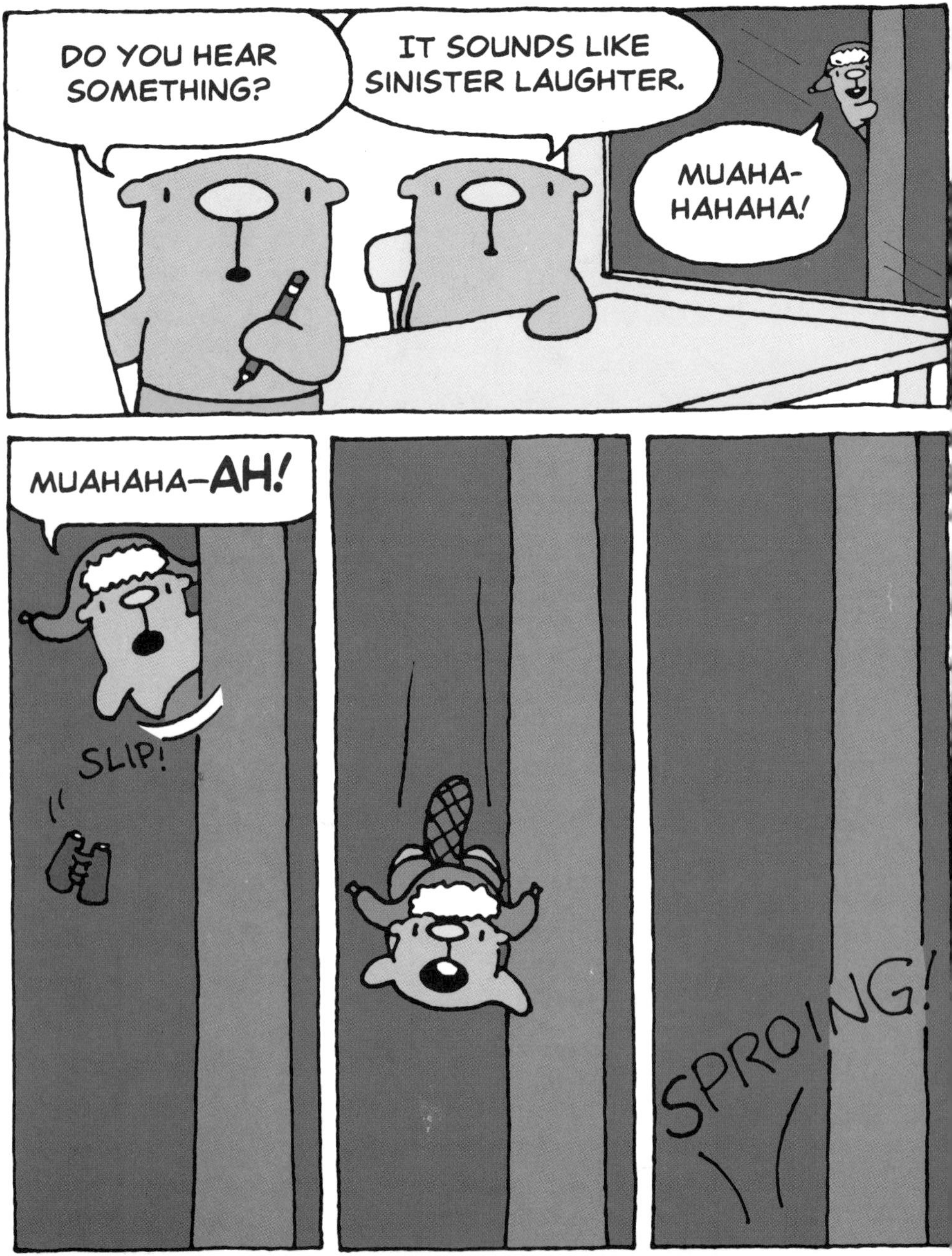
DO YOU HEAR SOMETHING?
IT SOUNDS LIKE SINISTER LAUGHTER.
MUAHA-HAHAHA!
MUAHAHA–AH!
SLIP!
SPROING!

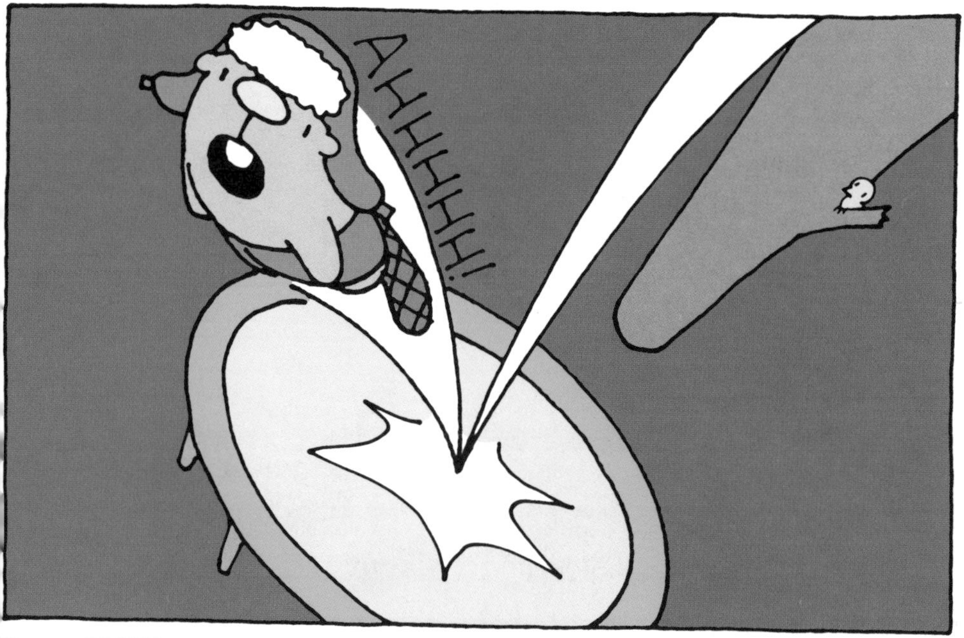
AHHHHHH!

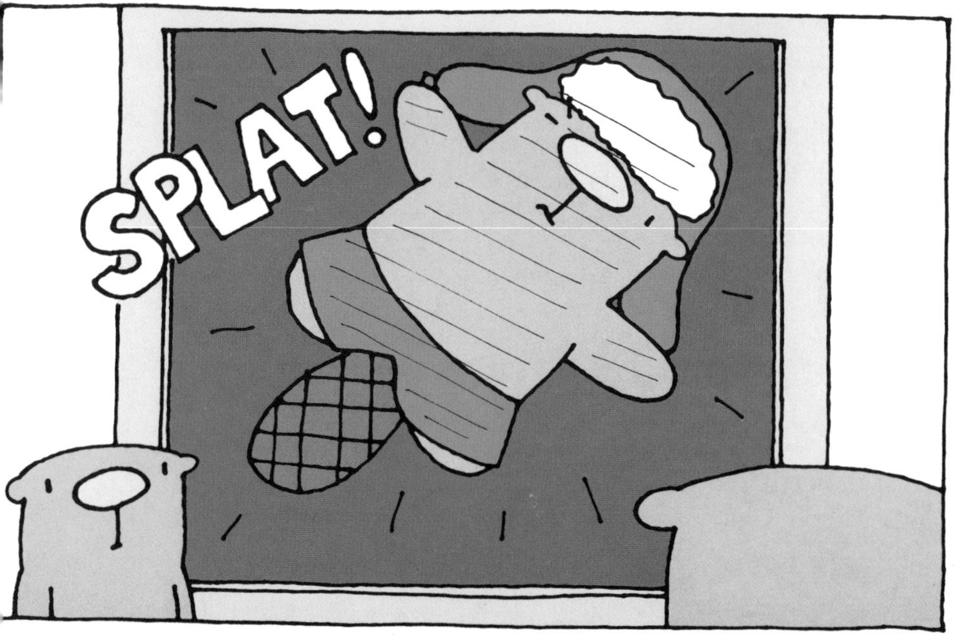
SPLAT!

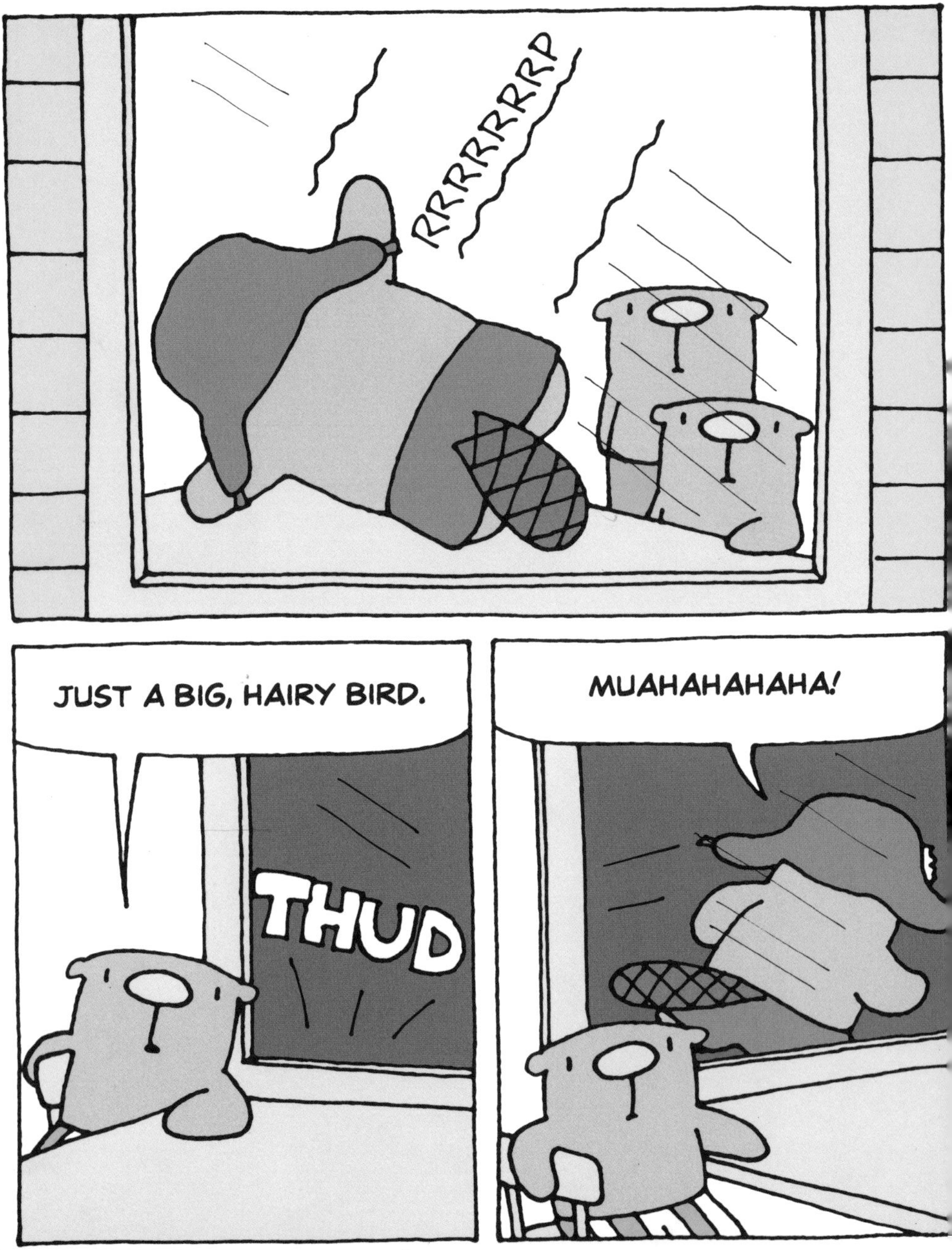
RRRRRRRRP
JUST A BIG, HAIRY BIRD.
THUD
MUAHAHAHAHA!

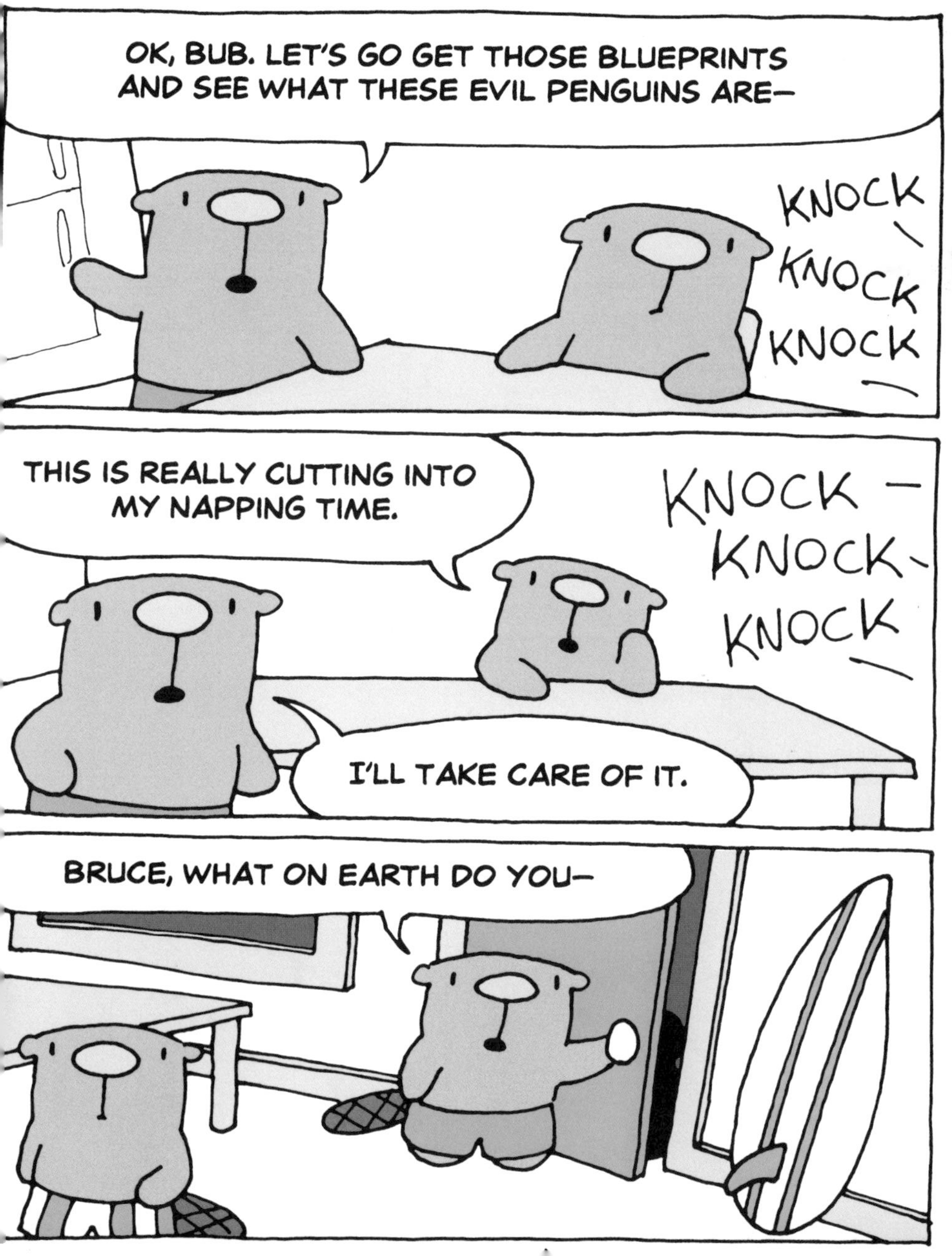

OK, BUB. LET'S GO GET THOSE BLUEPRINTS AND SEE WHAT THESE EVIL PENGUINS ARE—
KNOCK KNOCK KNOCK
THIS IS REALLY CUTTING INTO MY NAPPING TIME.
KNOCK KNOCK KNOCK
I'LL TAKE CARE OF IT.
BRUCE, WHAT ON EARTH DO YOU—

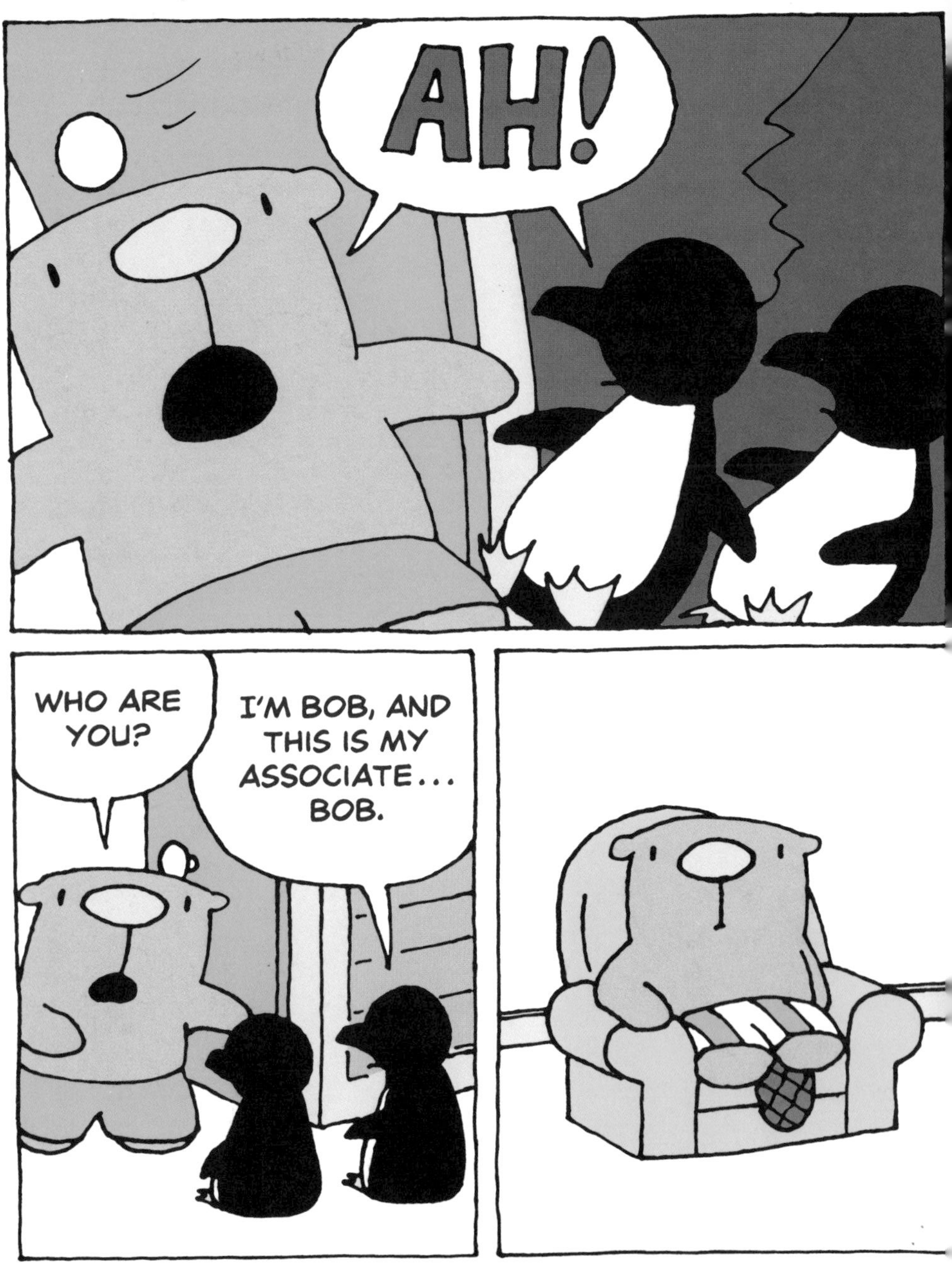
AH!
WHO ARE YOU?
I'M BOB, AND THIS IS MY ASSOCIATE... BOB.

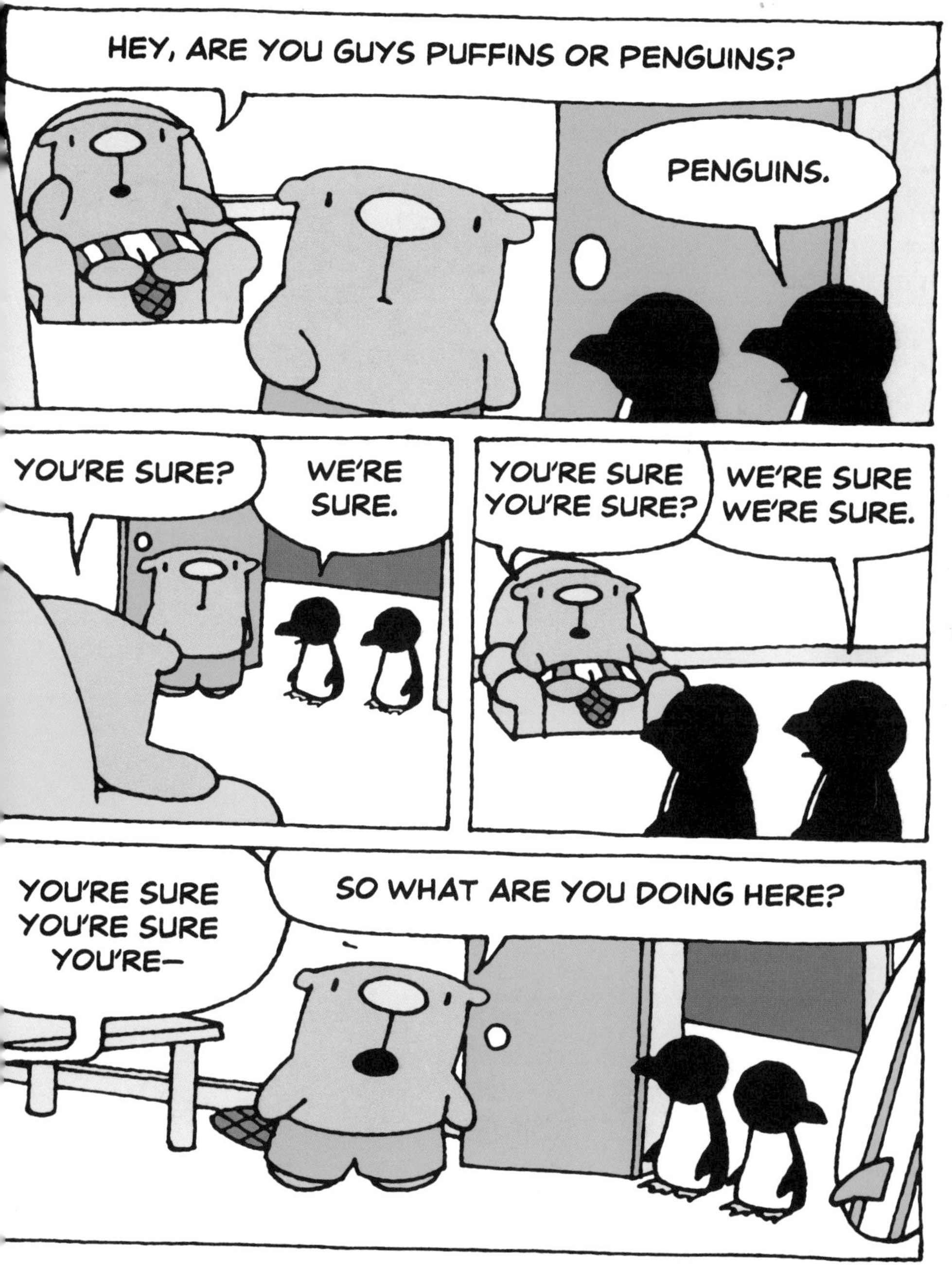
HEY, ARE YOU GUYS PUFFINS OR PENGUINS?
PENGUINS.
YOU'RE SURE?
WE'RE SURE.
YOU'RE SURE YOU'RE SURE?
WE'RE SURE WE'RE SURE.
YOU'RE SURE YOU'RE SURE YOU'RE–
SO WHAT ARE YOU DOING HERE?

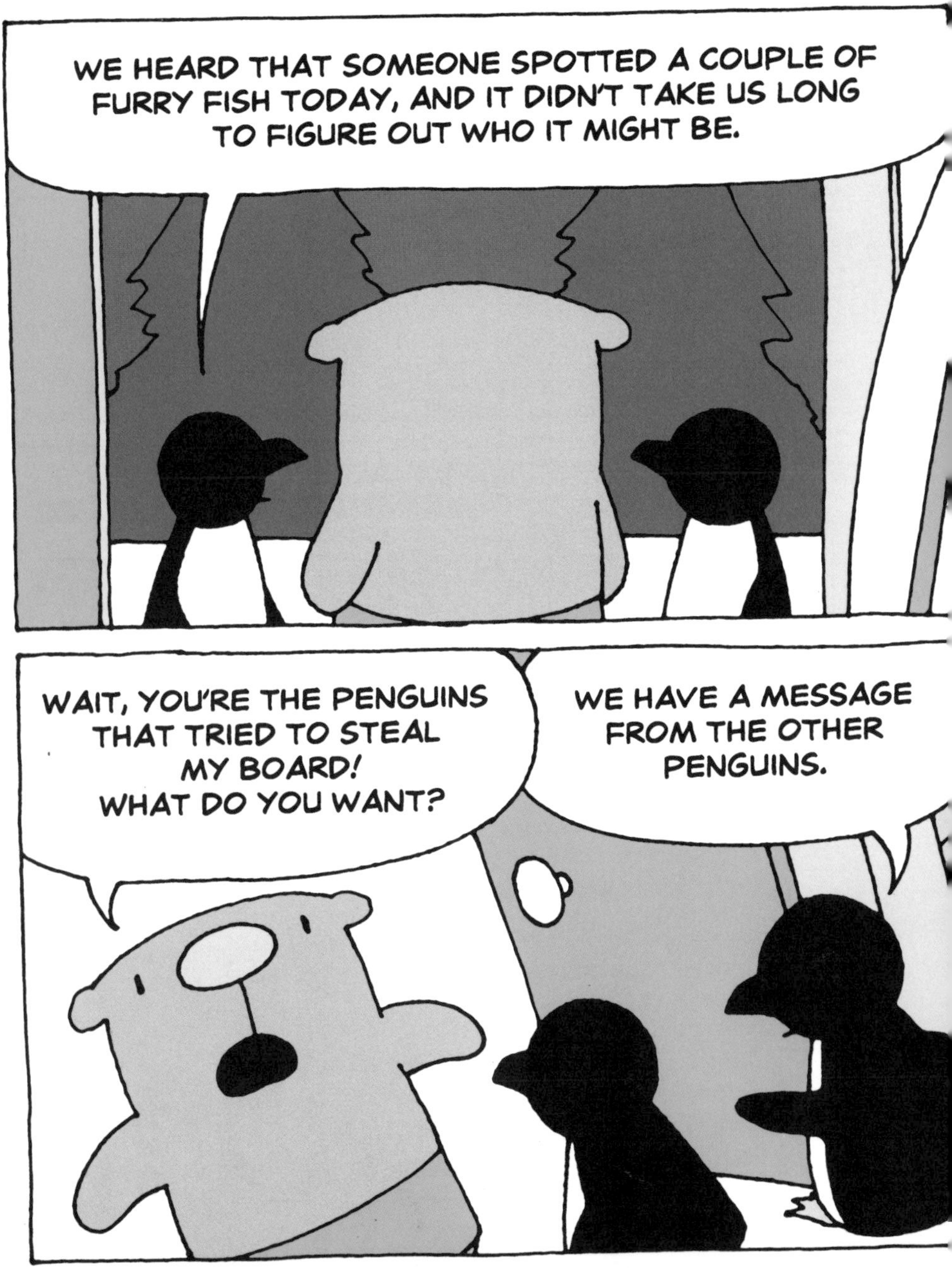
WE HEARD THAT SOMEONE SPOTTED A COUPLE OF FURRY FISH TODAY, AND IT DIDN'T TAKE US LONG TO FIGURE OUT WHO IT MIGHT BE.
WAIT, YOU'RE THE PENGUINS THAT TRIED TO STEAL MY BOARD! WHAT DO YOU WANT?
WE HAVE A MESSAGE FROM THE OTHER PENGUINS.

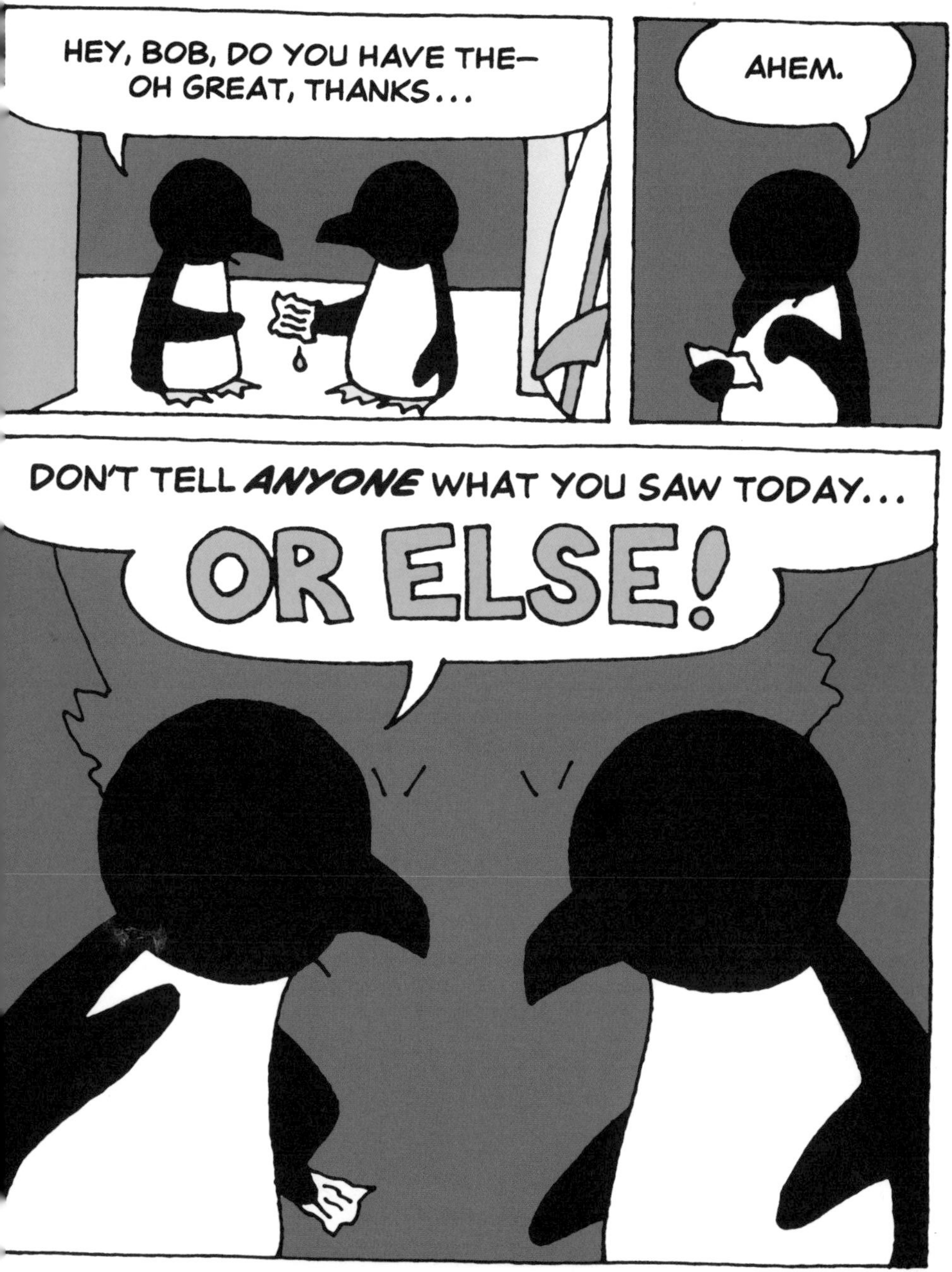
HEY, BOB, DO YOU HAVE THE—
OH GREAT, THANKS...
AHEM.
DON'T TELL ***ANYONE*** WHAT YOU SAW TODAY...
OR ELSE!

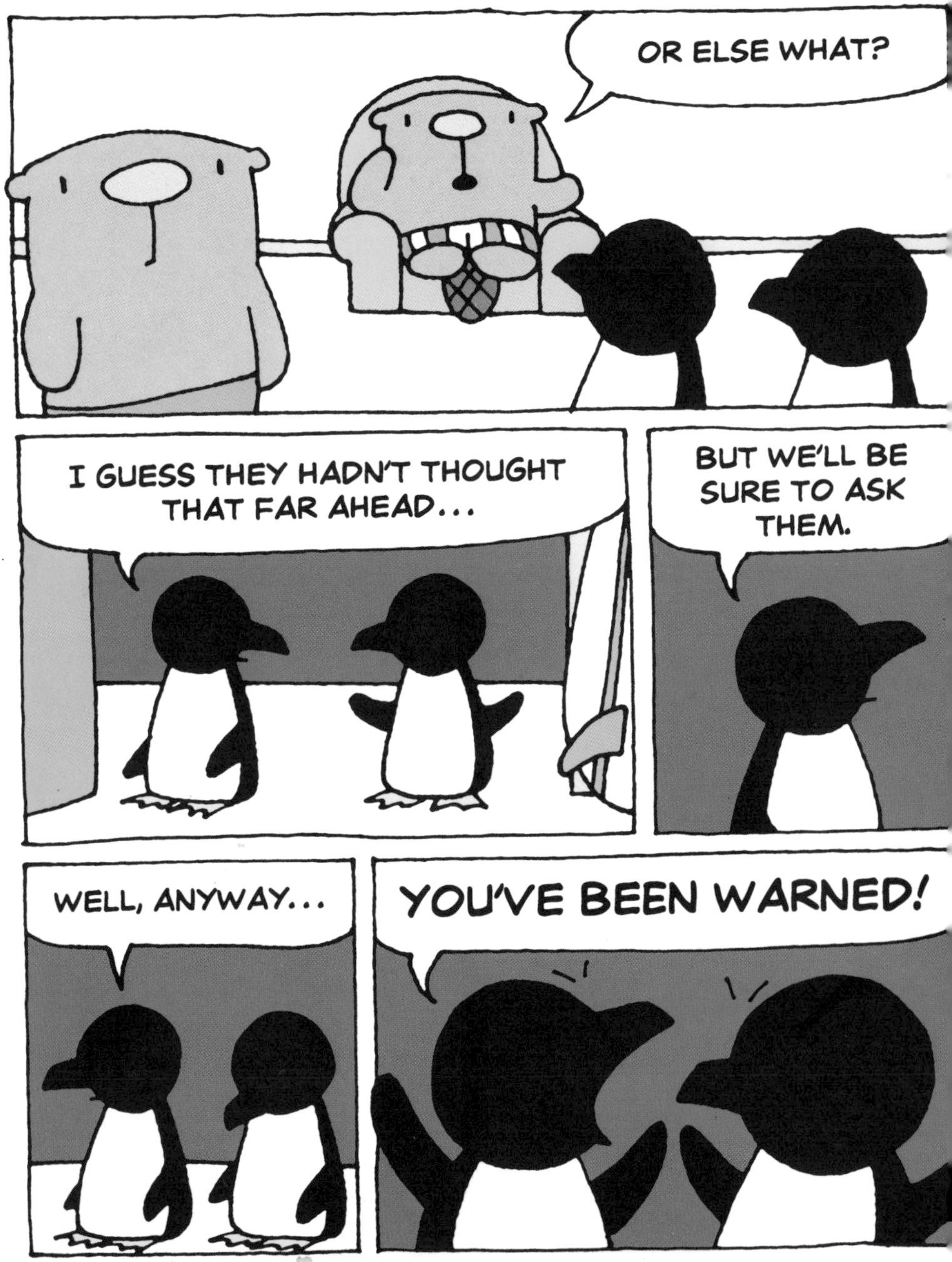
OR ELSE WHAT?
I GUESS THEY HADN'T THOUGHT THAT FAR AHEAD...
BUT WE'LL BE SURE TO ASK THEM.
WELL, ANYWAY...
YOU'VE BEEN WARNED!

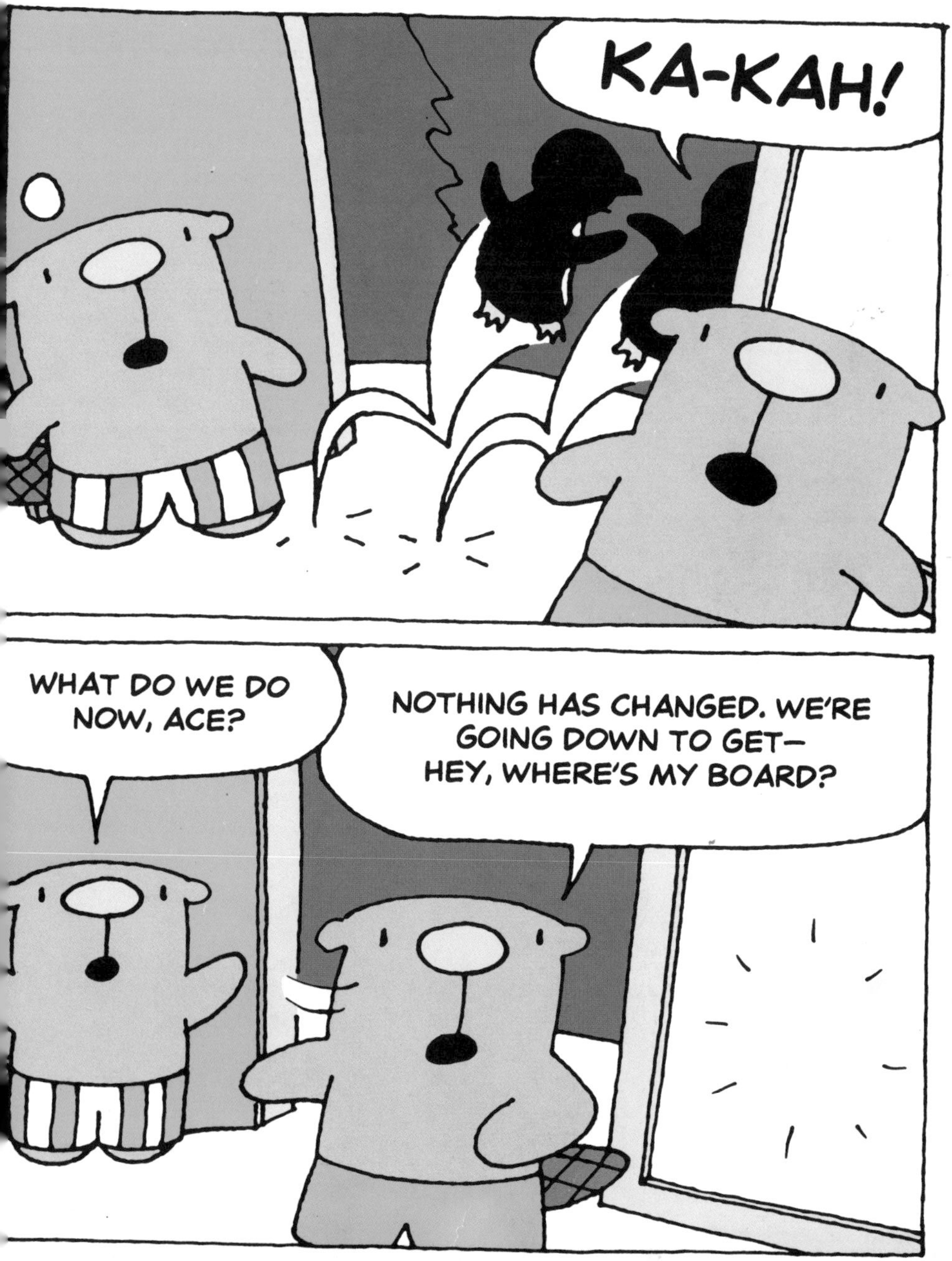
KA-KAH!
WHAT DO WE DO NOW, ACE?
NOTHING HAS CHANGED. WE'RE GOING DOWN TO GET— HEY, WHERE'S MY BOARD?

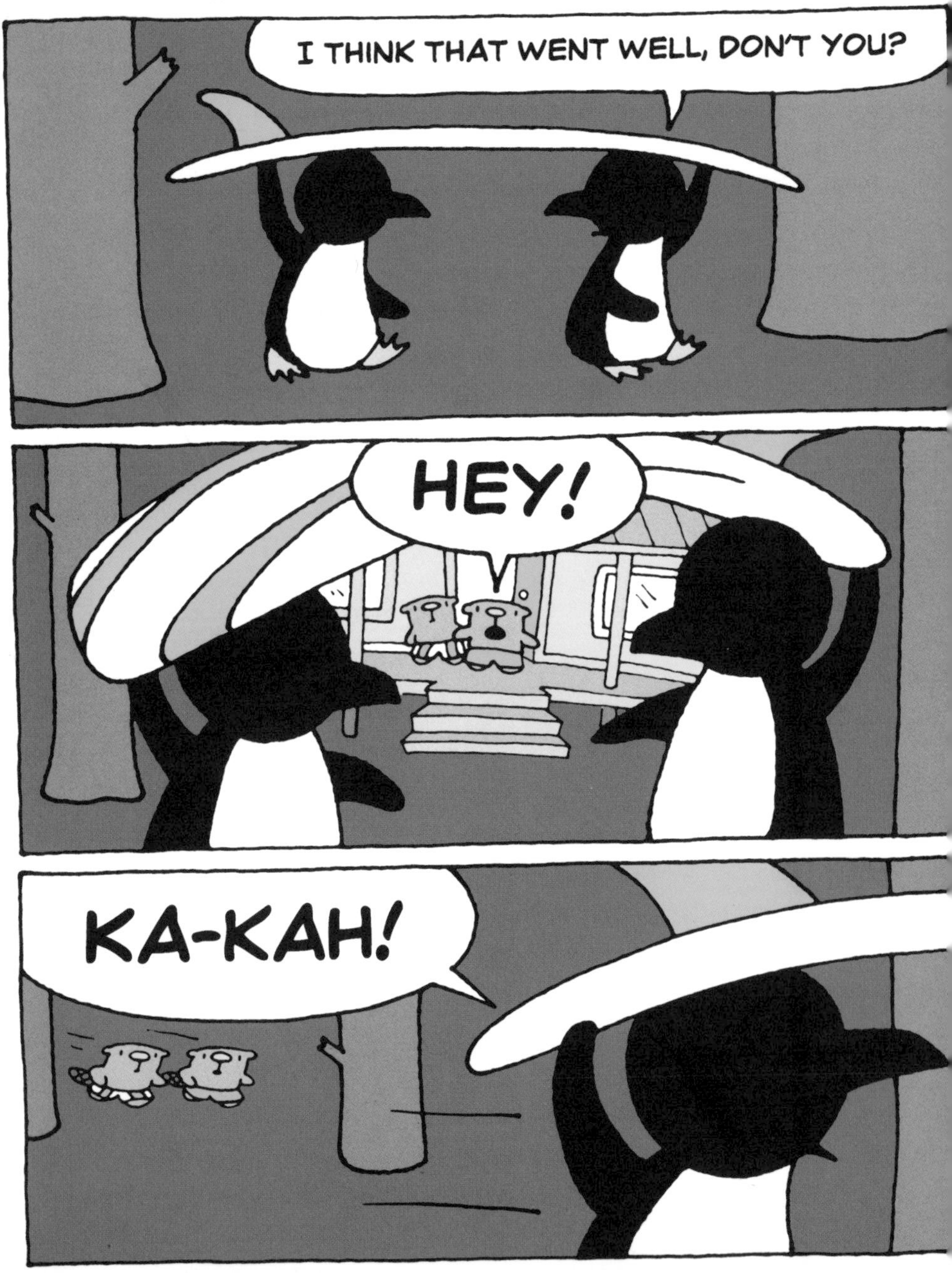
I THINK THAT WENT WELL, DON'T YOU?
HEY!
KA-KAH!

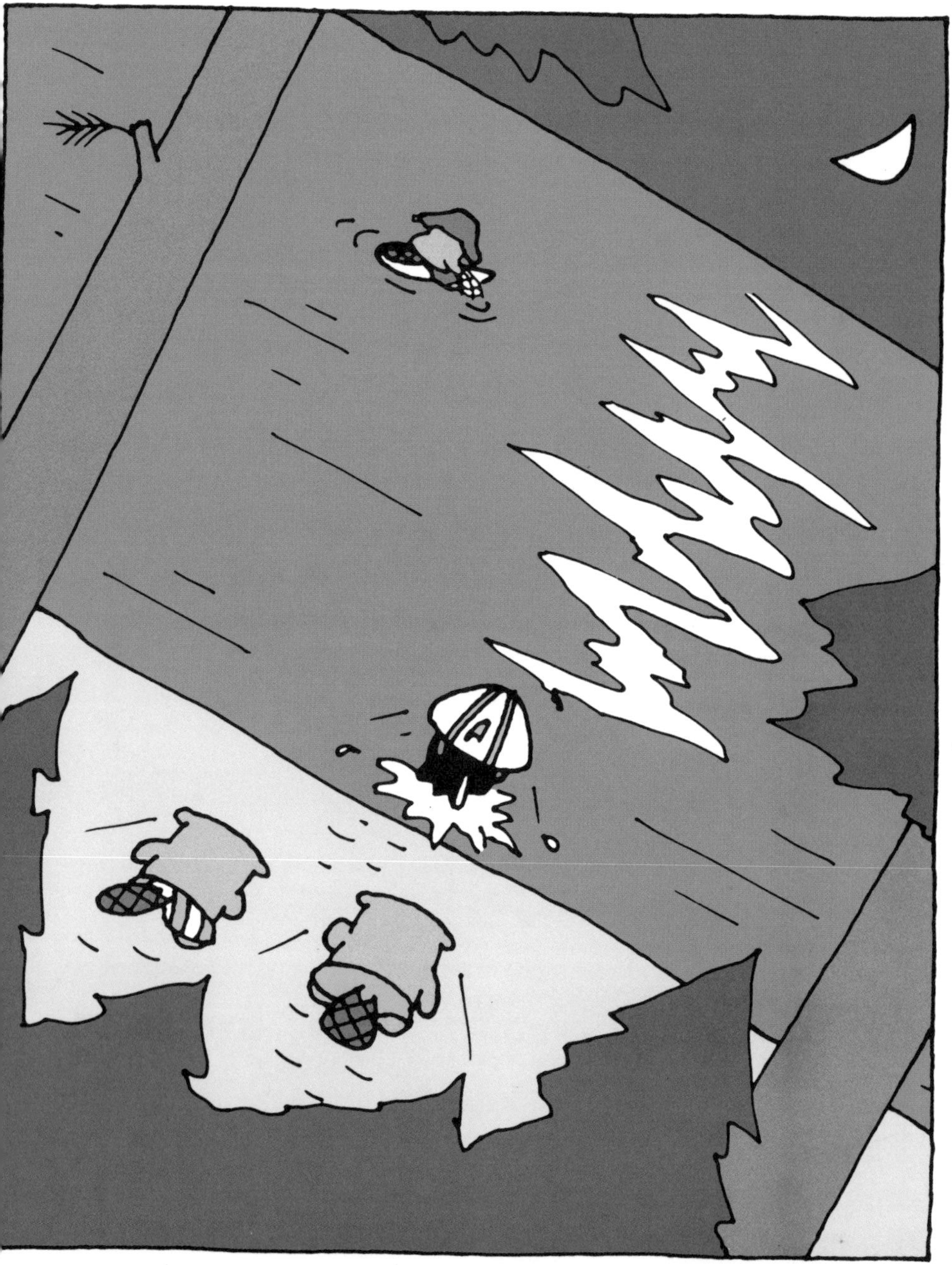

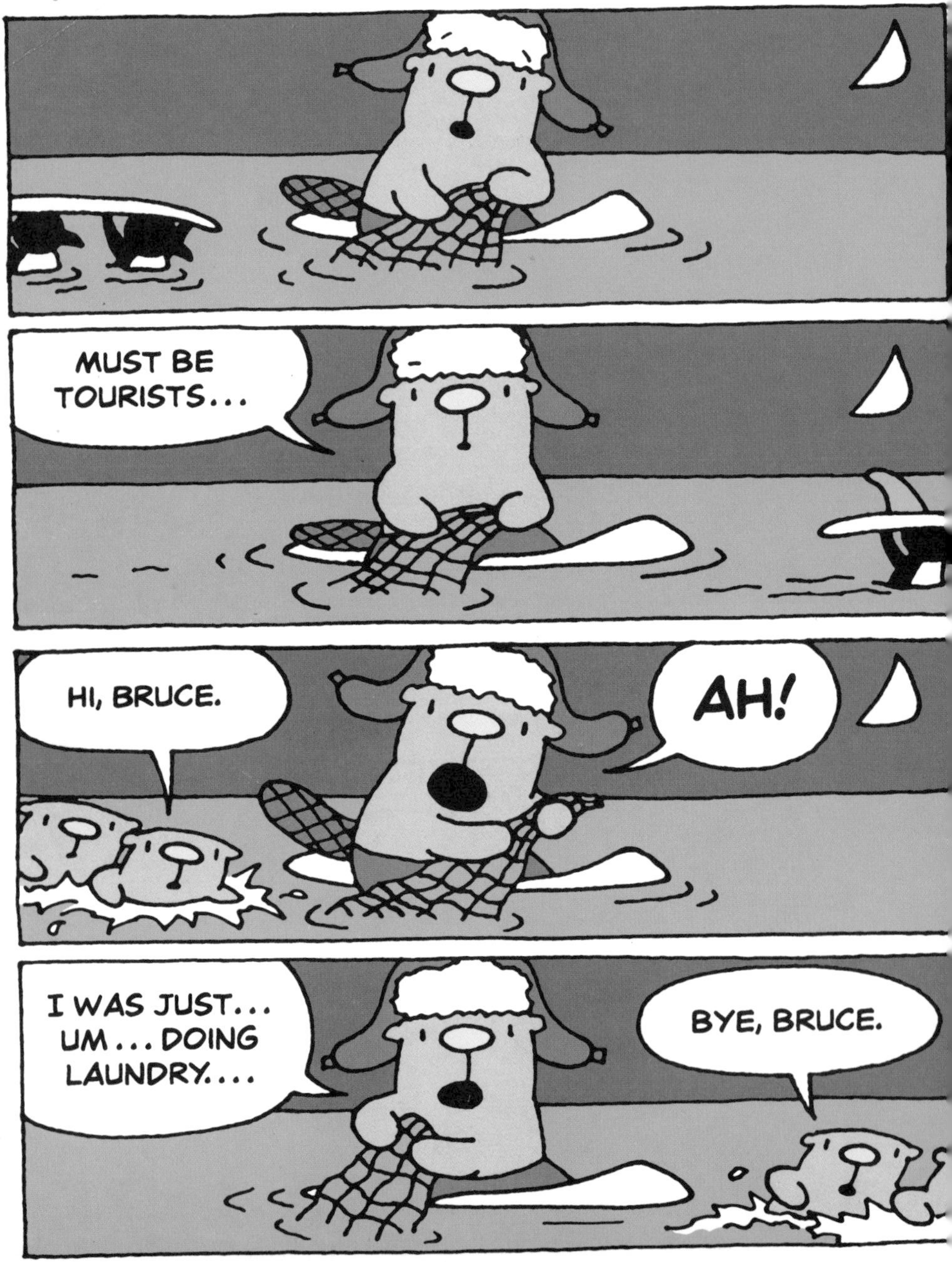
MUST BE TOURISTS...
HI, BRUCE.
AH!
I WAS JUST... UM... DOING LAUNDRY....
BYE, BRUCE.

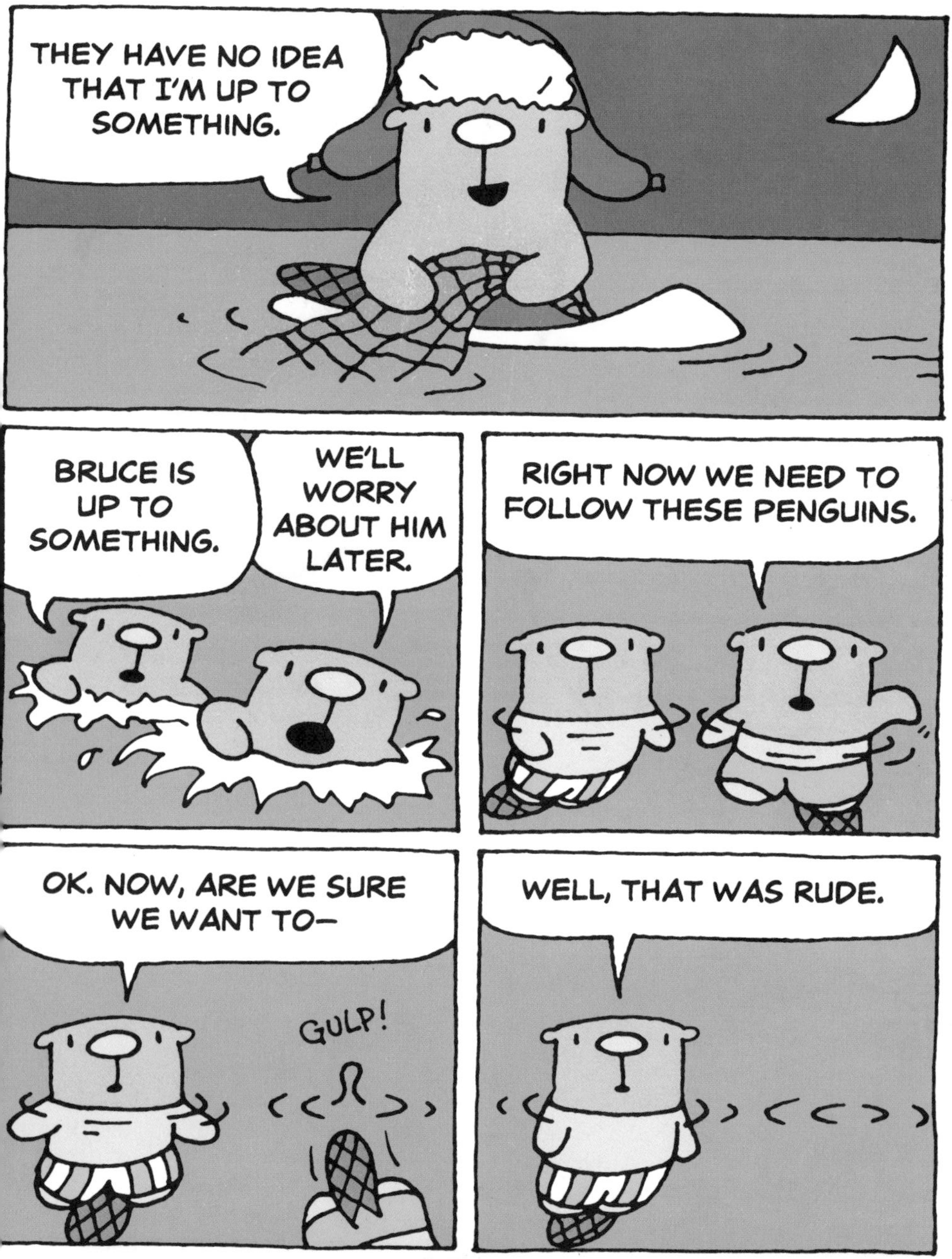

THEY HAVE NO IDEA THAT I'M UP TO SOMETHING.
BRUCE IS UP TO SOMETHING.
WE'LL WORRY ABOUT HIM LATER.
RIGHT NOW WE NEED TO FOLLOW THESE PENGUINS.
OK. NOW, ARE WE SURE WE WANT TO—
GULP!
WELL, THAT WAS RUDE.

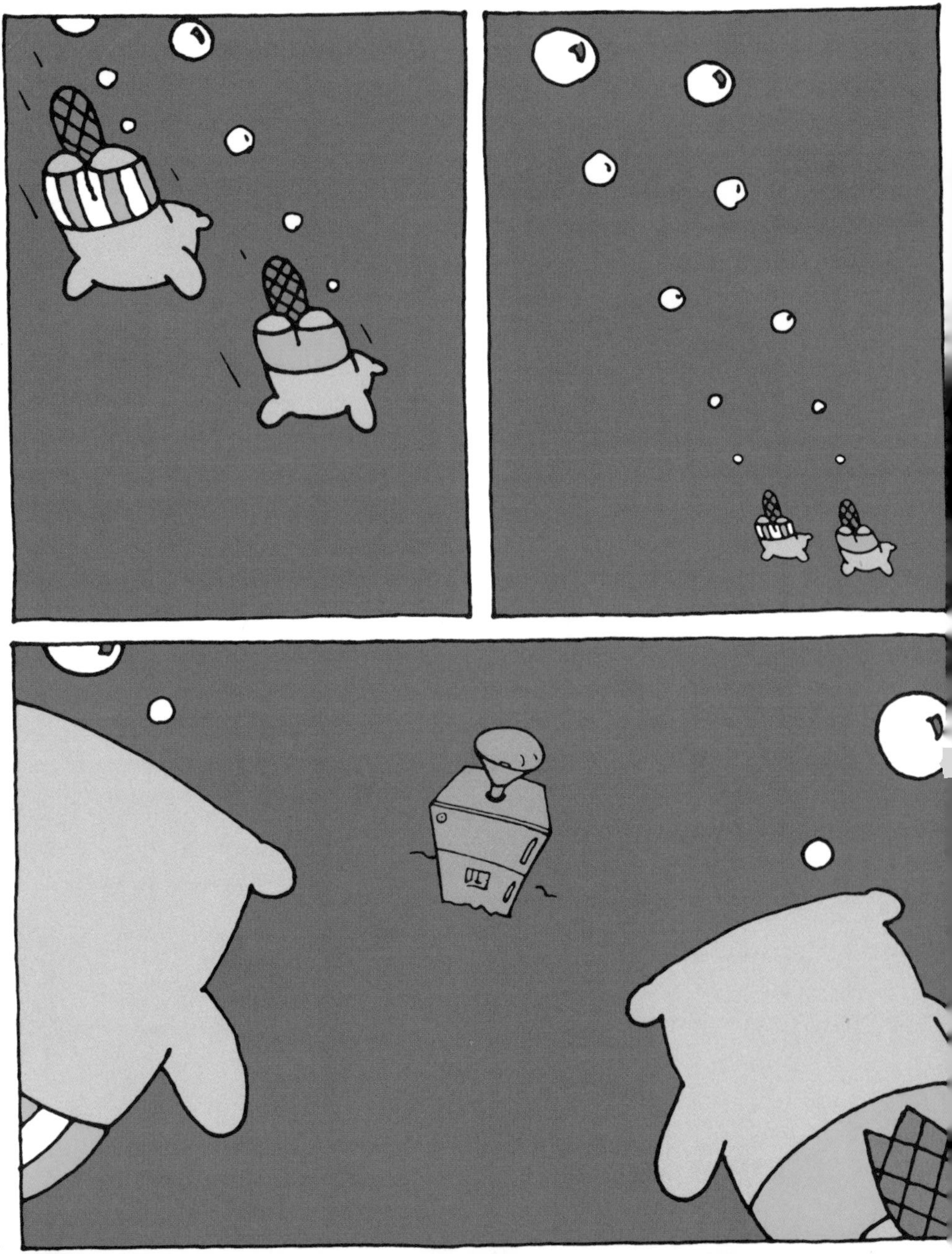

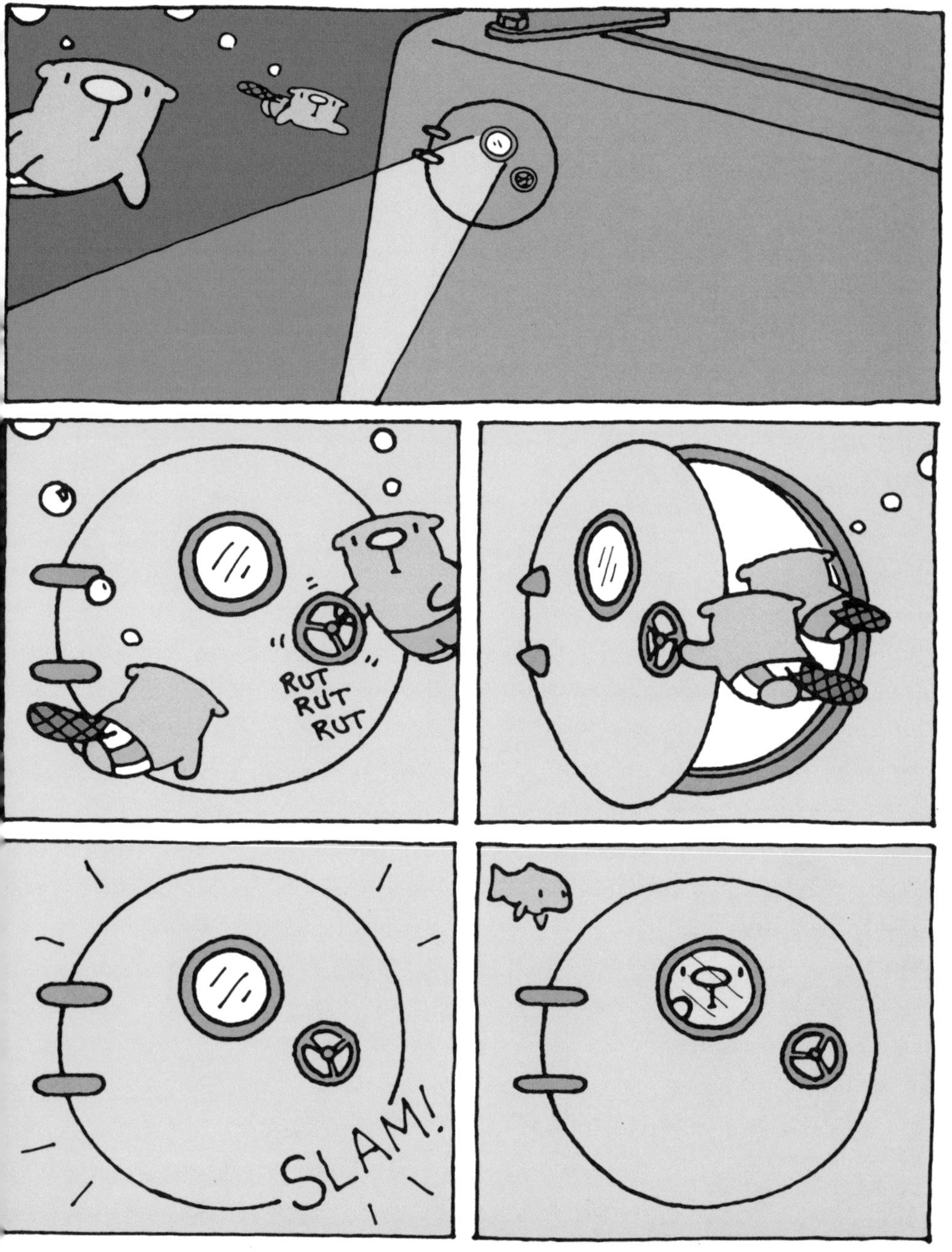
RUT
RUT
RUT
SLAM!

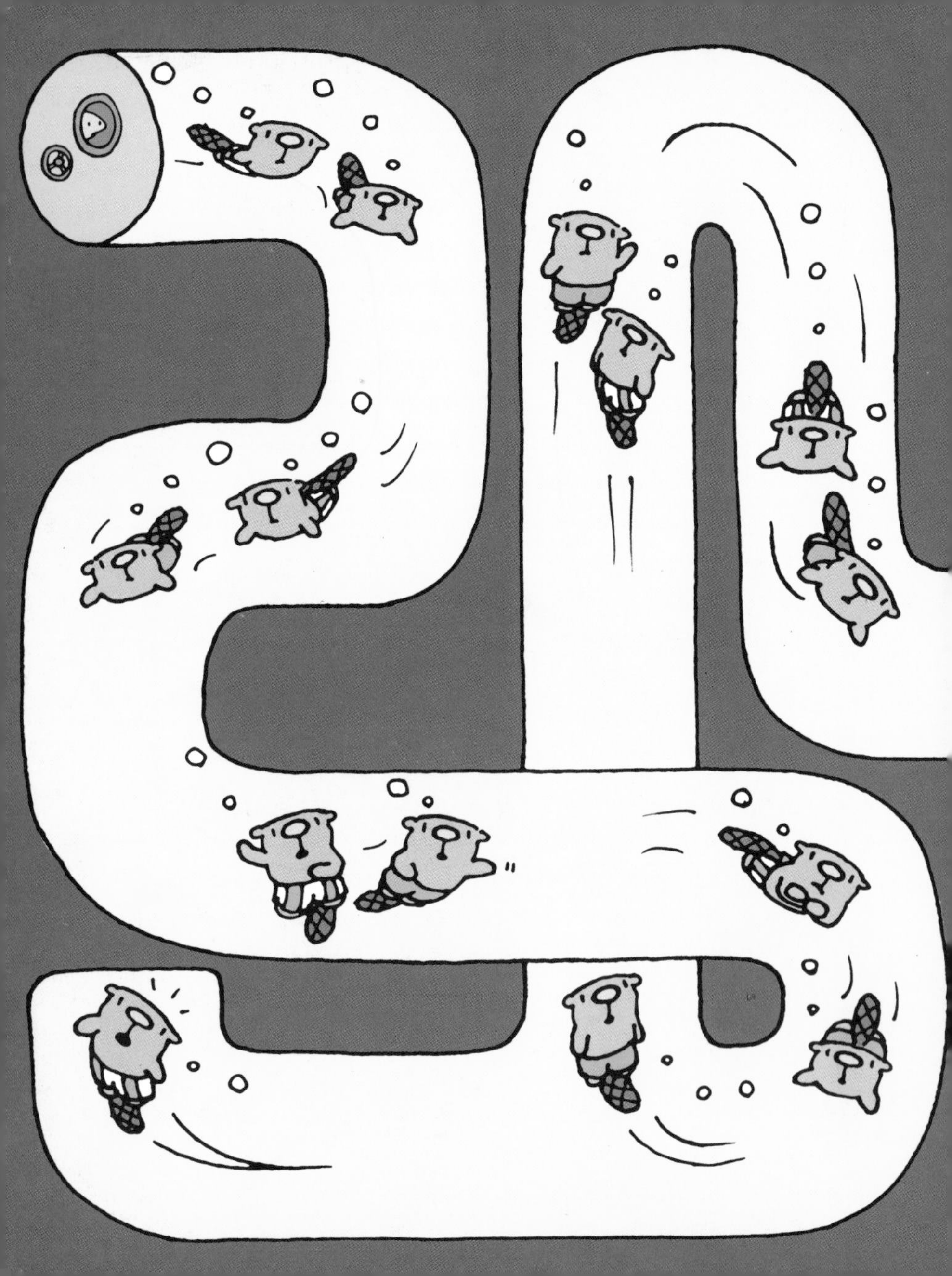

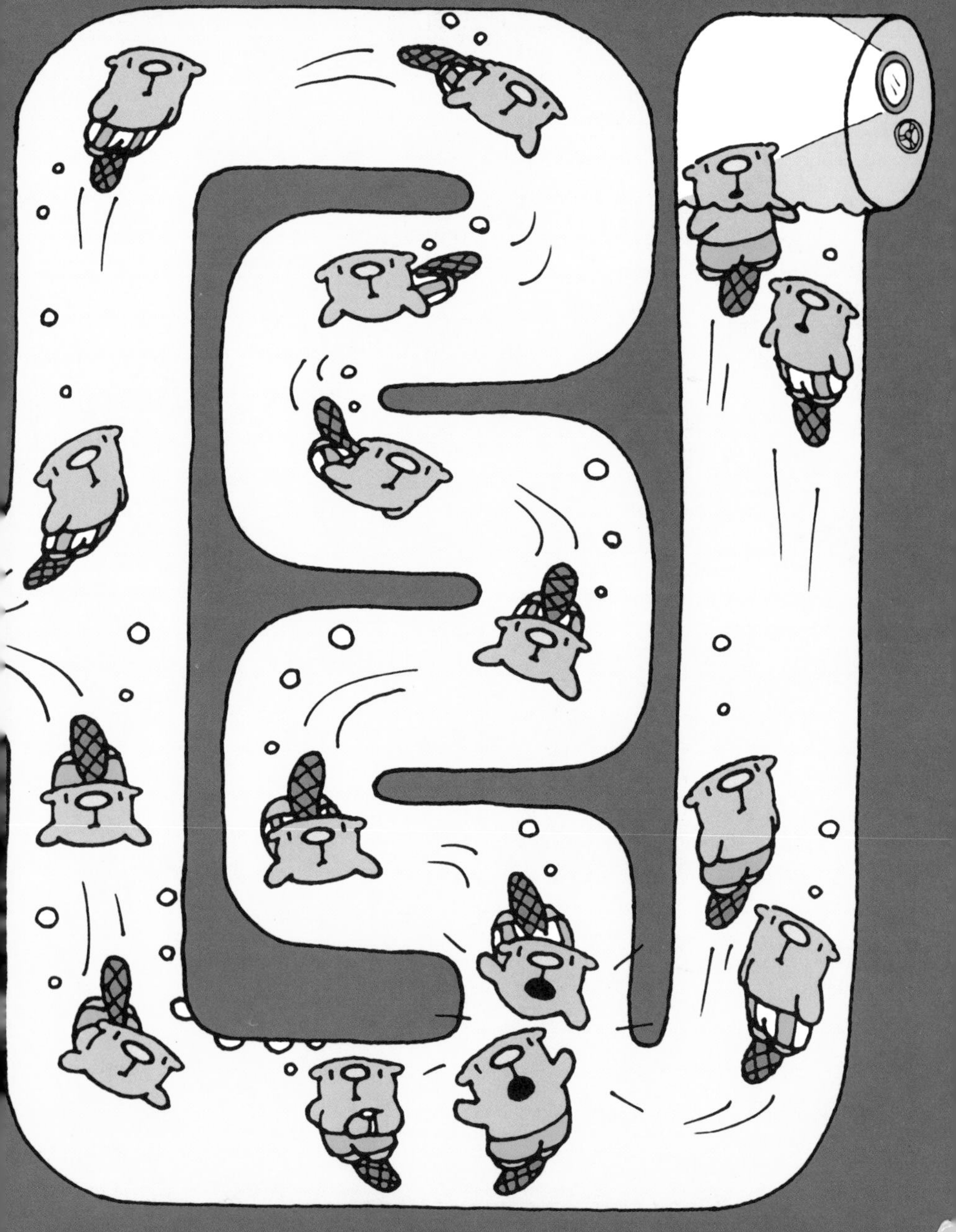

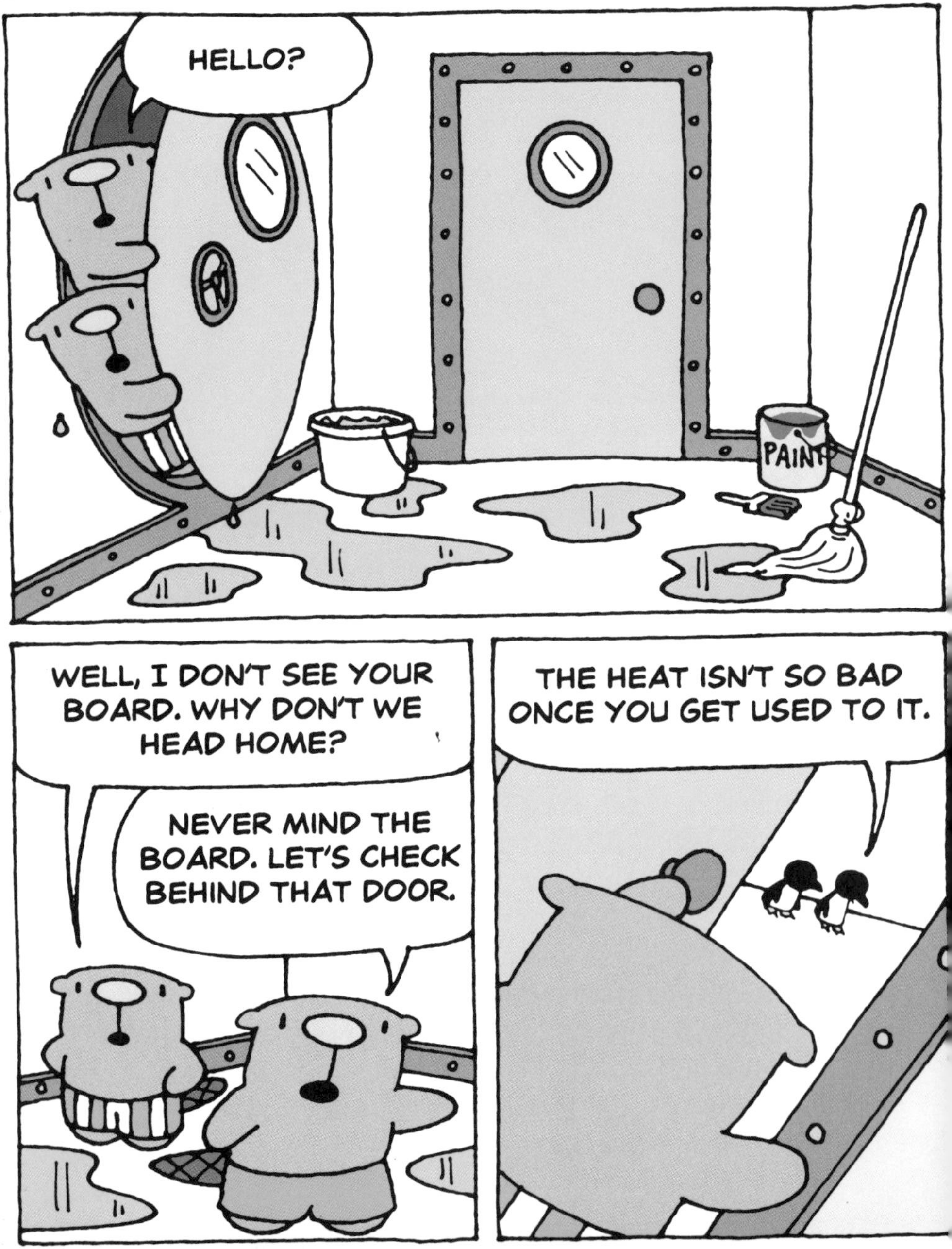
HELLO?
WELL, I DON'T SEE YOUR BOARD. WHY DON'T WE HEAD HOME?
NEVER MIND THE BOARD. LET'S CHECK BEHIND THAT DOOR.
THE HEAT ISN'T SO BAD ONCE YOU GET USED TO IT.
PAINT

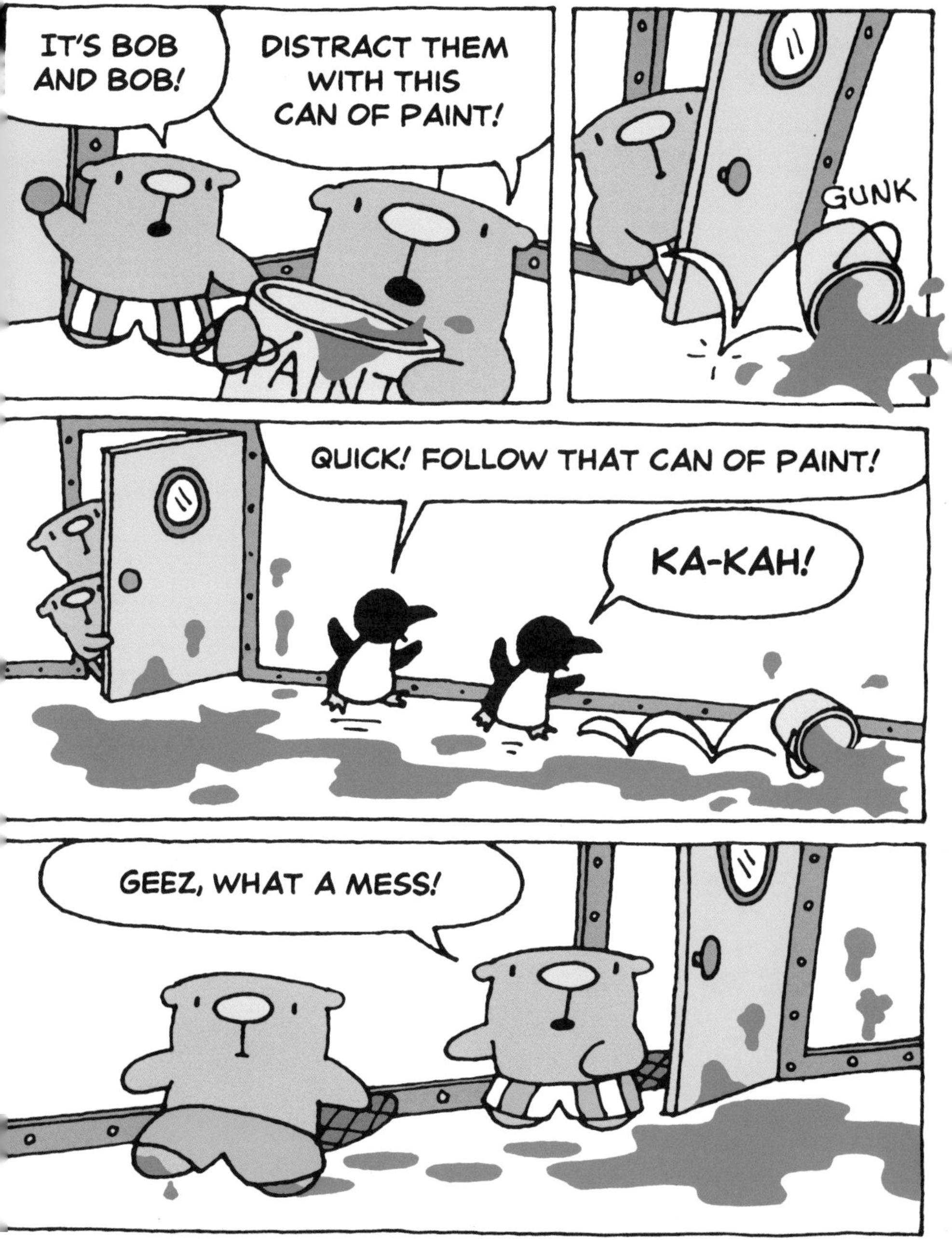
IT'S BOB AND BOB!
DISTRACT THEM WITH THIS CAN OF PAINT!
PAINT
GUNK
QUICK! FOLLOW THAT CAN OF PAINT!
KA-KAH!
GEEZ, WHAT A MESS!

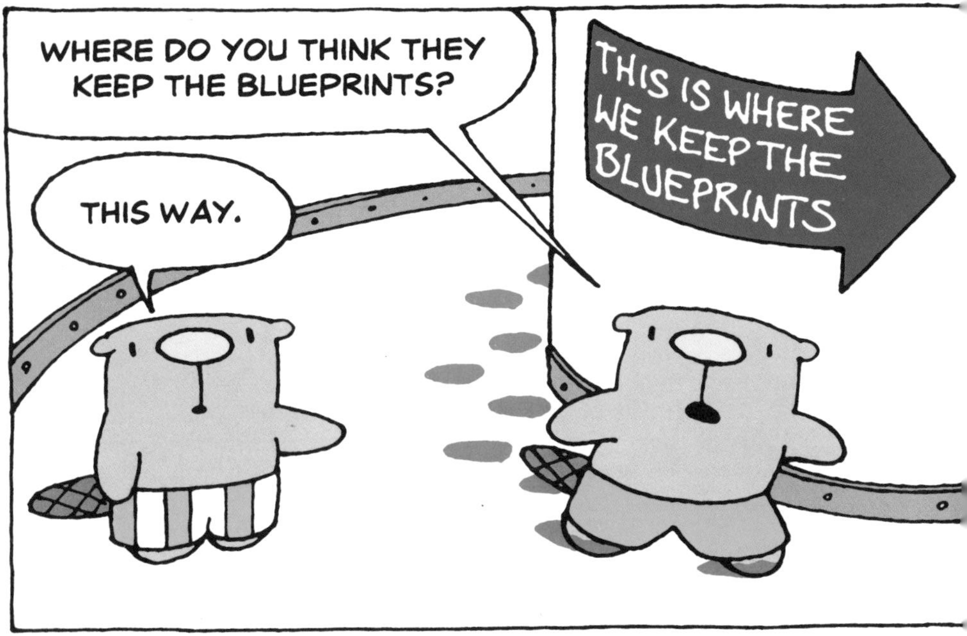
WHERE DO YOU THINK THEY KEEP THE BLUEPRINTS?
THIS WAY.
THIS IS WHERE WE KEEP THE BLUEPRINTS

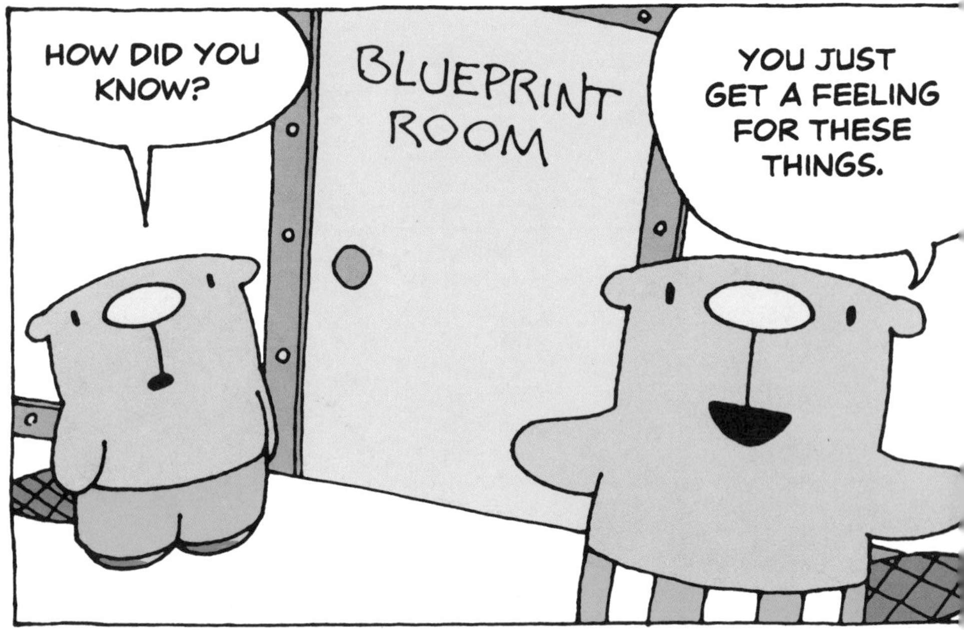
HOW DID YOU KNOW?
BLUEPRINT ROOM
YOU JUST GET A FEELING FOR THESE THINGS.

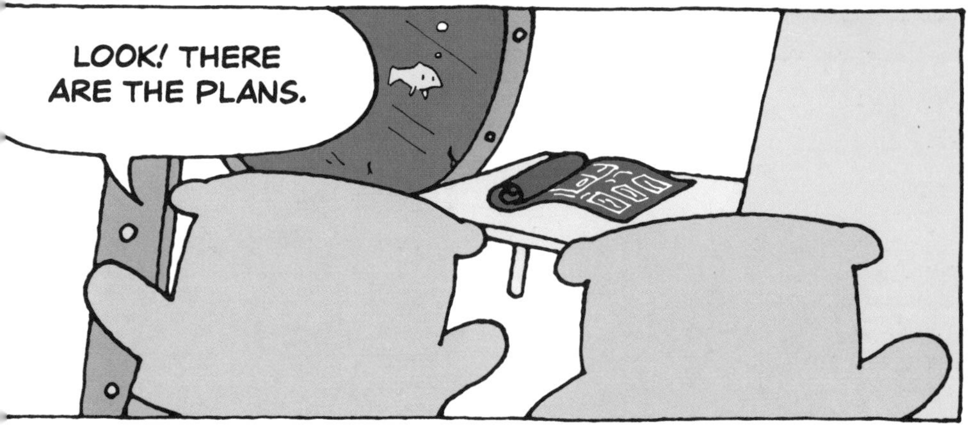
LOOK! THERE
ARE THE PLANS.

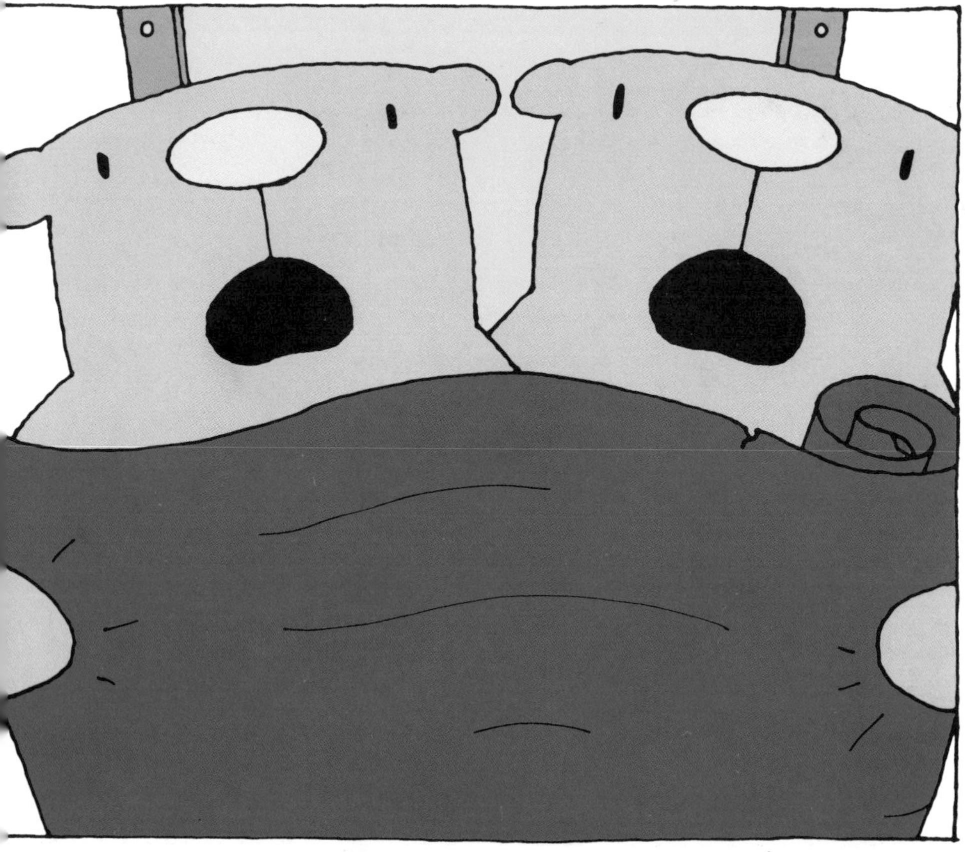

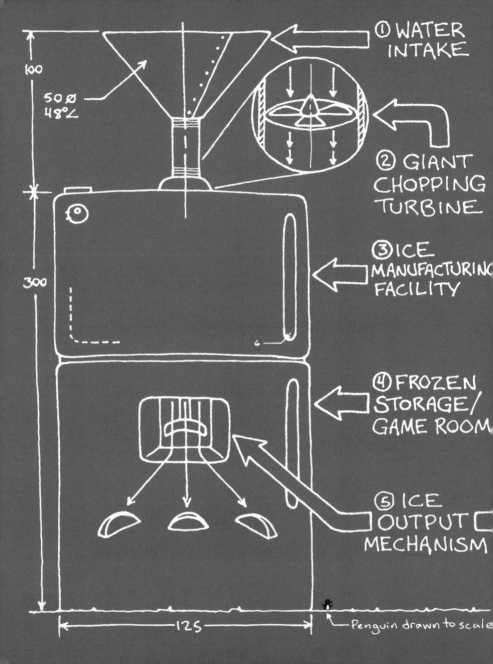

① WATER INTAKE

② GIANT CHOPPING TURBINE

③ ICE MANUFACTURING FACILITY

④ FROZEN STORAGE/ GAME ROOM

⑤ ICE OUTPUT MECHANISM

100

50⌀
48∠

300

125

Penguin drawn to scale

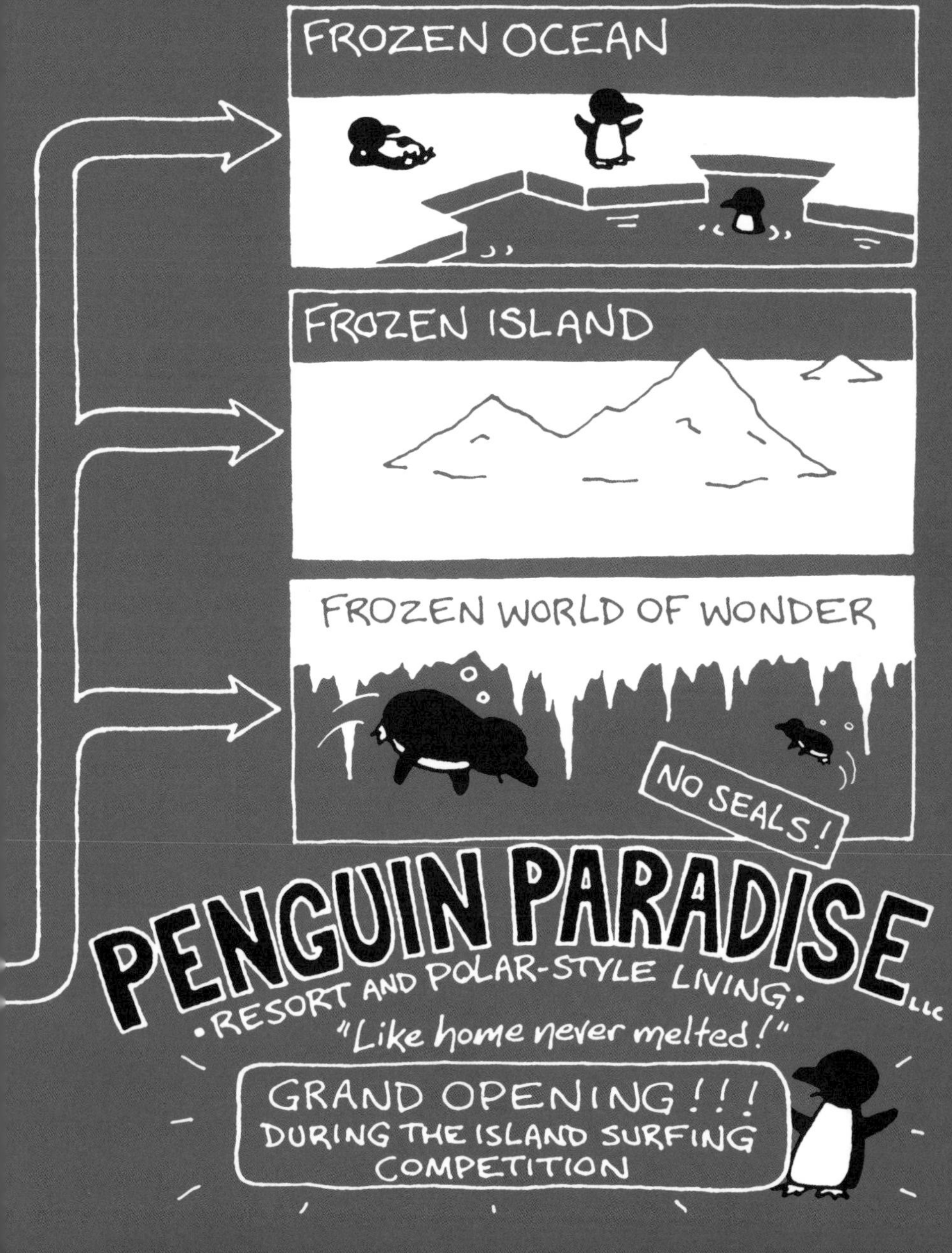
FROZEN OCEAN
FROZEN ISLAND
FROZEN WORLD OF WONDER
NO SEALS!
PENGUIN PARADISE LLC
•RESORT AND POLAR-STYLE LIVING•
"Like home never melted!"
GRAND OPENING!!!
DURING THE ISLAND SURFING COMPETITION

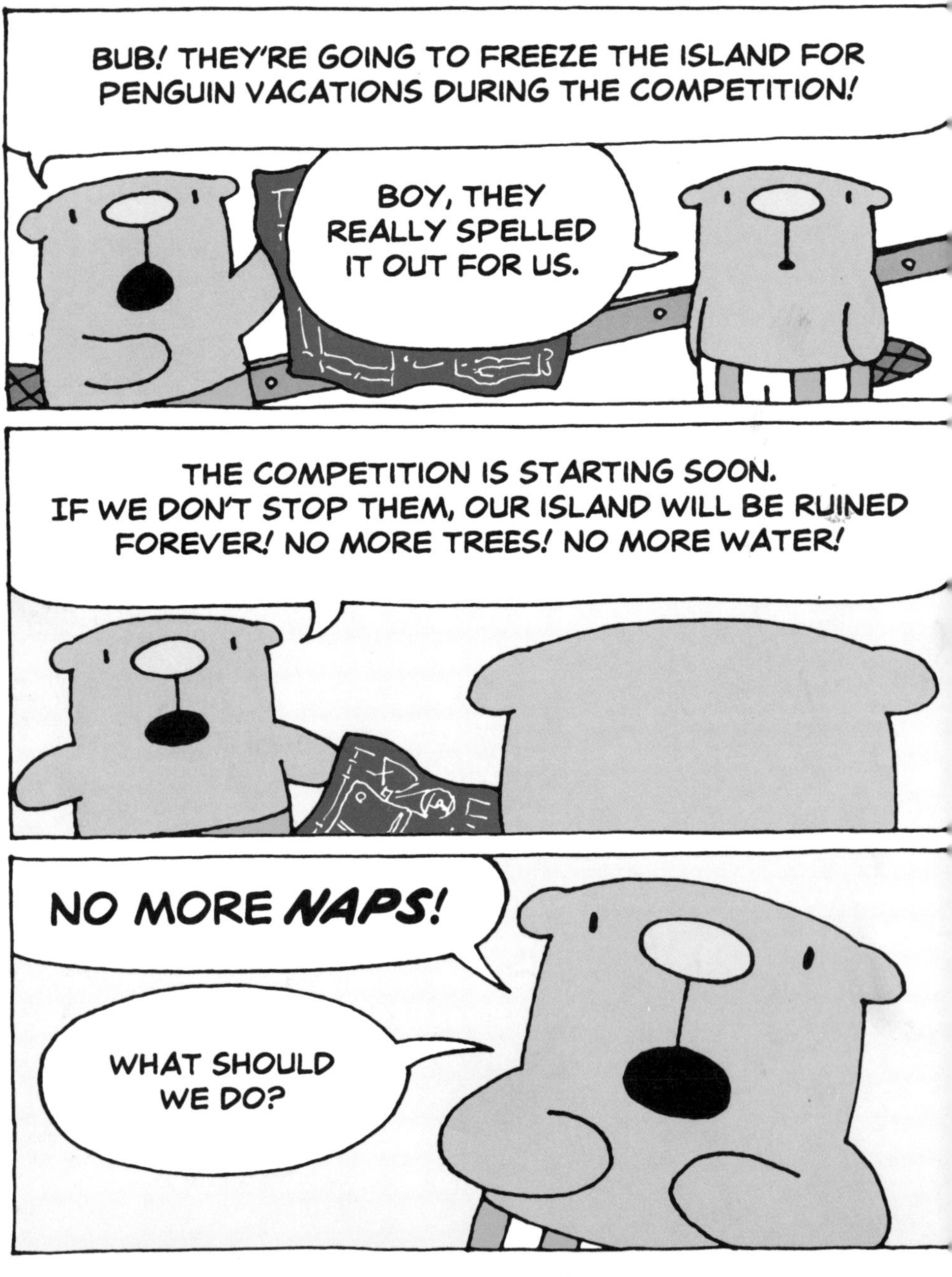
BUB! THEY'RE GOING TO FREEZE THE ISLAND FOR PENGUIN VACATIONS DURING THE COMPETITION!
BOY, THEY REALLY SPELLED IT OUT FOR US.
THE COMPETITION IS STARTING SOON. IF WE DON'T STOP THEM, OUR ISLAND WILL BE RUINED FOREVER! NO MORE TREES! NO MORE WATER!
NO MORE *NAPS*!
WHAT SHOULD WE DO?

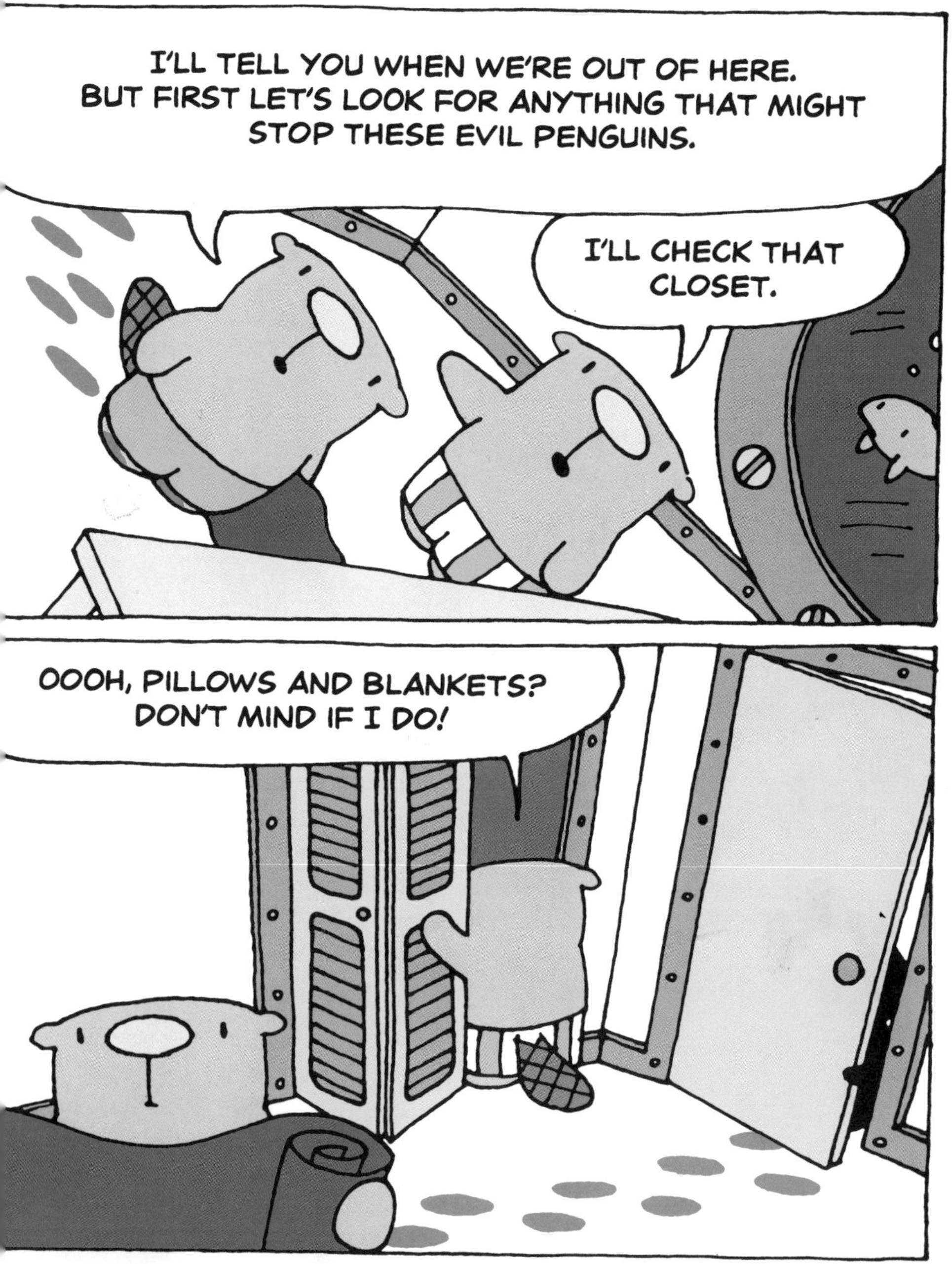
I'LL TELL YOU WHEN WE'RE OUT OF HERE. BUT FIRST LET'S LOOK FOR ANYTHING THAT MIGHT STOP THESE EVIL PENGUINS.
I'LL CHECK THAT CLOSET.
OOOH, PILLOWS AND BLANKETS? DON'T MIND IF I DO!

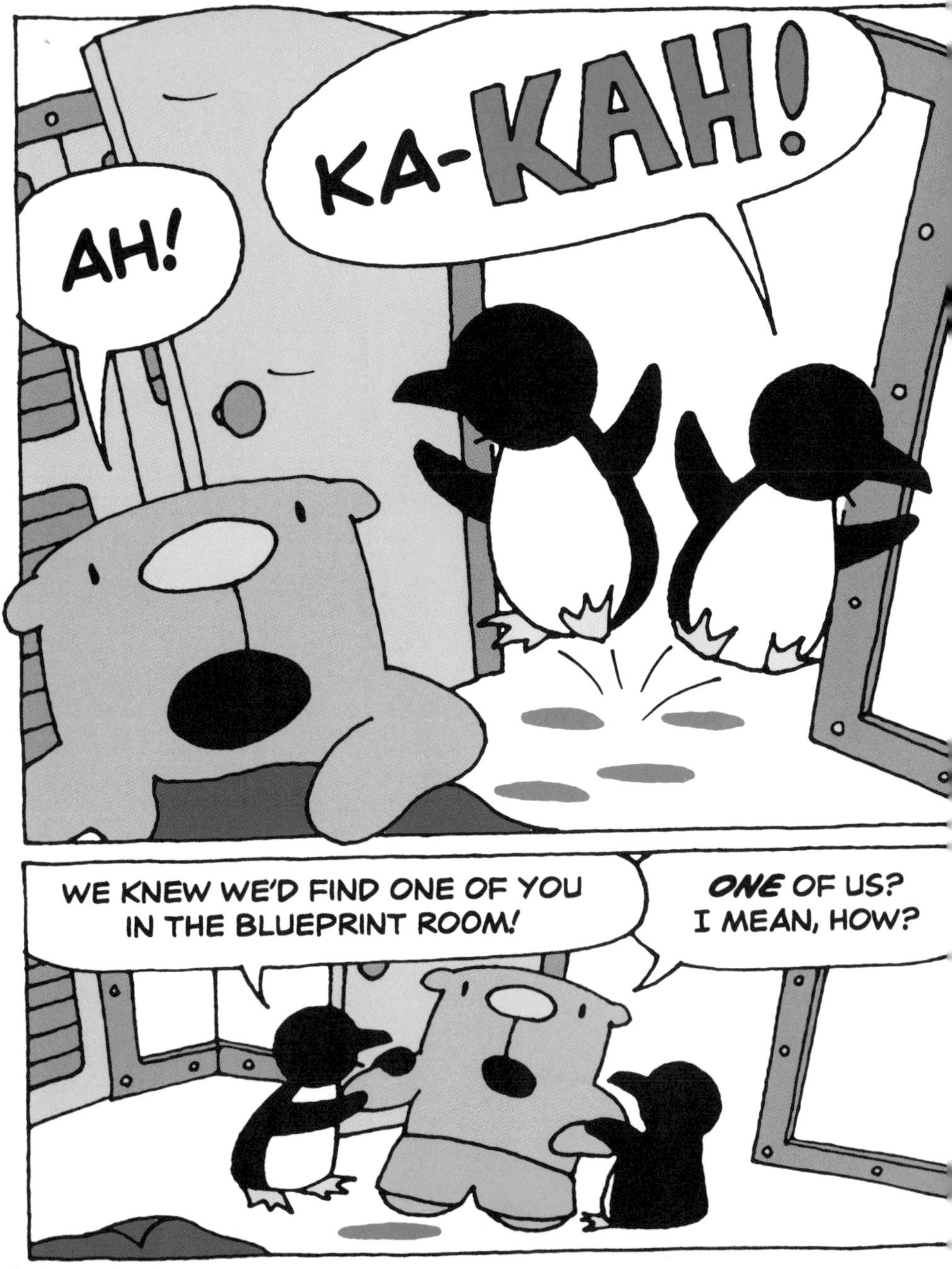
KA-KAH!
AH!
WE KNEW WE'D FIND ONE OF YOU IN THE BLUEPRINT ROOM!
ONE OF US? I MEAN, HOW?

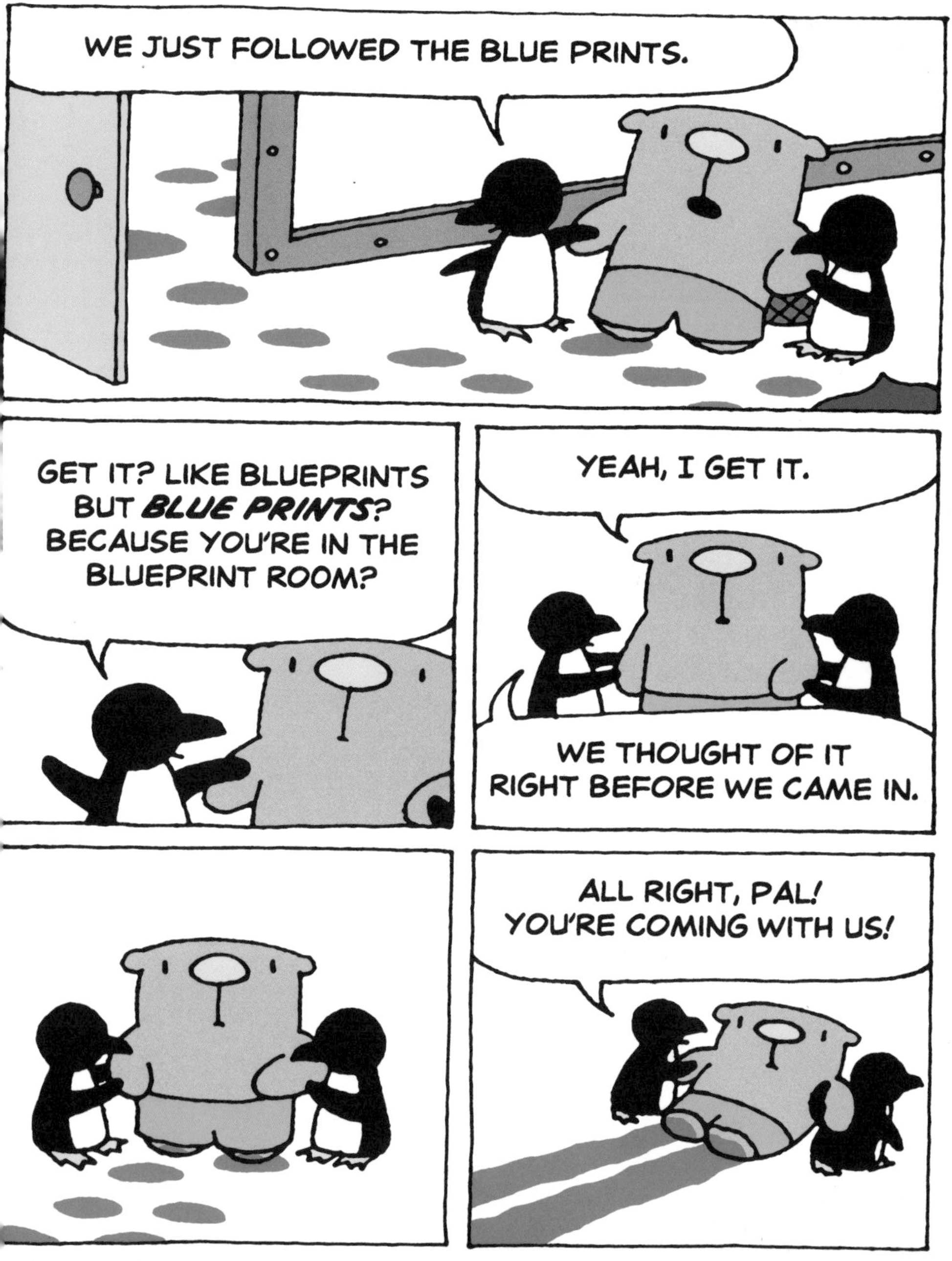
WE JUST FOLLOWED THE BLUE PRINTS.
GET IT? LIKE BLUEPRINTS BUT ***BLUE PRINTS***? BECAUSE YOU'RE IN THE BLUEPRINT ROOM?
YEAH, I GET IT.
WE THOUGHT OF IT RIGHT BEFORE WE CAME IN.
ALL RIGHT, PAL! YOU'RE COMING WITH US!

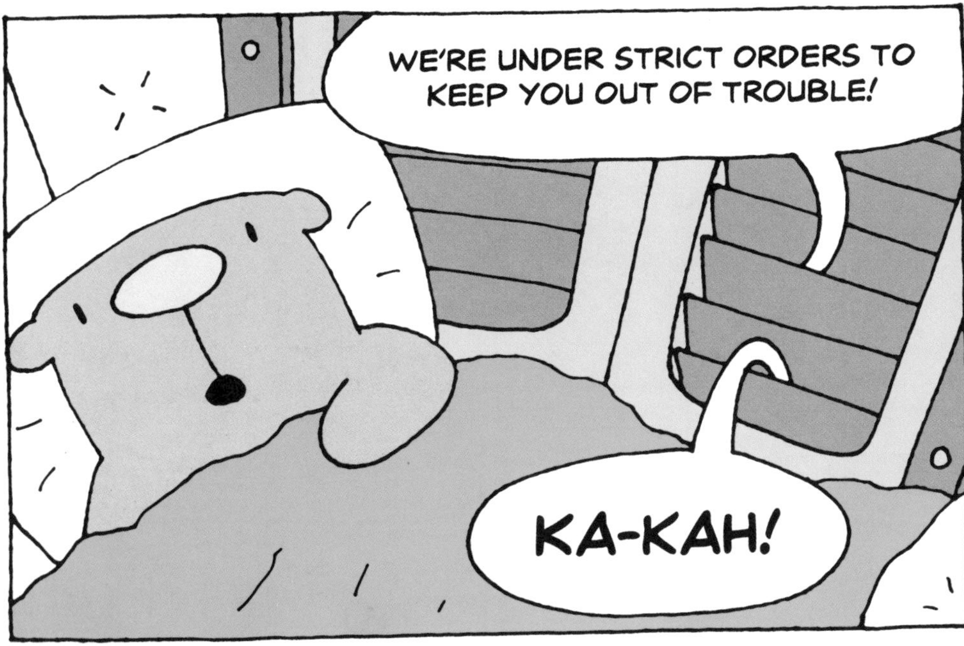
WE'RE UNDER STRICT ORDERS TO KEEP YOU OUT OF TROUBLE!
KA-KAH!
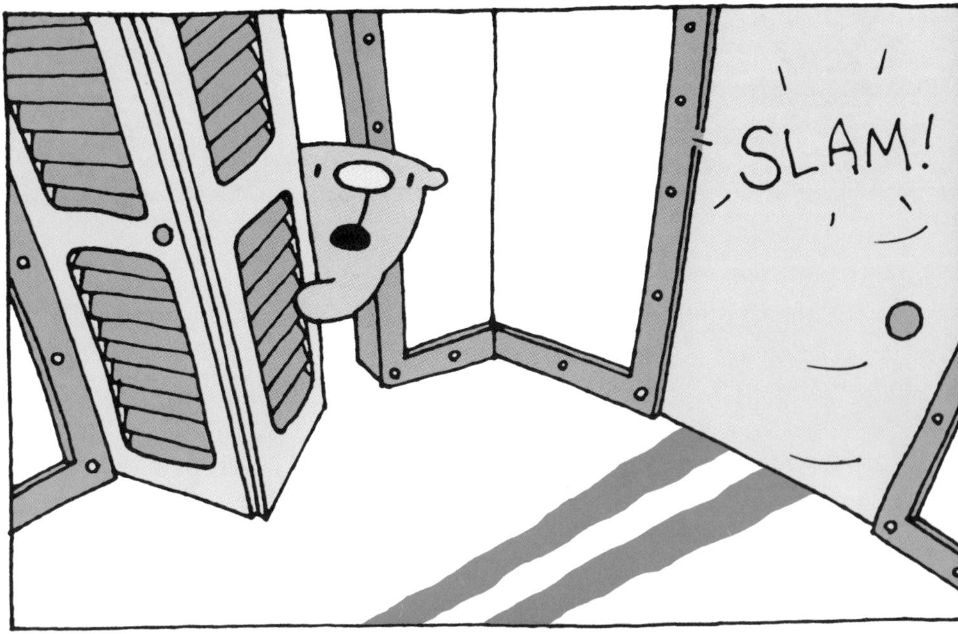
SLAM!

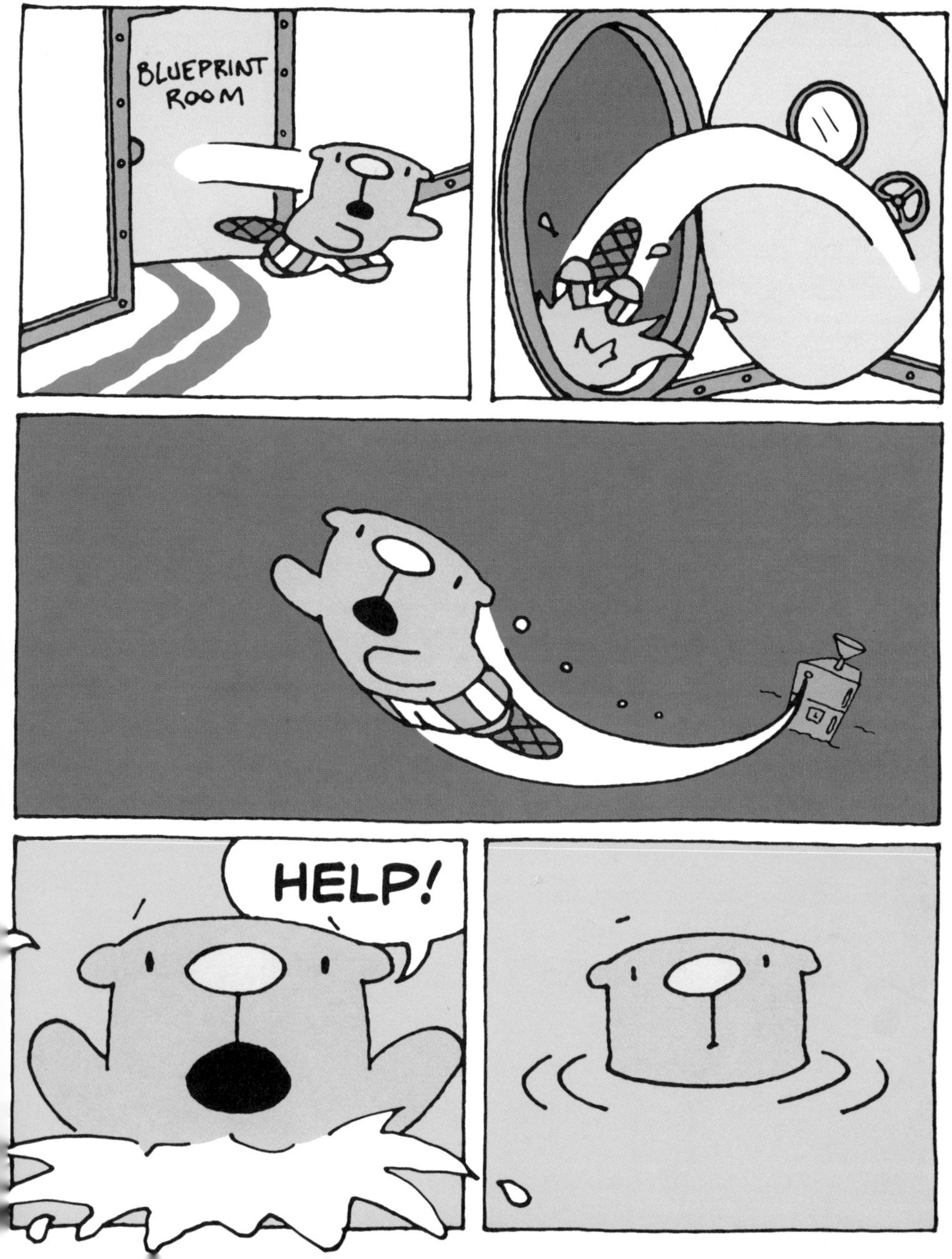
BLUEPRINT ROOM
HELP!

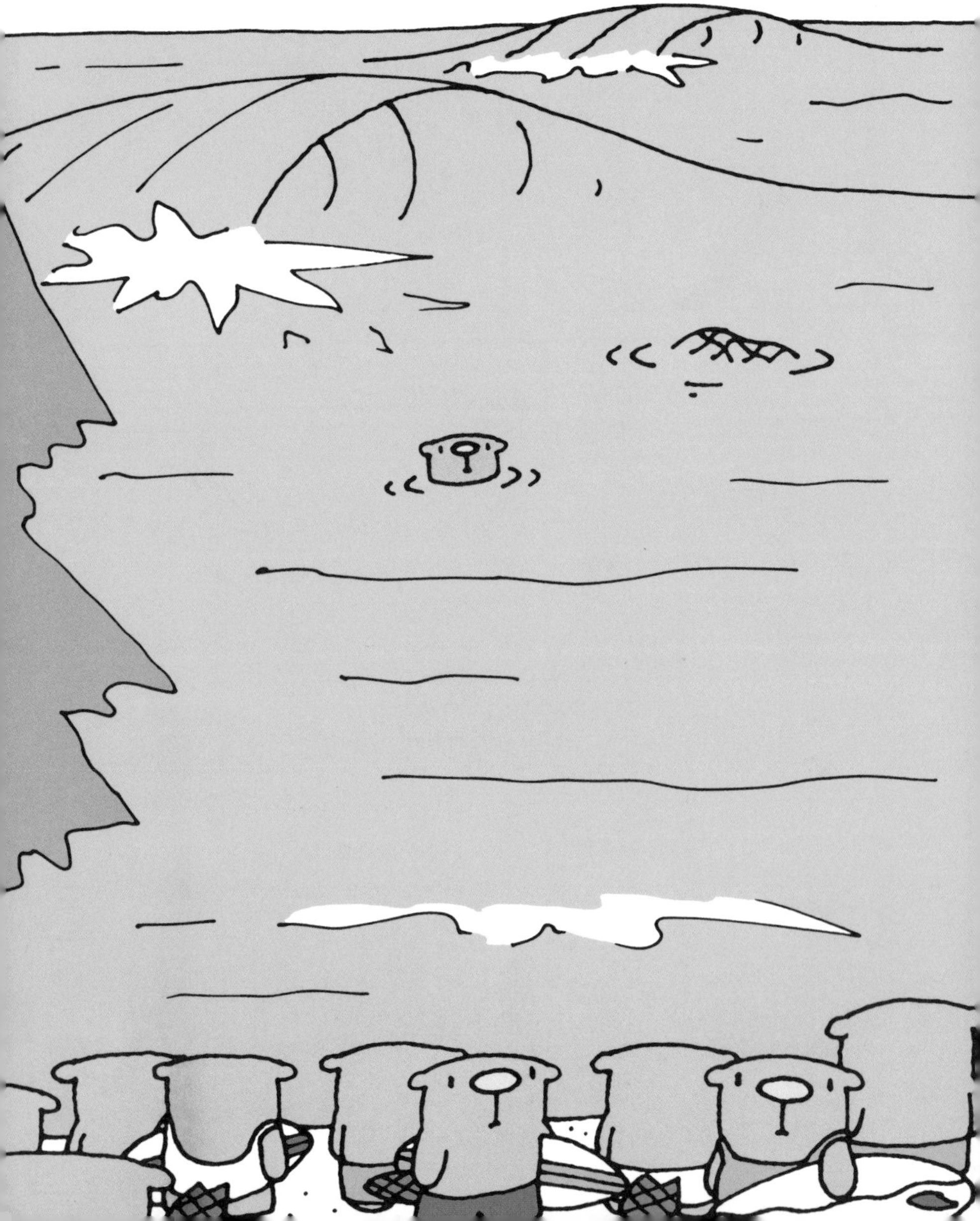

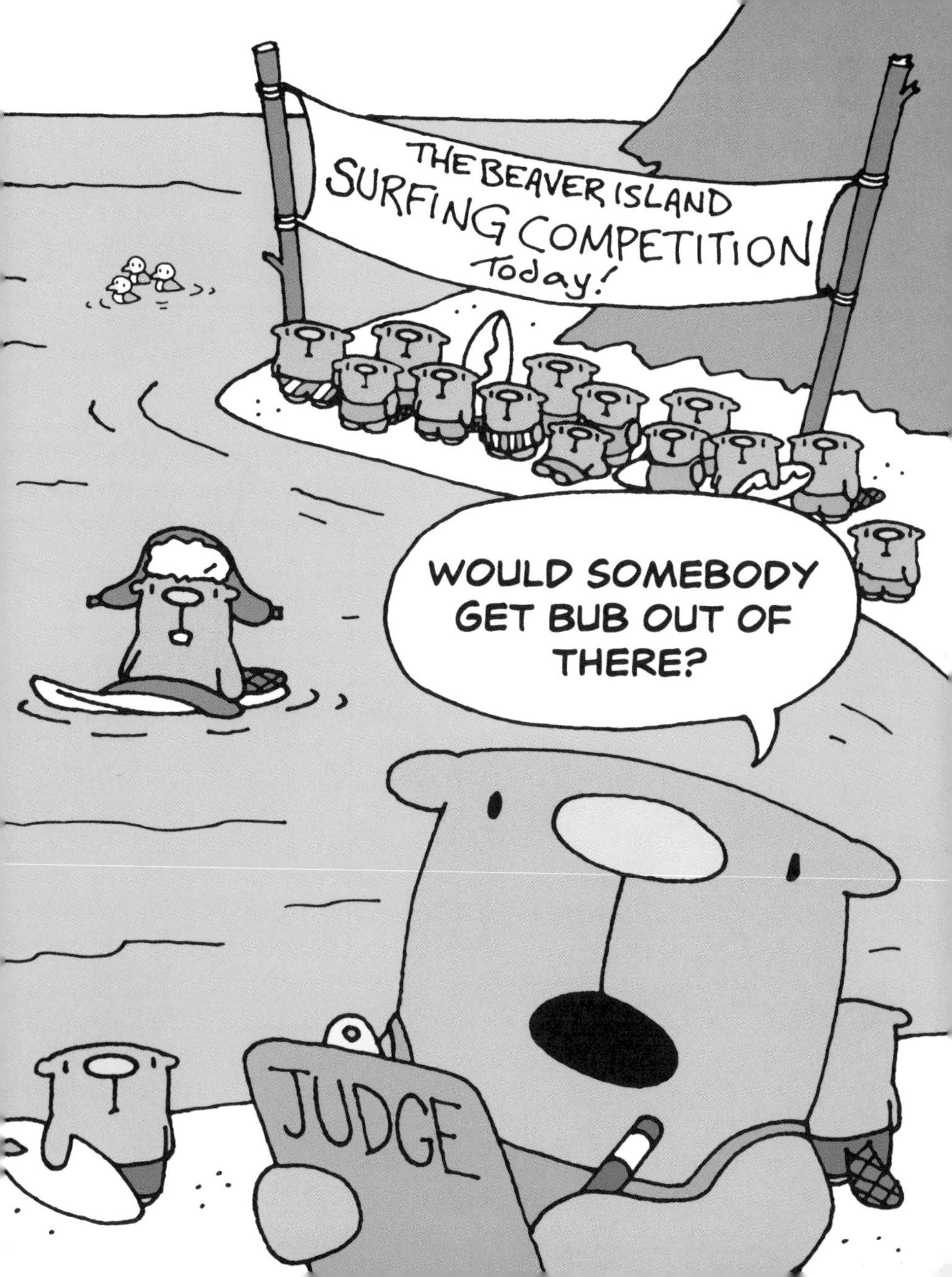
THE BEAVER ISLAND
SURFING COMPETITION
Today!
WOULD SOMEBODY GET BUB OUT OF THERE?
JUDGE

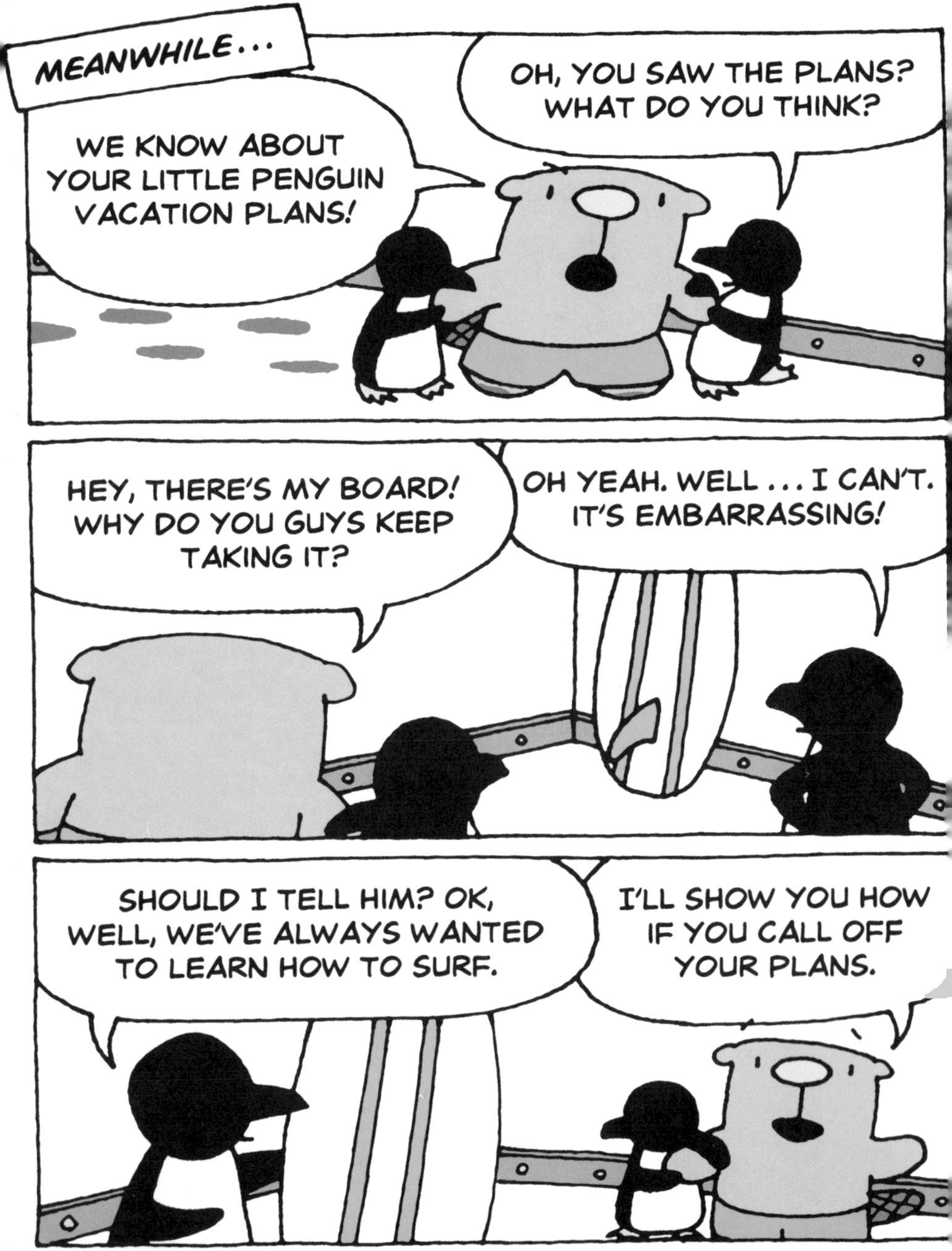
MEANWHILE...
WE KNOW ABOUT YOUR LITTLE PENGUIN VACATION PLANS!
OH, YOU SAW THE PLANS? WHAT DO YOU THINK?
HEY, THERE'S MY BOARD! WHY DO YOU GUYS KEEP TAKING IT?
OH YEAH. WELL . . . I CAN'T. IT'S EMBARRASSING!
SHOULD I TELL HIM? OK, WELL, WE'VE ALWAYS WANTED TO LEARN HOW TO SURF.
I'LL SHOW YOU HOW IF YOU CALL OFF YOUR PLANS.

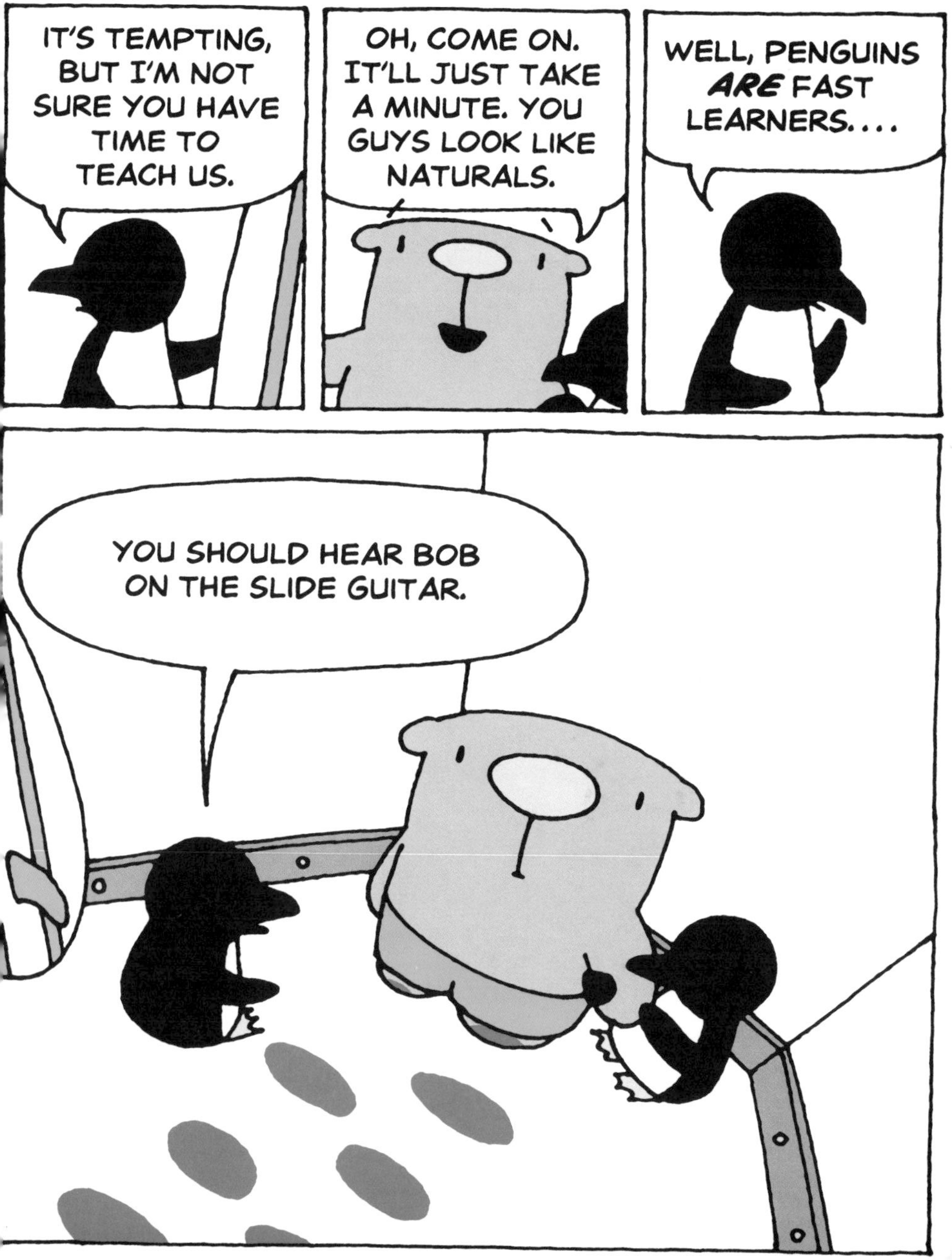
IT'S TEMPTING, BUT I'M NOT SURE YOU HAVE TIME TO TEACH US.
OH, COME ON. IT'LL JUST TAKE A MINUTE. YOU GUYS LOOK LIKE NATURALS.
WELL, PENGUINS *ARE* FAST LEARNERS. . . .
YOU SHOULD HEAR BOB ON THE SLIDE GUITAR.

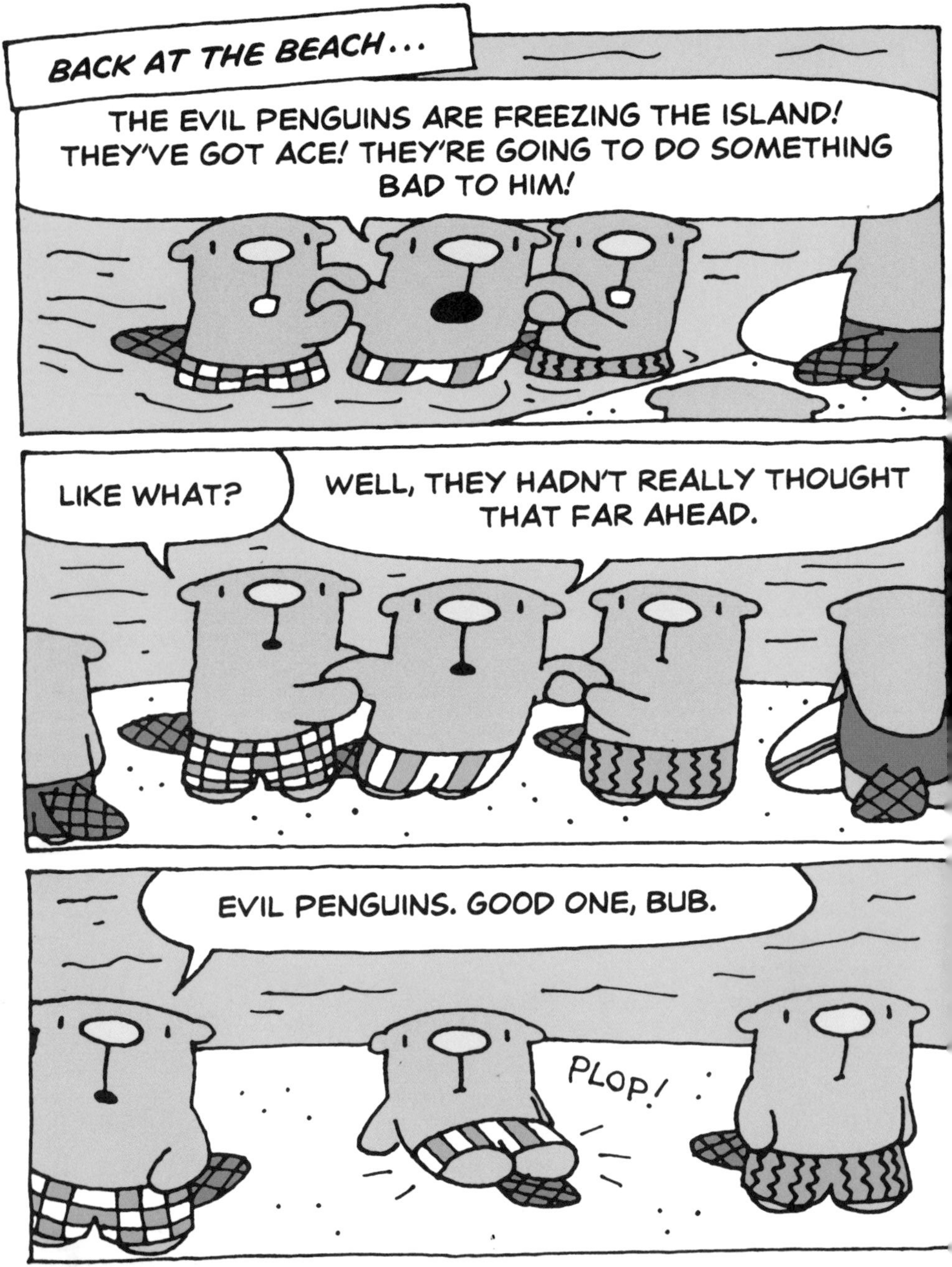
BACK AT THE BEACH...
THE EVIL PENGUINS ARE FREEZING THE ISLAND! THEY'VE GOT ACE! THEY'RE GOING TO DO SOMETHING BAD TO HIM!
LIKE WHAT?
WELL, THEY HADN'T REALLY THOUGHT THAT FAR AHEAD.
EVIL PENGUINS. GOOD ONE, BUB.
PLOP!

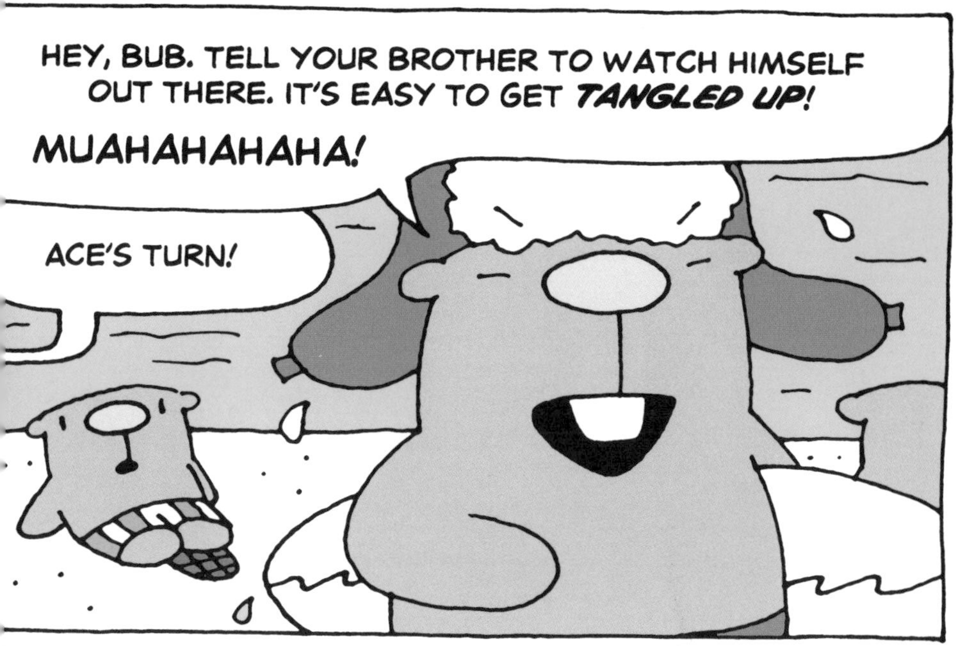
HEY, BUB. TELL YOUR BROTHER TO WATCH HIMSELF OUT THERE. IT'S EASY TO GET *TANGLED UP!*
MUAHAHAHAHA!
ACE'S TURN!

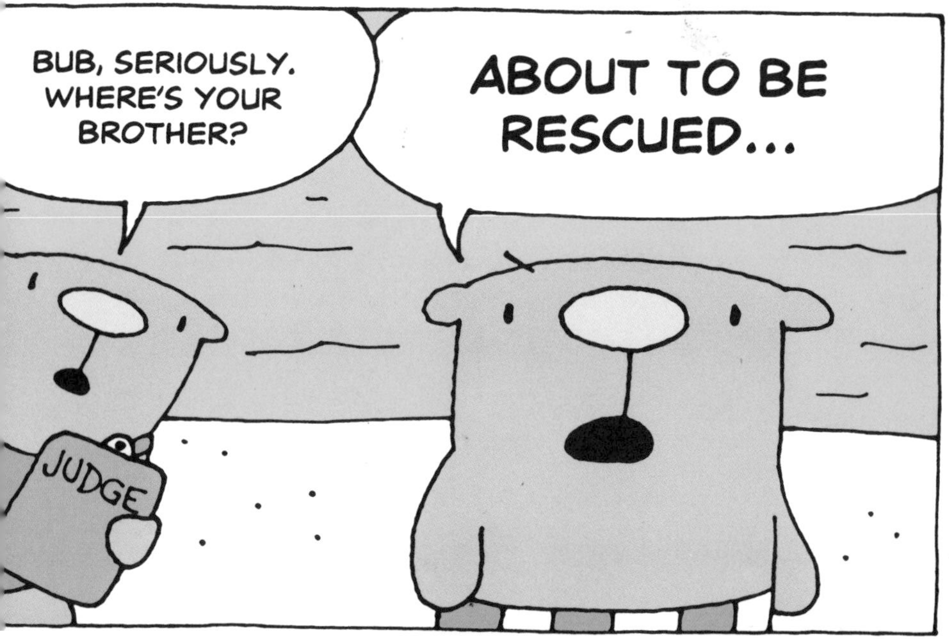
BUB, SERIOUSLY. WHERE'S YOUR BROTHER?
ABOUT TO BE RESCUED...
JUDGE

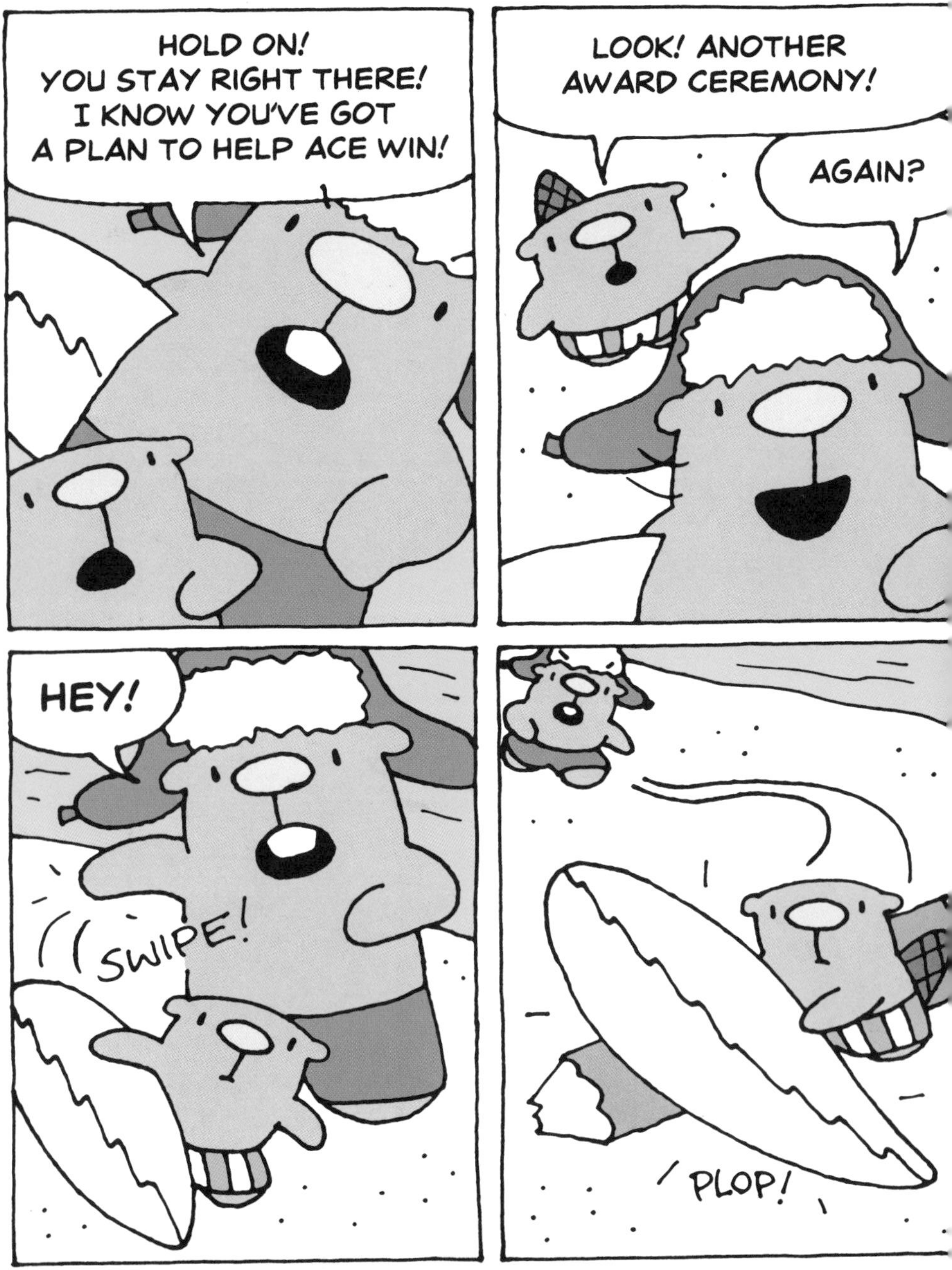
HOLD ON!
YOU STAY RIGHT THERE!
I KNOW YOU'VE GOT
A PLAN TO HELP ACE WIN!
LOOK! ANOTHER
AWARD CEREMONY!
AGAIN?
HEY!
SWIPE!
PLOP!

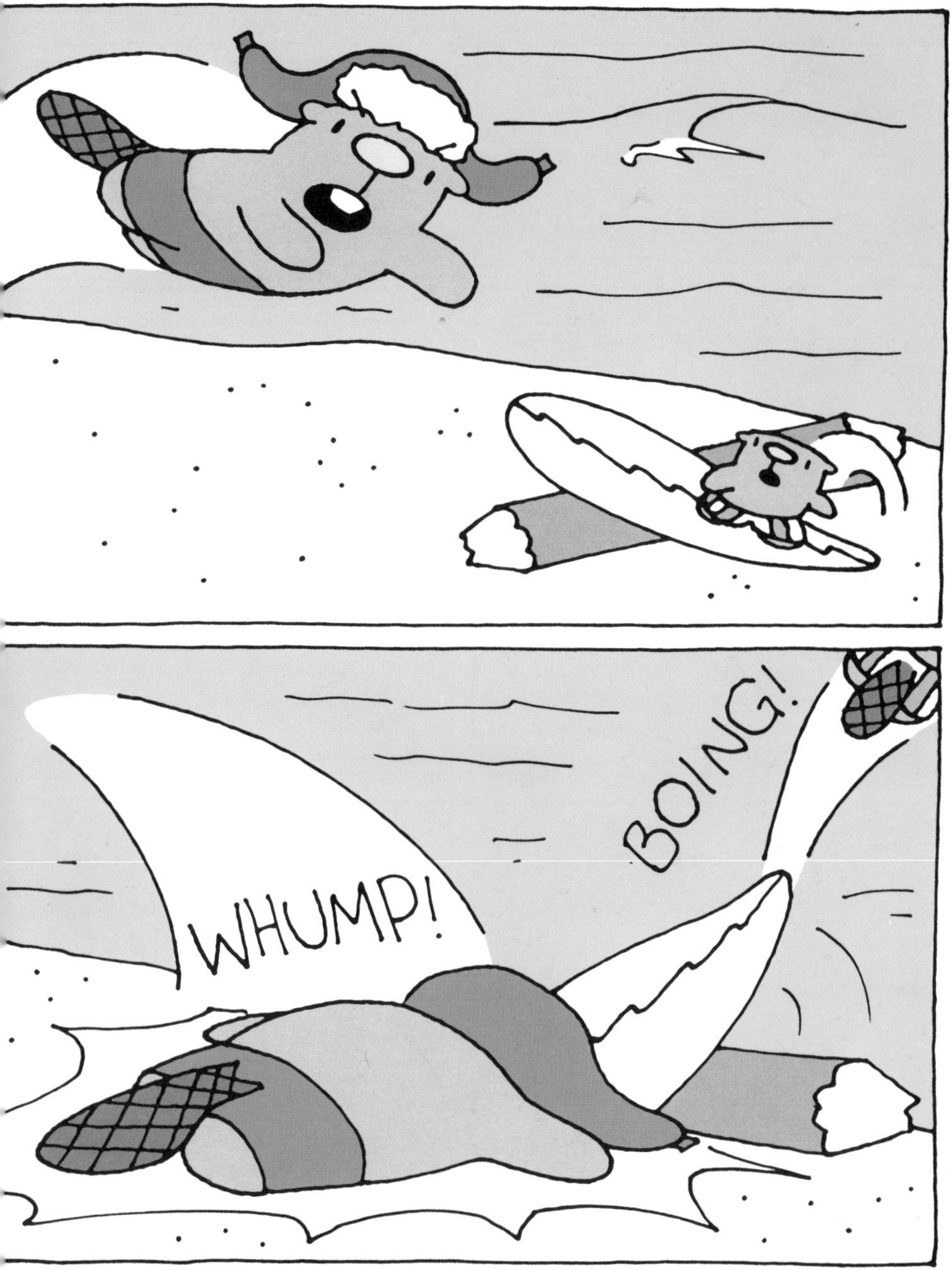
WHUMP!
BOING!

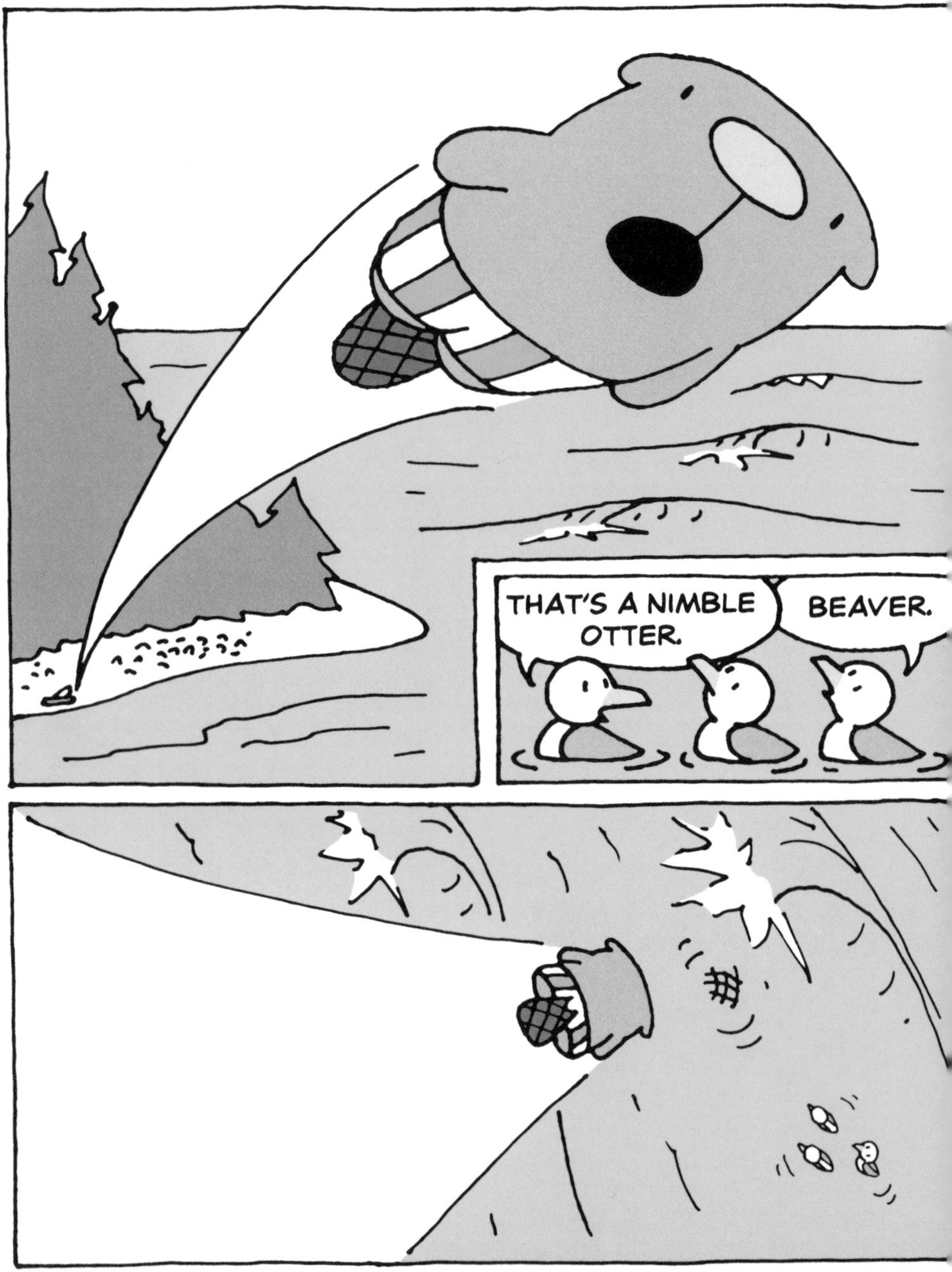
THAT'S A NIMBLE OTTER.
BEAVER.

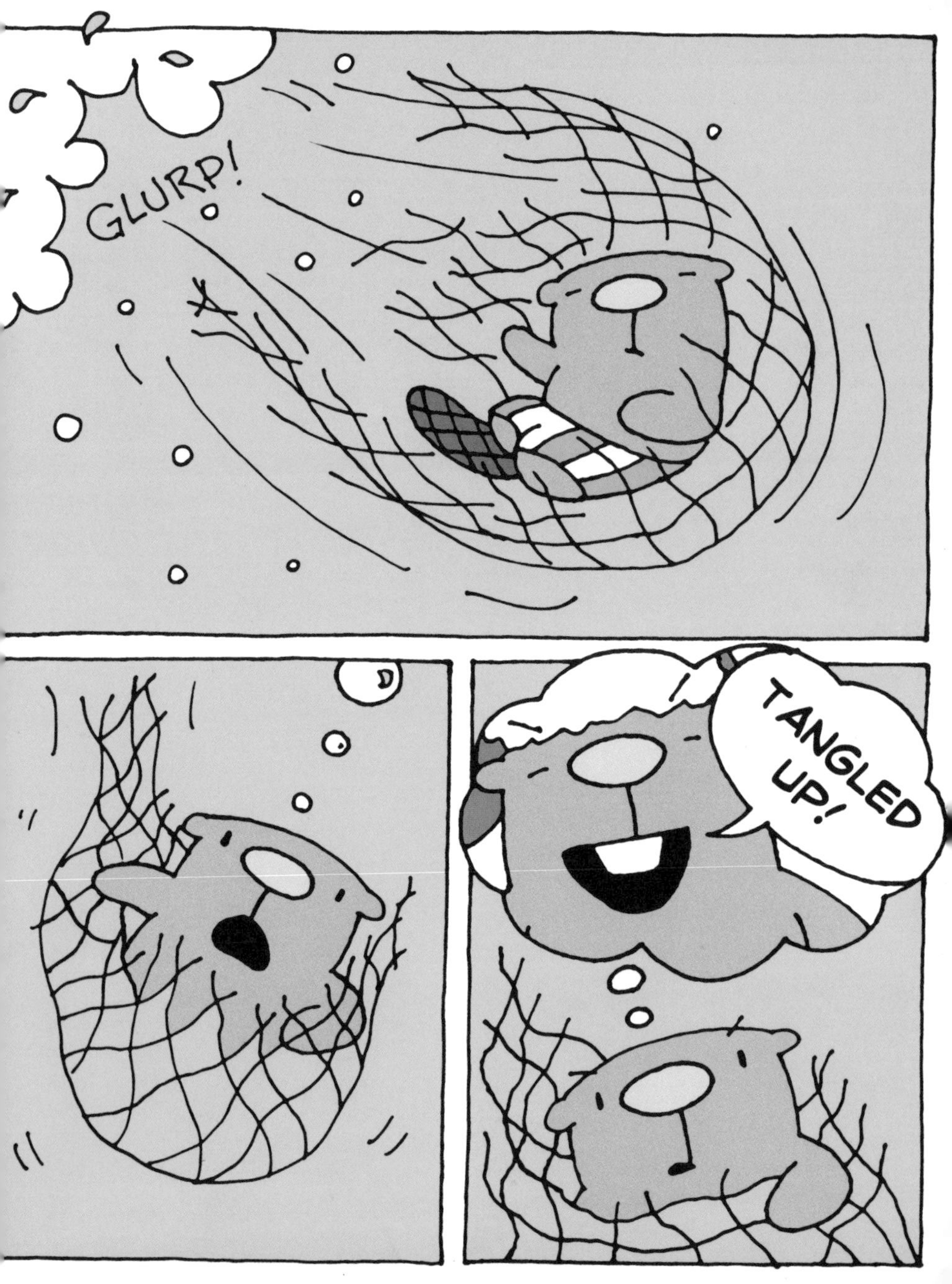
GLURP!
TANGLED UP!

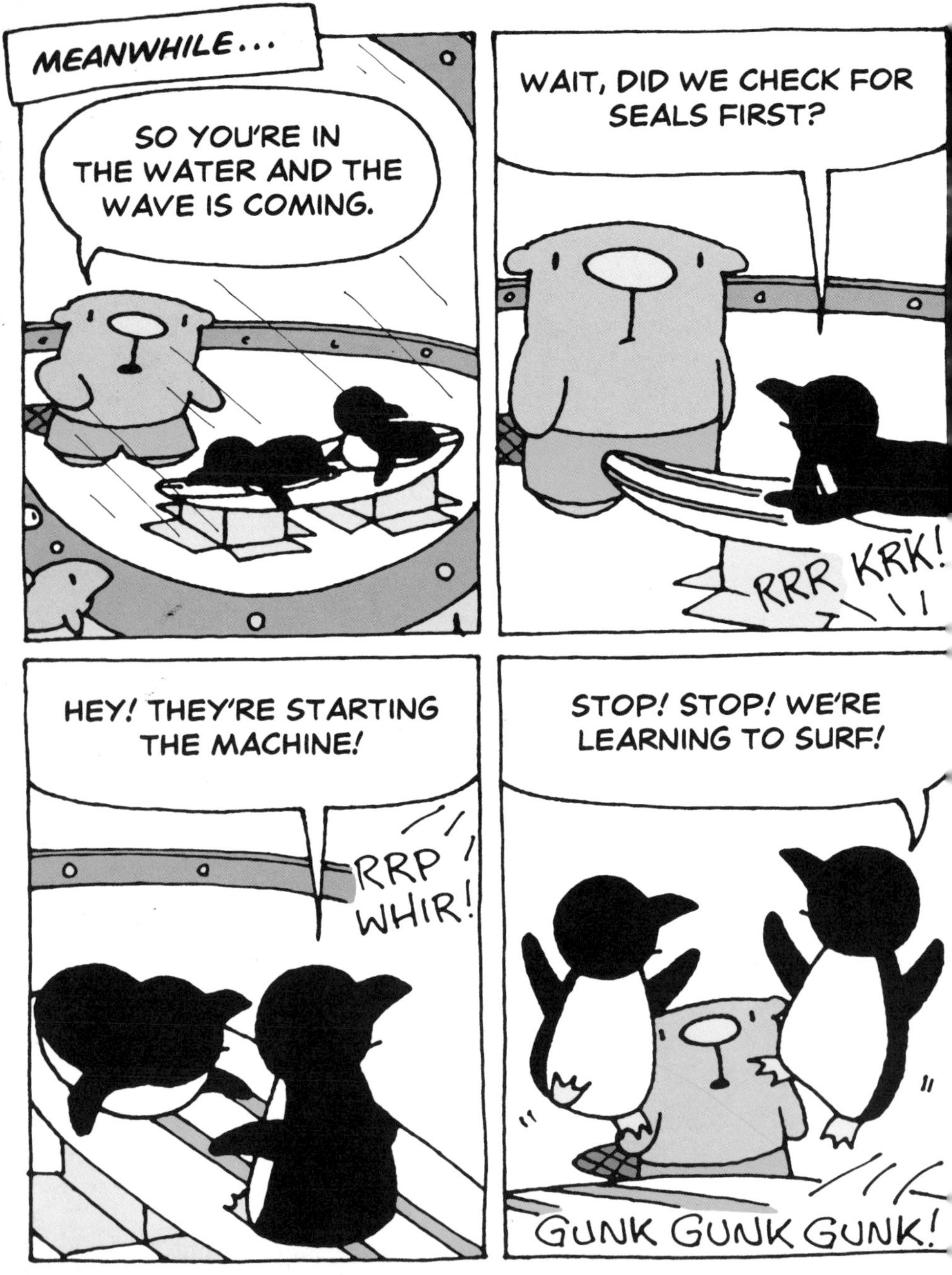
MEANWHILE...
SO YOU'RE IN THE WATER AND THE WAVE IS COMING.
WAIT, DID WE CHECK FOR SEALS FIRST?
RRR KRK!
HEY! THEY'RE STARTING THE MACHINE!
RRP WHIR!
STOP! STOP! WE'RE LEARNING TO SURF!
GUNK GUNK GUNK!

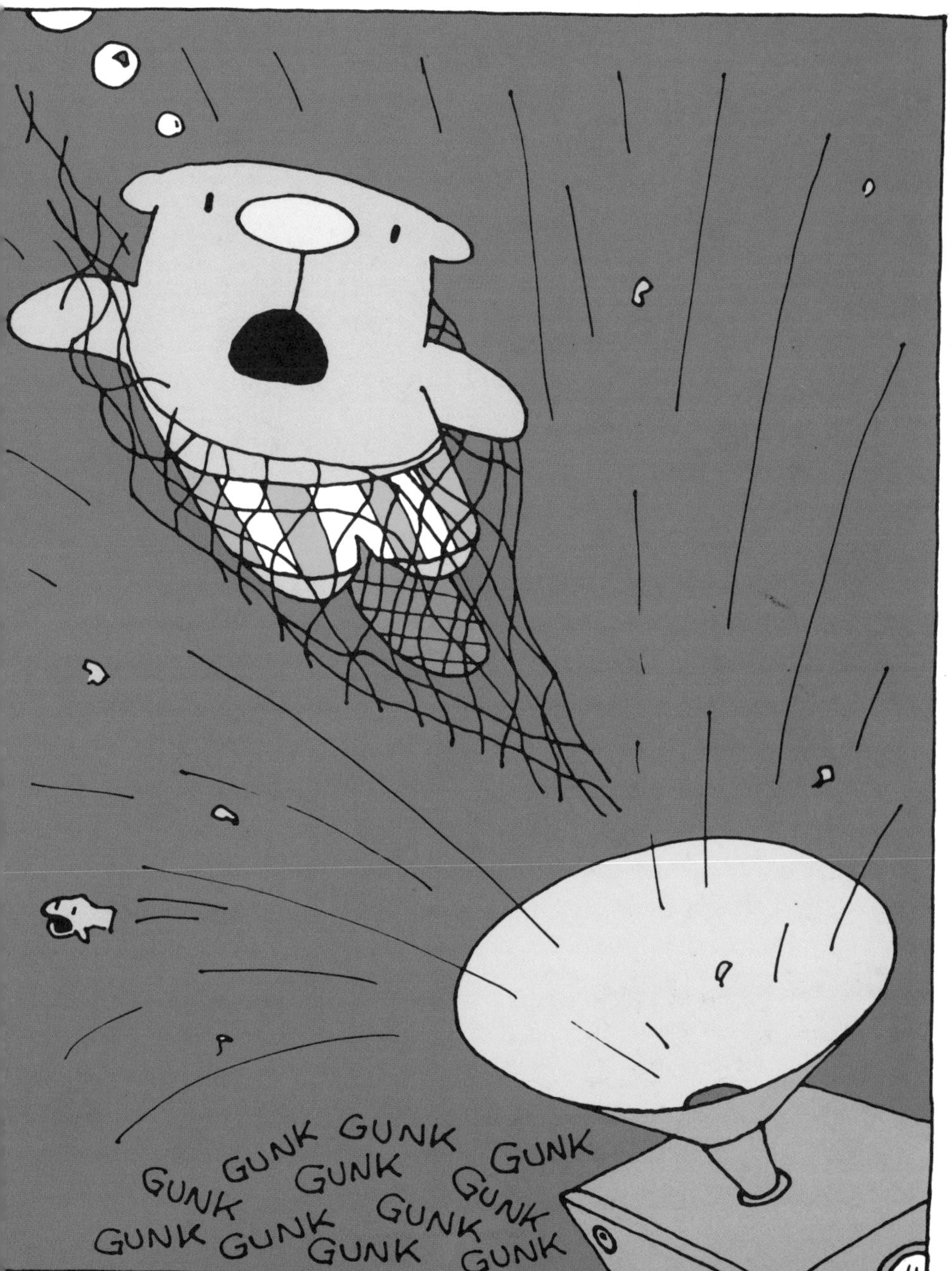
GUNK GUNK GUNK
GUNK GUNK GUNK
GUNK
GUNK GUNK GUNK GUNK

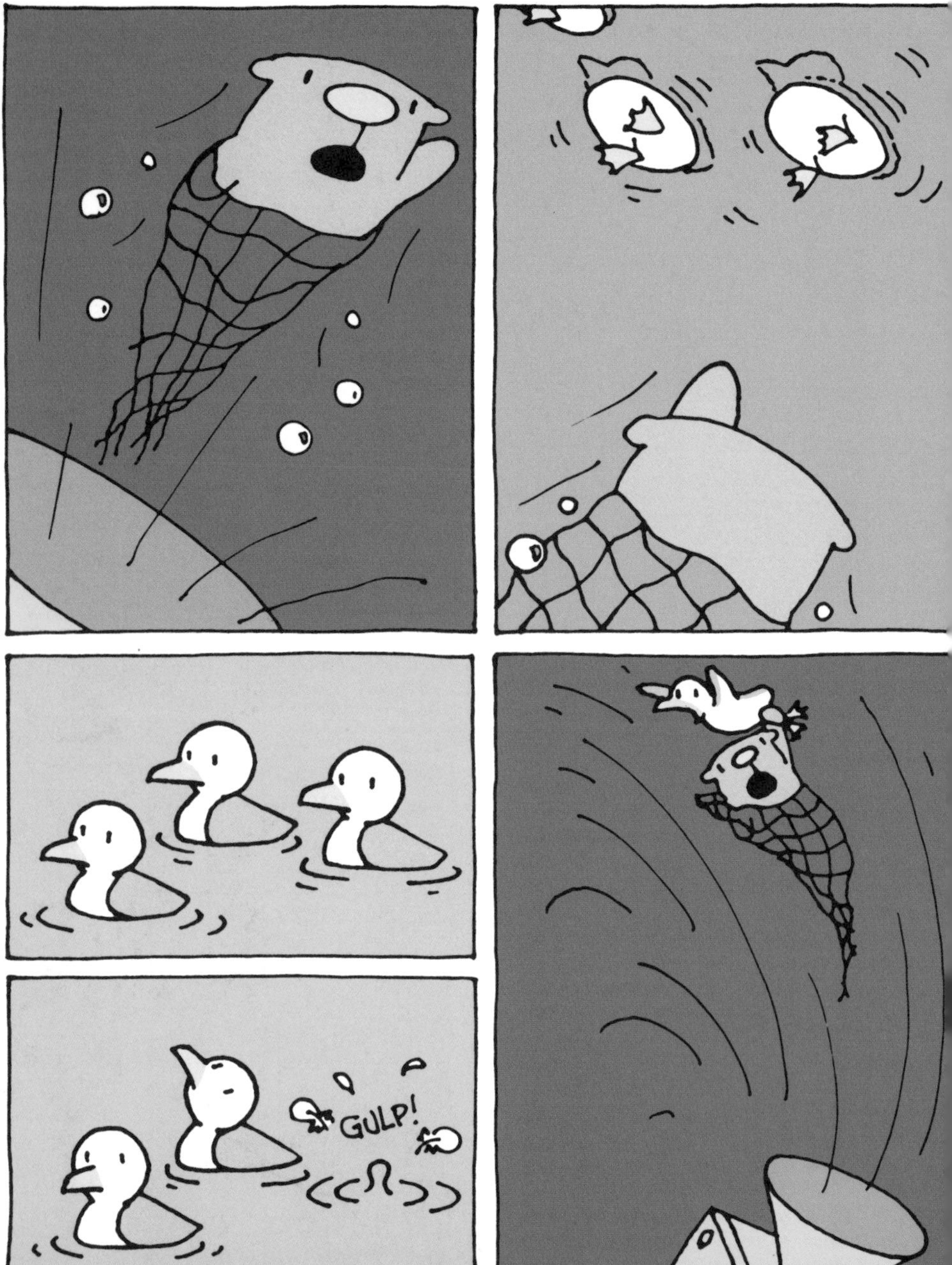
GULP!

SNIP!
SNIP!
SNIP!

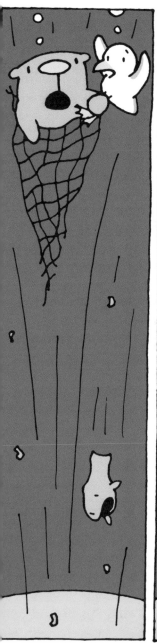

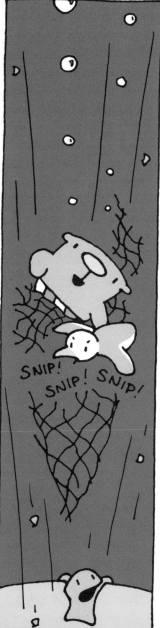

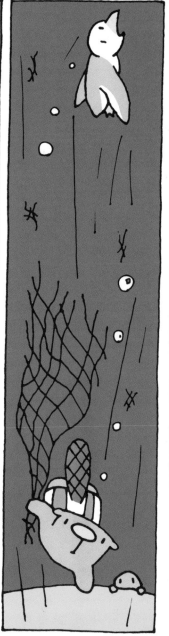

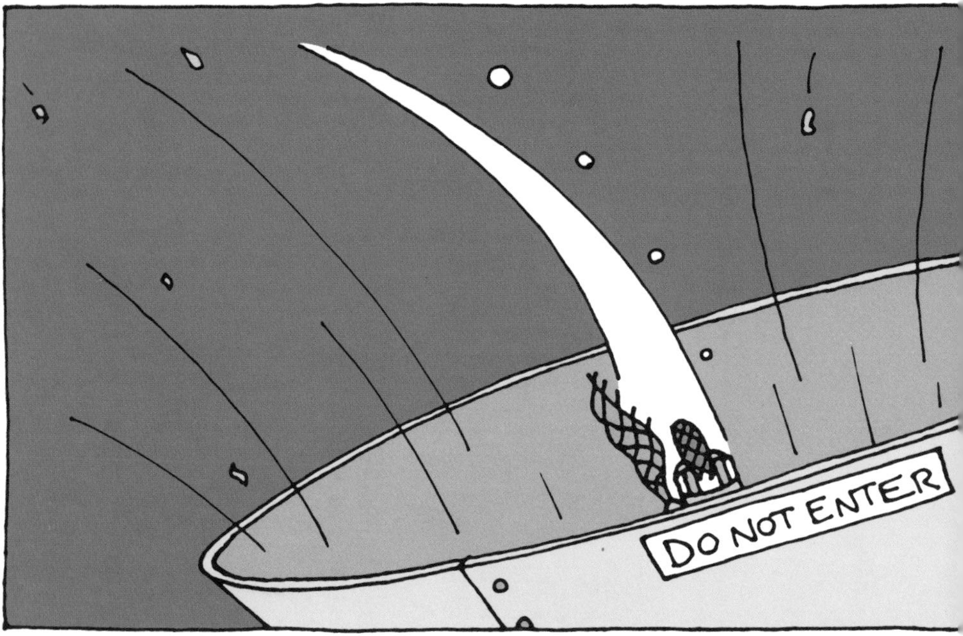
DO NOT ENTER
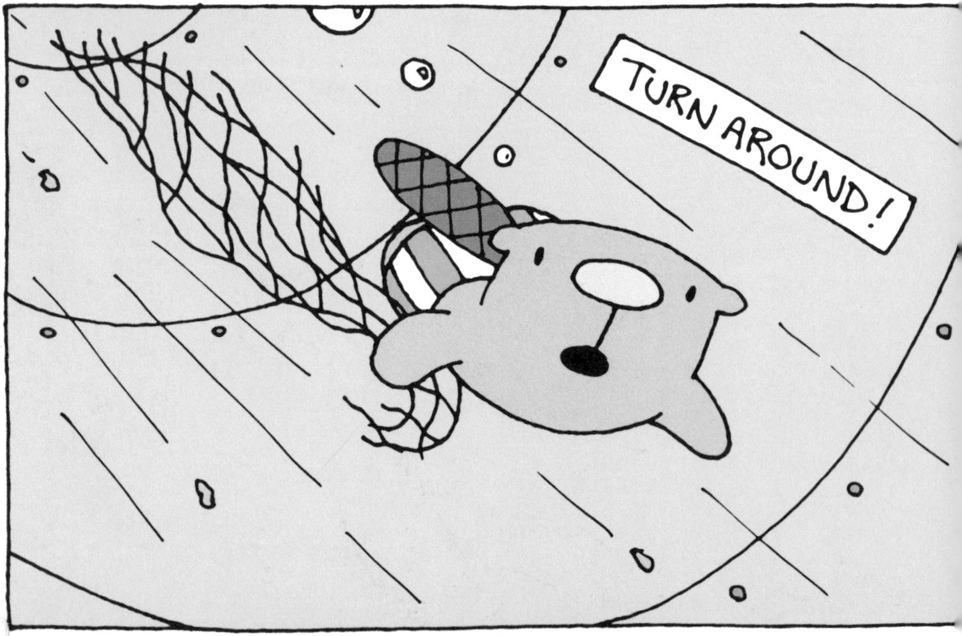
TURN AROUND!

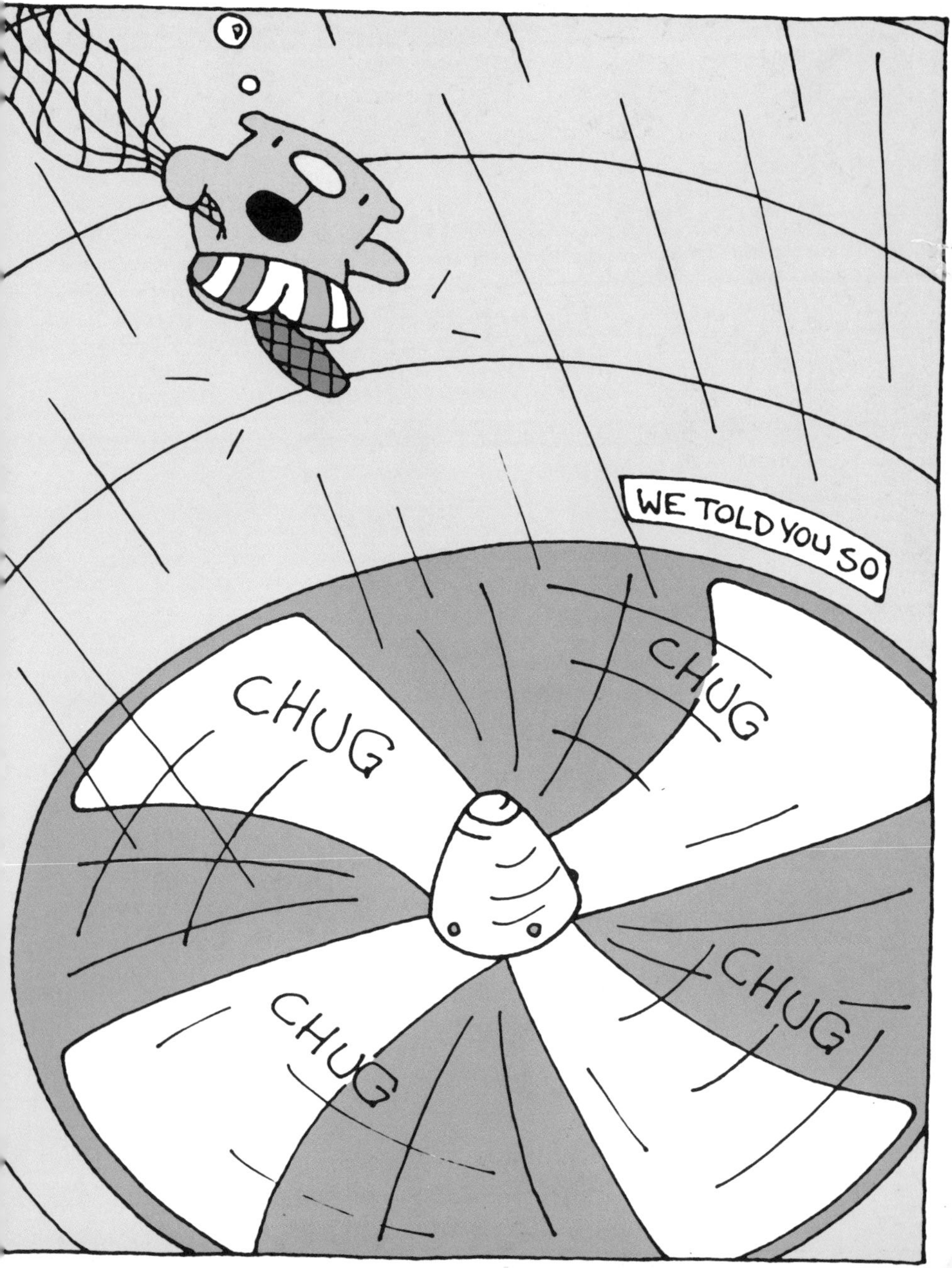
WE TOLD YOU SO
CHUG
CHUG
CHUG
CHUG

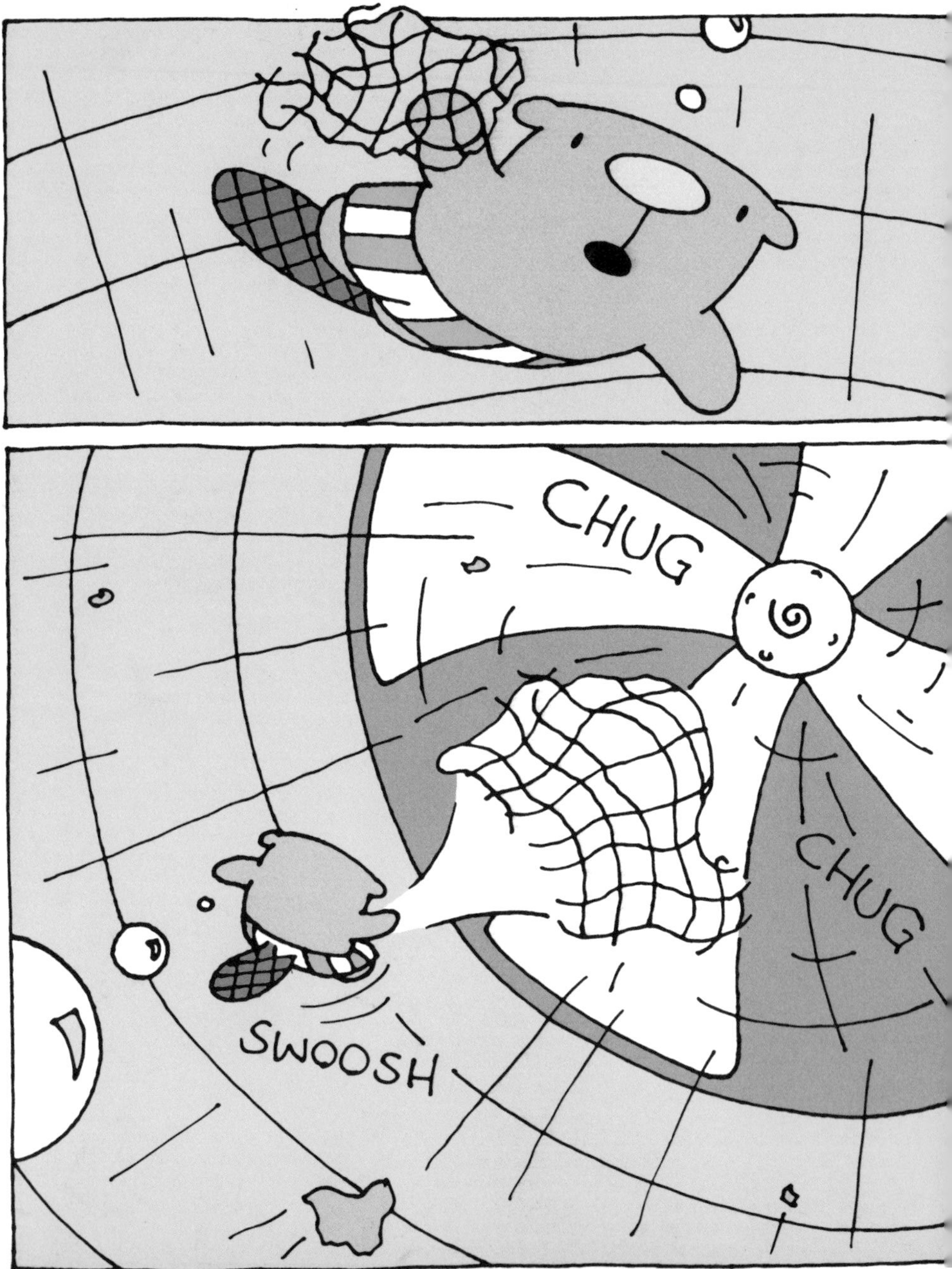
CHUG
CHUG
SWOOSH

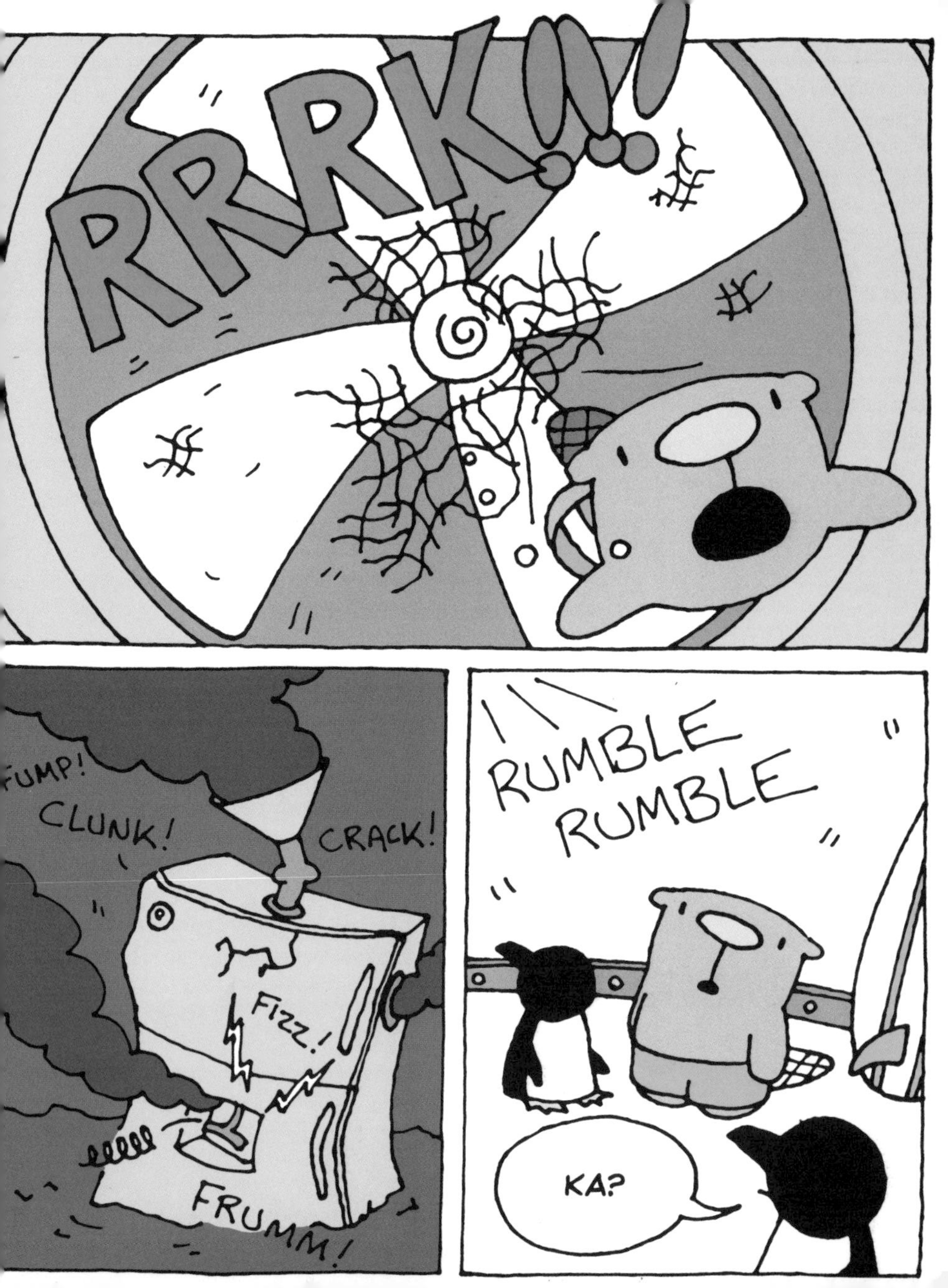
RRRK!!!
FUMP!
CLUNK!
CRACK!
FIZZ!
FRUMM!
RUMBLE
RUMBLE
KA?

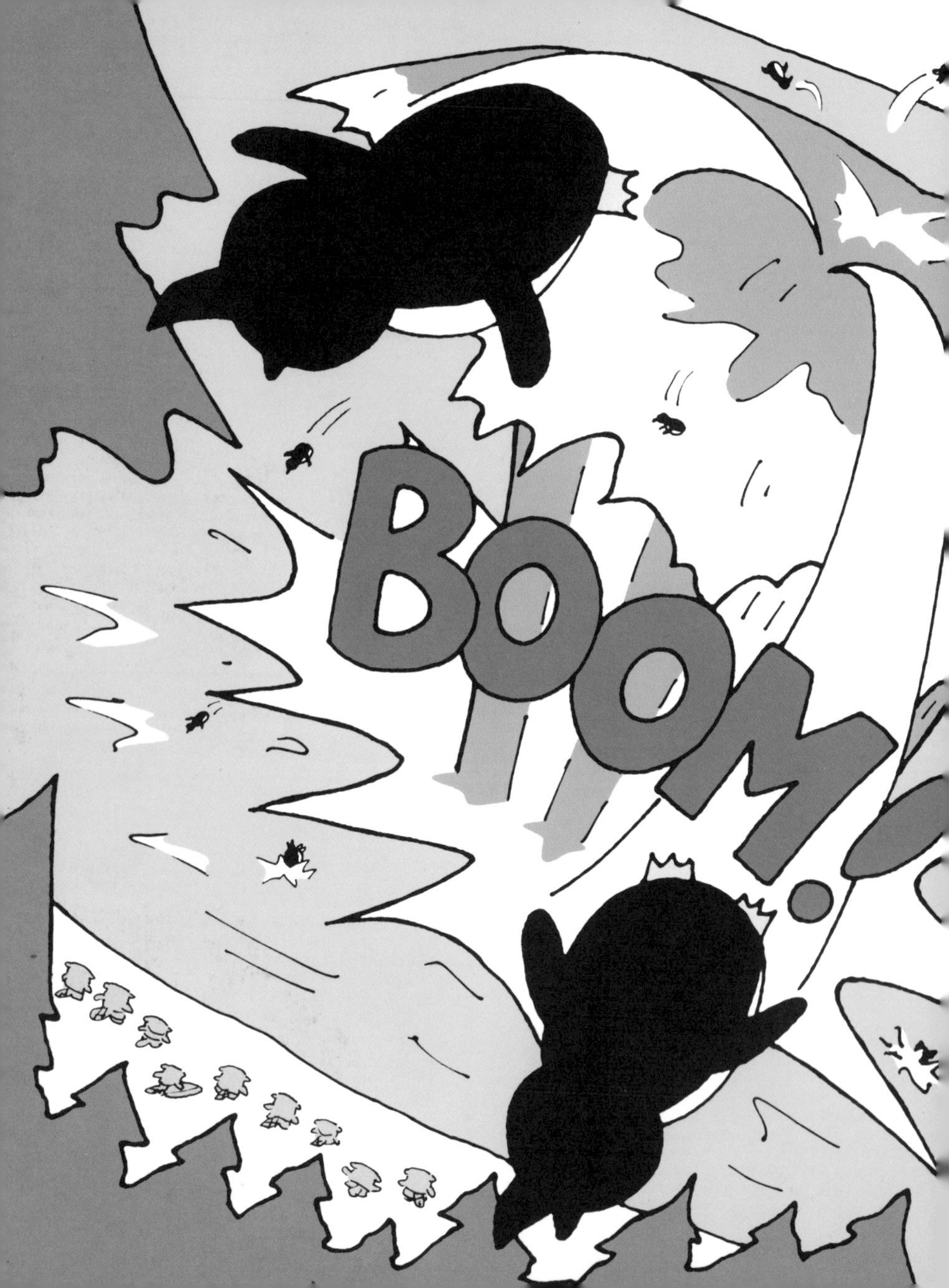
BOOM!

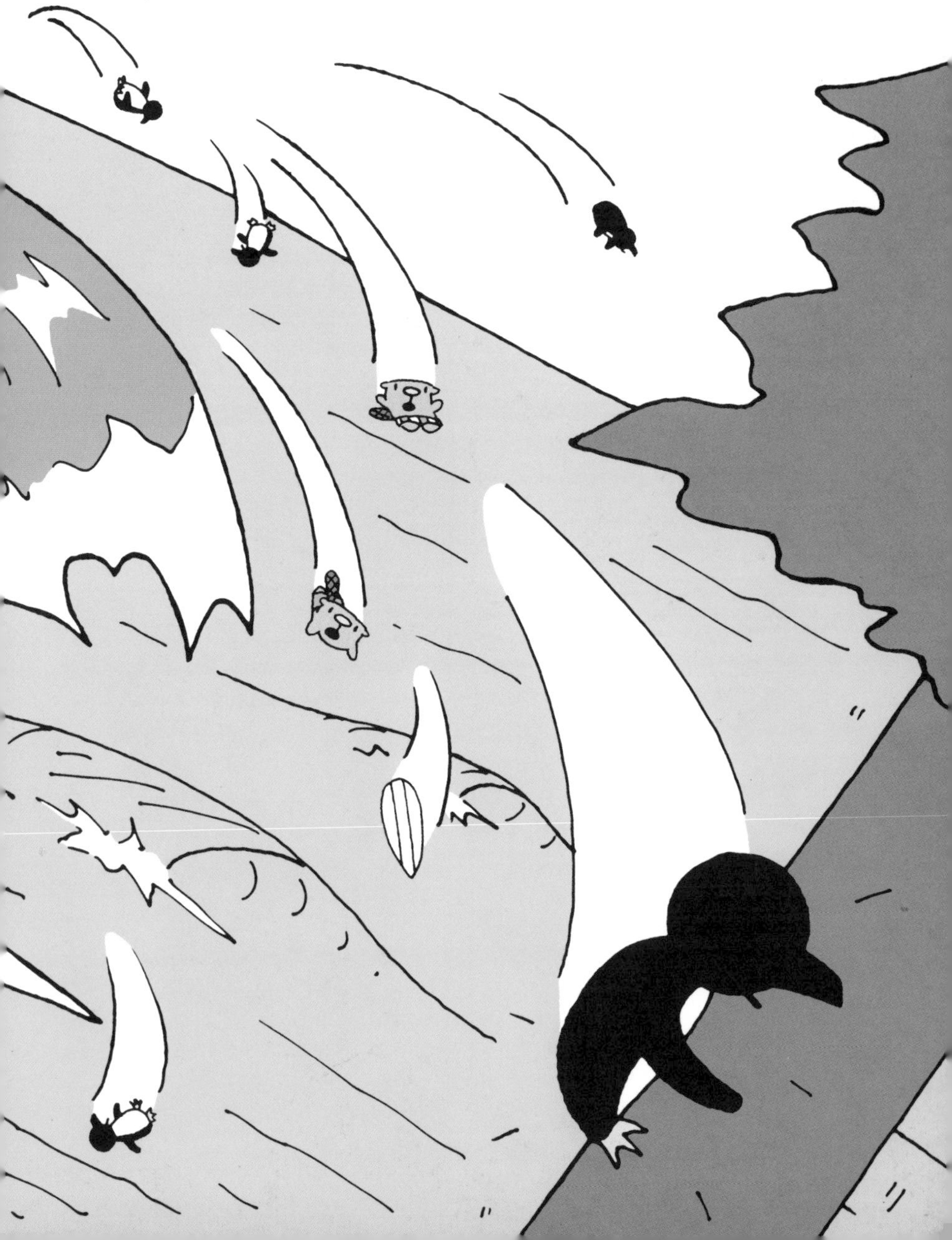

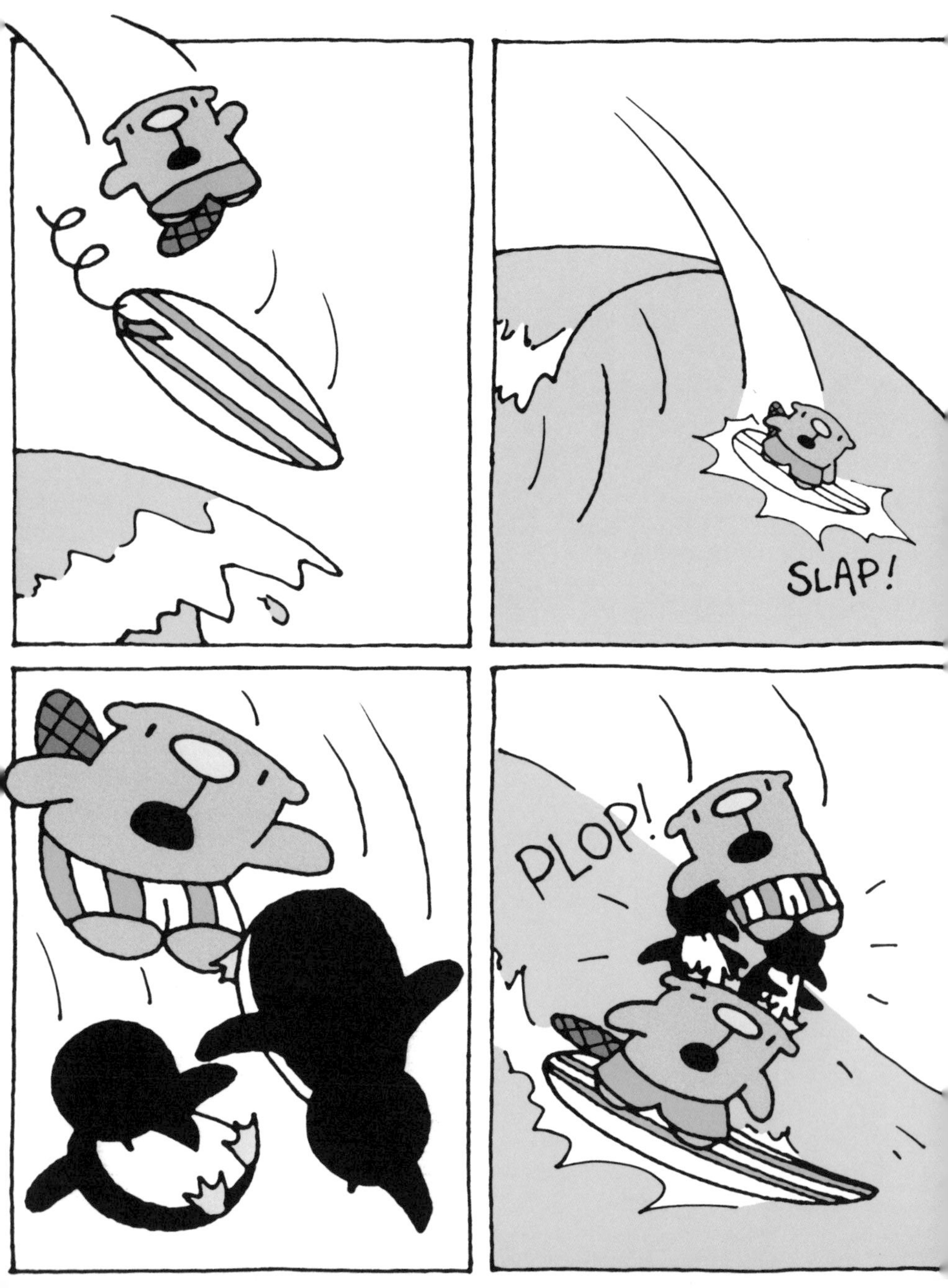
SLAP!
PLOP!

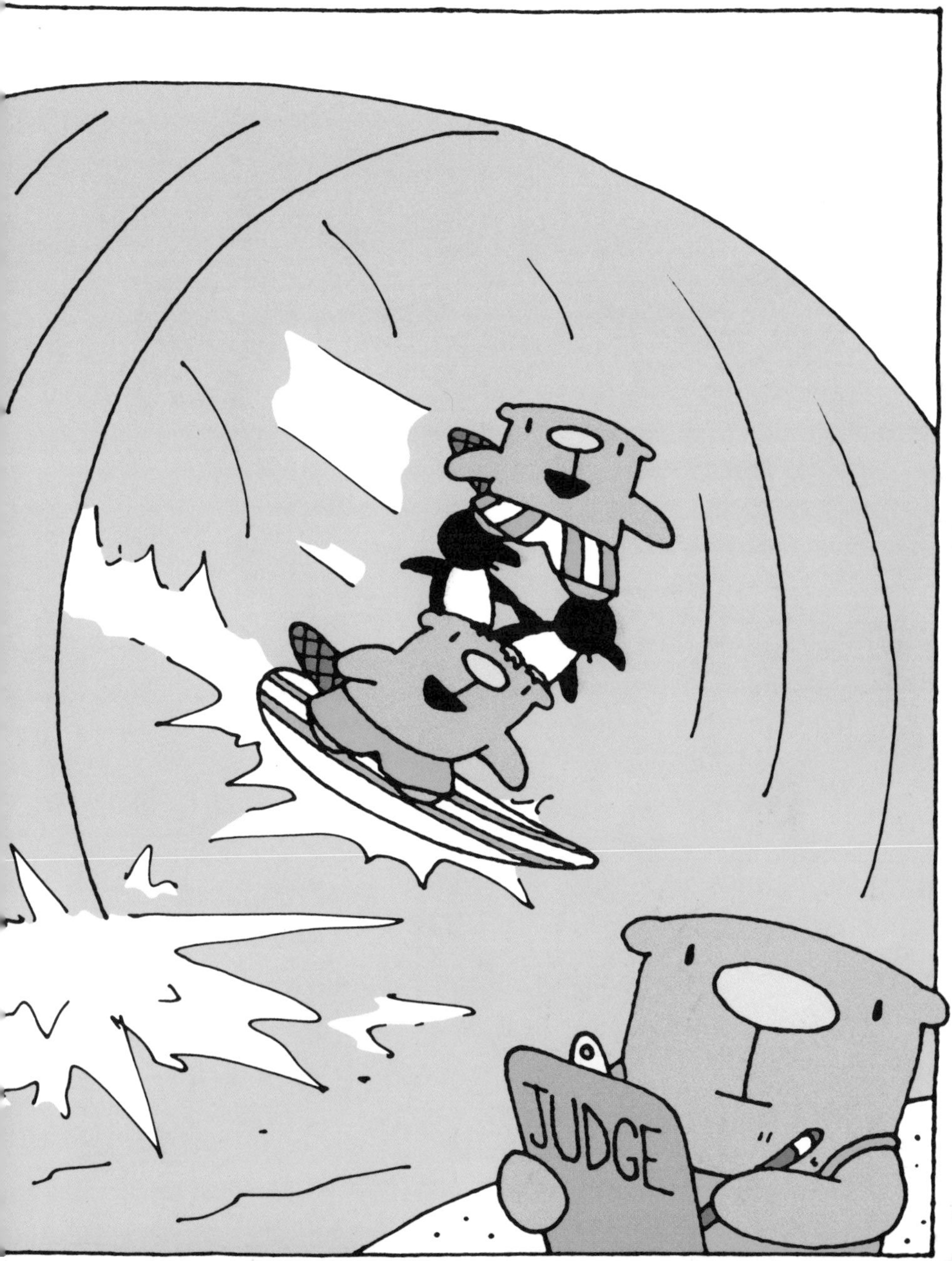
JUDGE

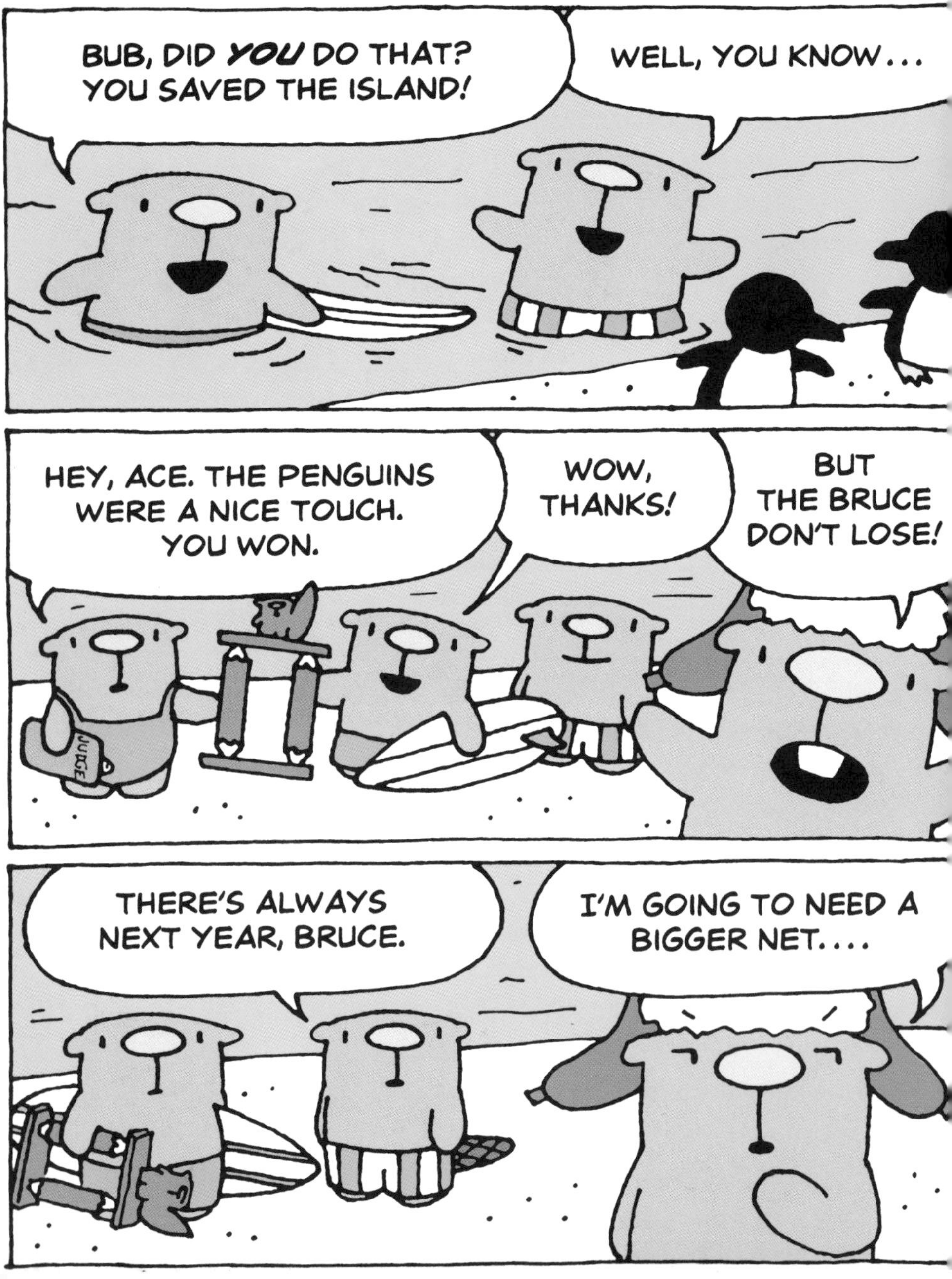
BUB, DID *YOU* DO THAT? YOU SAVED THE ISLAND!
WELL, YOU KNOW...
HEY, ACE. THE PENGUINS WERE A NICE TOUCH. YOU WON.
WOW, THANKS!
BUT THE BRUCE DON'T LOSE!
JUDGE
THERE'S ALWAYS NEXT YEAR, BRUCE.
I'M GOING TO NEED A BIGGER NET....

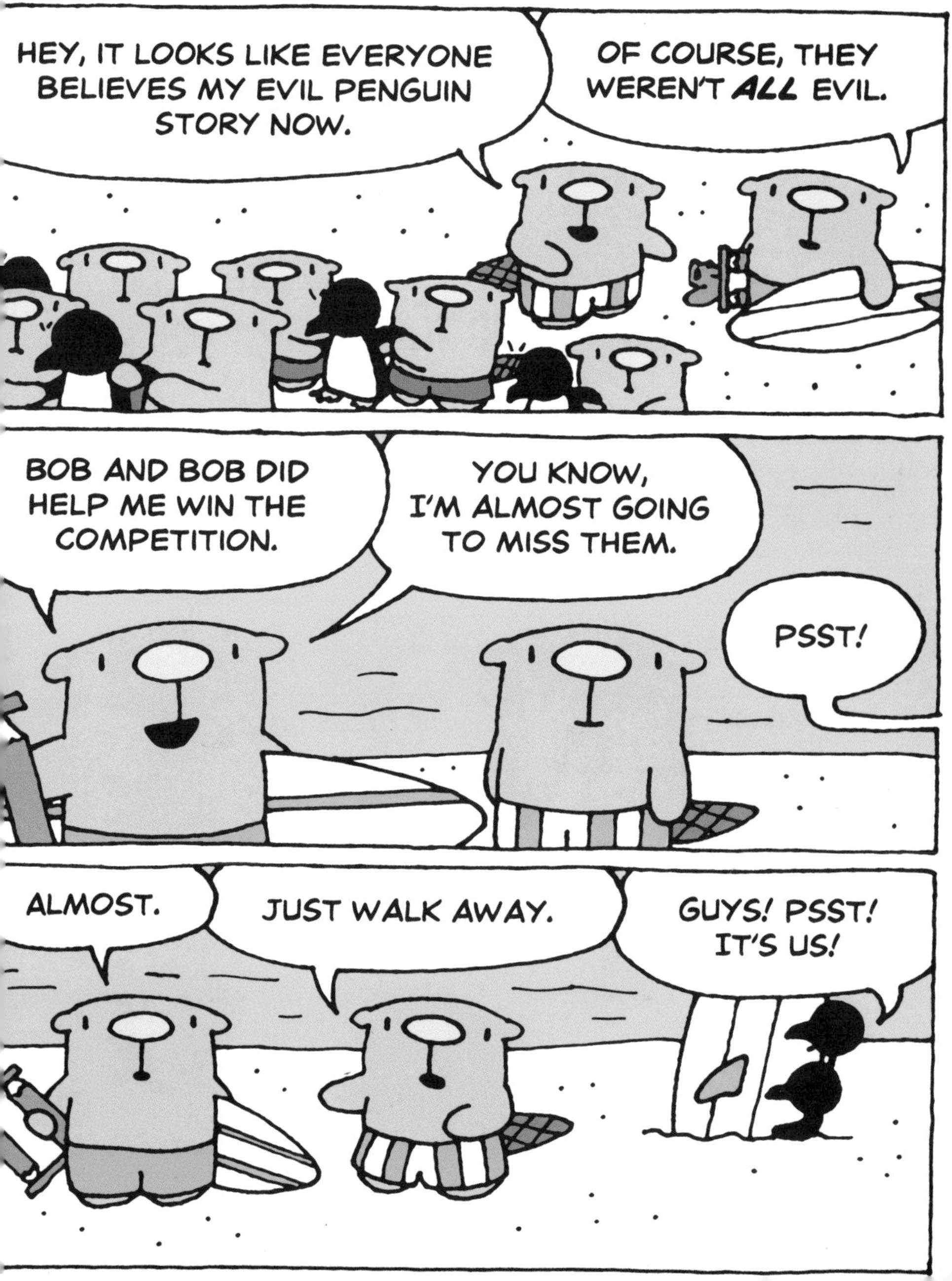
HEY, IT LOOKS LIKE EVERYONE BELIEVES MY EVIL PENGUIN STORY NOW.
OF COURSE, THEY WEREN'T ALL EVIL.
BOB AND BOB DID HELP ME WIN THE COMPETITION.
YOU KNOW, I'M ALMOST GOING TO MISS THEM.
PSST!
ALMOST.
JUST WALK AWAY.
GUYS! PSST! IT'S US!

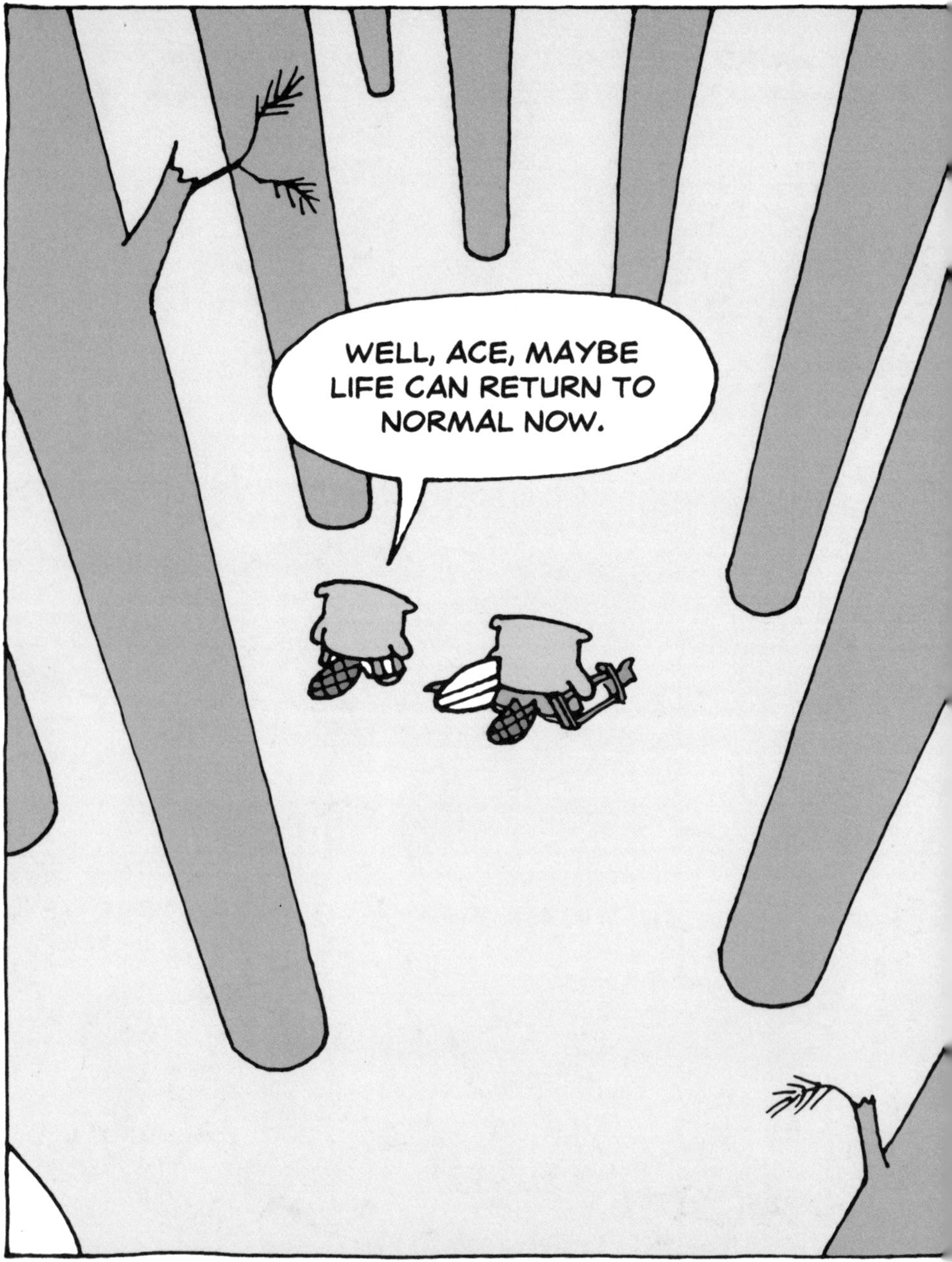
WELL, ACE, MAYBE LIFE CAN RETURN TO NORMAL NOW.

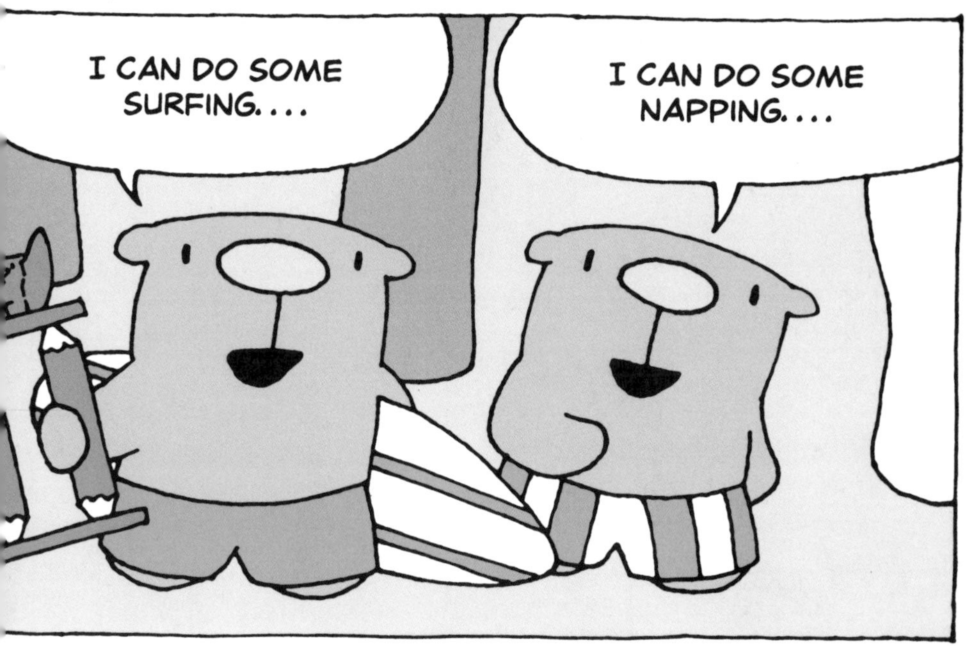
I CAN DO SOME SURFING....
I CAN DO SOME NAPPING....

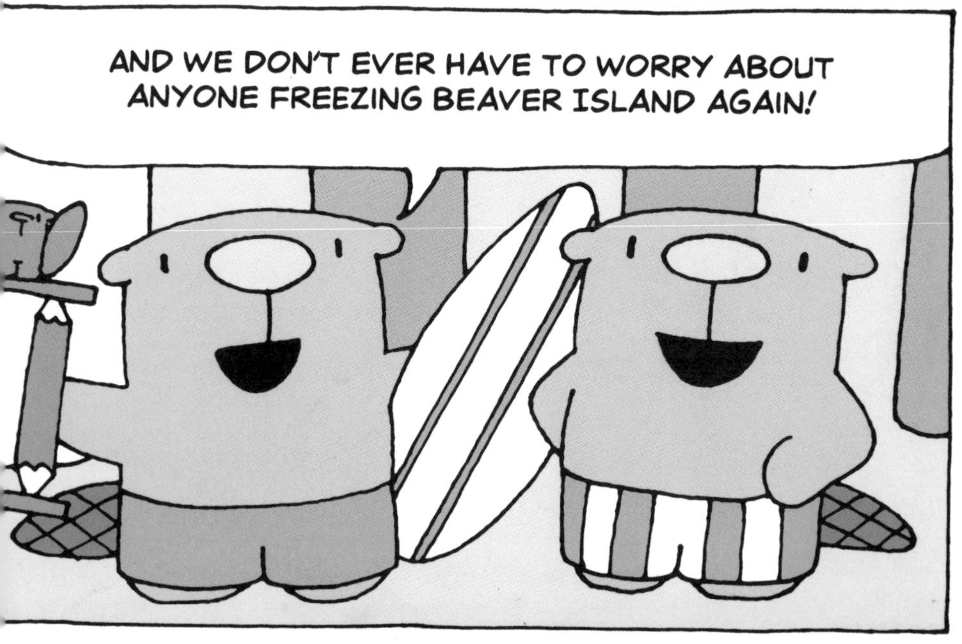
AND WE DON'T EVER HAVE TO WORRY ABOUT ANYONE FREEZING BEAVER ISLAND AGAIN!

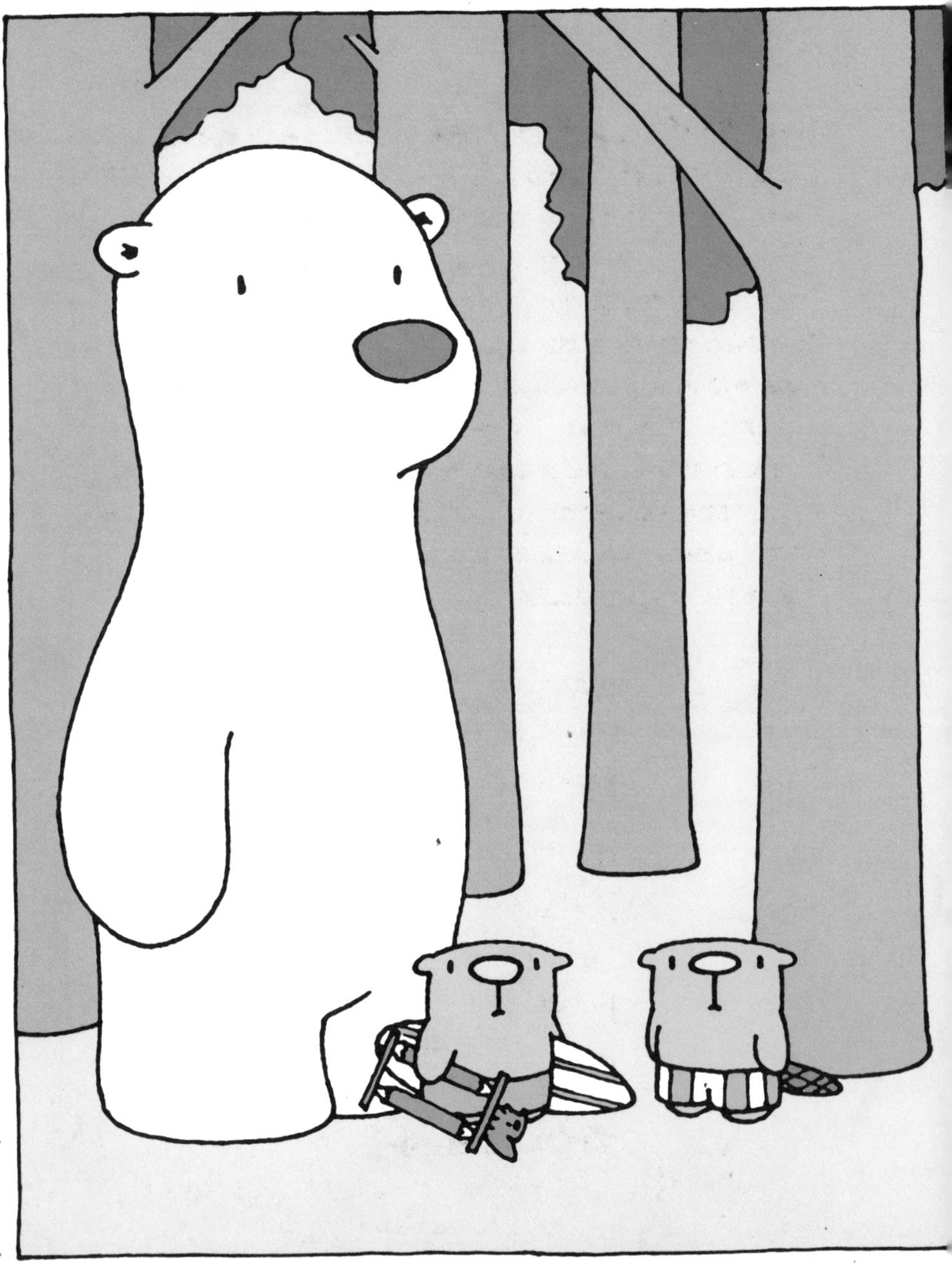